THE FAMILY B

Acknowledgements

This debut crime novel was conceived during the Corona Virus lockdown. It came about as a result of my grandson, Scott, suggesting I should write a crime novel. It would give me something to occupy my time, and engage my brain, he said. He suggested the name of a hero – Joe Mozart. He had thrown down the gauntlet.

Having previously written a children's story in the first lockdown I felt compelled to write a grown up story in my second attempt. I thought about it and said to myself, why not. So Mozart was born.

I would be writing of what I knew, and of some of the experiences I had over twenty seven years as a detective. Not all the experiences are mine. Some were those of friends and ex-colleagues, whose stories I have adapted and used in the text. However a great deal is from my imagination, based on collective experiences.

DEDICATION

I am deeply indebted to my wife, for putting up with hours of isolation, as I wrote and rewrote plots. At least this left her to pursue her own hobby of quilting in peace.

I am also deeply indebted to my particular friend Dave, who not only is a friend but an ex-colleague, whom I have based a character in the story on. He has been a constant source of information, encouragement and detail, and volunteered to be my critic and editor, as did his wife Sue who valiantly stuck to her editing although she would not normally enjoy a crime novel with descriptions of such graphic violence. Many of their amendments and suggestions have been included and I am grateful for their valued input.

It is my hope that you, the reader may enjoy the tale. If you do, perhaps Mozart will rise again.

Jeff Murray

January 2021

The family business

Chapter One

The man was tied to a chair in a white walled , windowless room, with a searing white light overhead which even penetrated the cloth bag over his head. His sweat soaked shirt had been torn open to the waist, and pain showed in his every body movement as he jerked and struggled against his bonds in time with the blows. His tormenters stood over him, pounding him on his chest and legs with lengths of rubber hose, but his screams were muffled by the dirty cloth tied across his mouth and the hood over his head. He writhed in pain. Would the torment ever end, there seemed no end coming. He had been in this position for hours, and the pain came in waves as he jerked to the rhythm of the blows. The floor around him was puddled with sweat and the frequent dousing of water which had been thrown over him when he showed signs of slipping into unconsciousness. He had soiled himself, with urine soaking his trousers.

The harsh voice by his ear demanded ," You owe us money. We want it."

He tried to speak, but all he could manage was a grating croak through the confines of the spittle soaked rag jammed in his mouth. "I haven't got it," he tried to mouth through the pain. The beating continued, the two men standing over him taking it in turns to hit him again and again.

"Where's the money. When are we getting it" came the demand.

Again the man croaked "I haven't got it. I can and will get it, give me time."

"You've had weeks. You know our terms" came the voice to his right. "Cash within the week. You've had a month."

"I can get it. I will get it, I'll pay you interest, but please stop. I can't take any more. Please, please".

One more blow, and the man slipped into unconsciousness. He didn't feel the needle entering his vein. He woke up with his hands and feet tied. He was free of the chair but still couldn't see. He still had the hood over his head and he could feel that he was now lying in water on a soft surface, like mud. He was in the open air, he could feel the cold air. He was freezing. His trousers were wet, his shirt was wet, and he started to tremble. He had no shoes on. He was sore all over his upper body, he could feel his lips mashed and sticking to his teeth. He heard a ships siren and sounds of the sea as his senses started to revive. He felt it was night. He dare not move as his captors were still there, and he was helpless. He couldn't shout, the gag was still in place and anyway his throat was dry and all he could do was make whimpering noises.

The voices came again. "Leave him there, the tide will be in soon and he will drown. Nobody is going to hear him. Nobody's going to find him. He's done for. Let's go." He then heard the sound of the men walking away, car doors slamming, a vehicle starting up, and the sound of the engine fading as it drove away.

He was lying in about six inches of very cold water, listening to the sounds of ships, and water lapping close by. Was the tide coming in. Could he get away before the water flooded over him. Could he avoid drowning. He struggled against his bonds, hoping the water would loosen the rope which secured him, and he worked his jaw to get rid of the rag in his mouth. His struggles came to nothing. He was helpless. He tried to wriggle away from the incoming water, but only managed to scrape his already sore body along the ground. It seemed that he had been there for hours, when suddenly he heard a vehicle. Had they come back, should or could he attract attention. Could he get out of his predicament. He saw light through the material of the hood as it swung over him. He heard car doors open and footsteps as they approached.

He heard a male and a female voice. "Is that a body" said a female voice. "It's moving" said the man.

Hands grabbed him at the shoulders, and pulled him sideways out of the water, then pulled him up to a sitting position. The hood was whipped off his head, and he sat shivering and blinking in the headlight glare of a car. He was sitting in a puddle. He was alive.

The man asked, "Who did this to you. You look beat up" as the ropes around his wrists and feet were loosened. The rag was removed from his mouth. All he could croak was "Water, please, water."

The man got a bottle of water from the car and he gulped it down. "Thanks" he said, "That's a life saver. "

The male from the car said, "What's happened. Why are you tied up and sitting in a puddle." " It's a long story" said the man, "I'm freezing. Where am I." The man from the car said, "You are near Barking Creek. The Thames is just over there," nodding to his right. "How did you get here and who tied you up." "As I said, it's a long story, and its best that you don't know. Is there any way you can give me a lift."

The man from the car helped him to his feet and he staggered as if drunk. The man held him to steady him on his feet, causing pain to sweep across his body, and his knees to buckle. The man from the car said, "Take it easy. You need hospital. We will take you." He then said to the girl, "Get the blanket from the car".

With the blanket around his shoulders, the man was half dragged and half walked to the car, where he was put in the back seat. His whole body was raw and he was wracked with pain. He had black eyes, his torso had long welts across it, and written in big bold letters in red lipstick were the words WE WILL BE BACK. He was bloodied, bruised, his lips were mashed and he was nauseous as he lay trembling. He felt the car move, he was so tired and fell into a troubled doze. He awoke to lights coming from a large building, and felt hands pulling him from the car, and putting him on a wheeled trolley. He opened his eyes a crack and saw he was being wheeled into a hospital, the trolley stopped and he felt a prick in his arm. A wave of heat coursed through his body, and his hurts faded as consciousness left him. He was safe – for the time being.

Chapter two

The man slowly woke, his eyes seared by white light and a flash. He started to sit up, until he realized that he was warm, in a bed, in a room, and linked to a drip attached to his arm and he was dressed in a loose fitting hospital gown. He slowly realized that he was not alone. Standing at the foot of the bed was a tall, dark haired, slender but muscular man, wearing a suit and tie, with penetrating blue eyes which seemed to bore into his very soul. This was not a man to mess with. He had a look of sardonic amusement on his intelligent face, and as he walked around the bed he moved with the grace of a stalking panther. He emanated strength and vitality.

He said, "You're awake at last. Let me introduce myself. I am Detective Inspector Joe Mozart and you have a story to tell me. Let's start with your name."

The man said, "John Green." Mozart said, "No, I mean your real name." The man repeated John Green."

“Alright” said Mozart, “If that’s what you want me to call you. Where do you live.”

The man thought for a while and said, “I don’t have to tell you, do I.”

Mozart said, “No, you don’t, but, it is obvious that you have been in serious trouble. You have been seriously beaten, tied up and left half dead in a puddle on the shore of the Thames at Barking Creek, and I would like to know who did this to you, why, and why you had WE’LL BE BACK written in lipstick on your chest, which has come out very well on the photographs I have taken. You are obviously in some deep trouble, so much so, that your life appears to be in danger, and therefore this must be a matter for the Police. I am a Policeman and am asking you to cooperate. Tell me your story, and we can help you. This has the look of a punishment beating to me, which probably means you are in some very serious trouble and in way over your head”

The man hesitated and to gain time asked for water. Mozart handed him a glass and he gulped it down in one swallow, handing the glass back to Mozart before saying, “I’m not sure anyone can help me, I’m not sure I want help. My name is Green, I got involved in a fight outside a pub, and that's all I want to say."

Mozart looked at the man lying in the bed. " Some fight. They obviously want more of you, judging from the message they have left on your chest. But I believe you are not telling me anything like the truth. I don't suppose your name is Green. But what is plain is that your life is in danger and you have probably been beaten as a warning. That they put a message on your chest, and don't deny it because whilst you were asleep, as I said, I took some very clear photographs. You are obviously involved in something which has serious consequences for you, and if that's the case, we the police are more than interested, especially if it means preventing further harm to yourself and perhaps others. Who are you really?"

The man said, "That's all I've got to say. I'm very tired. I would like to sleep."

A nurse entered the room and said, "That's enough. He's had enough. Please go, he will need complete rest and treatment before any further questions."

Mozart said, "I will be back. There is a story here and I will get to the bottom of it." He then left the room, pointedly taking the glass that the man had handled whilst taking a drink, and placing it in an evidence bag as he left. Mozart then spoke at length to a uniformed police officer posted outside the door and walked out of the man's sight.

The nurse checked the man's temperature, checked his injuries, which were still raw and painful, then added a hypodermic to the drip, which gradually eased his pain, and sent him into a deep sleep. For the time being the man was safe and warm, and he had a bodyguard outside the room which gave him some comfort, but meant that the Police were determined to find out who he was and why he had been beaten and left lying in a riverside puddle, gagged, and tied hand and foot.

Joe Mozart had possession of the man's clothing, or the little that was left of it. He was in a side room of the hospital. The trousers, now dry, but torn and bloodied, were a standard size but the label showed an upmarket company in London's Saville Row and the shirt, again bloodied and torn revealed an upmarket label. Obviously the man was in a high income bracket. Mozart reflected that the man had a well- groomed appearance despite his injuries, and his voice was that of someone of culture and education. He was obviously not a rough sleeper or a labourer. His hands were soft, his nails professionally cared for, and the clothes he wore were bespoke, and well out of Mozart's price range. His type as a general rule rarely got involved in crime, so who was he and why had he been beaten.

The two people who had found the man at Barking Creek were waiting for Mozart in Matron's office. He wanted to speak to them both. John Brice and his girlfriend Sally O'Brian lived in the Barking area, and they had driven to Barking Creek courting when they spotted the man lying tied up in a puddle. They told Mozart that they had untied him and taken him to the hospital.

"Will you take me to where you found him please" said Mozart, "And then I will get you home."

The couple climbed into the back of Mozart's car and directed him to the spot where they had first seen the man. Mozart got a torch and examined the scene. He saw the puddle, about six inches deep, adjacent to the river, and he then spotted pieces of rope lying on the ground.

John Brice said, "That's the rope we took off him." Mozart then bagged the two lengths of rope in an evidence bag, and said, "I will have to have the scene examined in daylight. Hang on, I want to get the area preserved."

He radioed to the control room, and they waited until a Police Car was seen coming down the track. Mozart then briefed the car crew, telling them to remain on site until relieved, when the area could be examined by Scenes of Crime officers, in daylight. Mozart then made arrangements to have the car crew relieved at regular intervals, until daylight came. John Brice and Sally O'Brian were dropped at the hospital to pick up their car, and allowed to go home. Their night had been thoroughly spoiled, and they were now essential witnesses to what appeared to be a serious crime, shrouded in mystery. Who was the man, what was he involved in and who had beaten him so badly.

Chapter three

Jimmy "Gunner" Nolan's mobile rang. It was a withheld number. "Yes," he grunted in his usual rasping voice. "Nolan," said the voice. "The family want a meet."

This demand caused Nolan to start worrying. The family wanted to see him. Not good. He swallowed, "When and where". "Two hours. The Duke of Wellington, Whitechapel. Be there." The phone went dead.

Gunner Nolan phoned his brother John. "The family want a meet in two hours at the Duke of Wellington. I'll meet you there."

The Nolan brothers were known as the Whitechapel Cartel, a grandiose name they had thought up to impress their clientele. They were drug dealers, supplying the City of London, the west end night club scene, and had organized drug lines into neighbouring counties. It was a very lucrative trade and had made them wealthy. They ruled their empire with terror and violence, having carved it out over the last few years. They had the scars to prove it. They had fought their way to the top of their profession, and were embedded in the Whitechapel area, their native territory. Both were hard men, well known to the police, brought up in a criminal family and had served their criminal apprenticeship in the school of hard knocks. They survived by their wits and muscle. They had done time in prison, but rarely, considering the number of criminal pies they had their fingers into. They were making a good living, and they always made sure that they collected on bad debts. Their overnight activities, where they had dumped one of their late paying clients into a puddle at Barking Creek, was one example of how they enforced their business. Their livelihood depended on one source. The family. They were the wholesalers. The suppliers of the Nolan brother's product. Without them they would not exist, and they ruled by extreme violence and intimidation. A summons from the family was not to be ignored. It didn't pay to upset them. Many had tried and had disappeared. Hard men some of them. Rumours came back there were many well fed pigs on farms around the home counties and many, so called hard men, left crippled as a result of upsetting the family.

Two hours later the Nolan brothers entered the Duke of Wellington pub. The pub was almost empty at this time of the morning. They were well known to the landlord, who produced two whiskies as soon as they entered. He also nodded towards a man sitting alone at a table near the window. The brother's took their drinks and stood in front of the table. The man they saw was unknown to them. He was middle aged, smartly dressed in a suit, and had a grey raincoat on the chair next to him. He looked like a businessman or lawyer. He did not invite them to sit.

He said, in a quiet and neutral voice, "The family are upset with you. You have taken some initiatives they do not like."

"Like what" said Gunner, belligerently. "You have put a man they have an interest in in hospital, and this may compromise the family, as he has been, shall we say, employed for some time by them, to carry out certain financial functions. In doing so, he has syphoned off certain amounts as an unauthorized fee, and he may well have certain records which could compromise the family at what is a particularly delicate time for them. They are not pleased with you. We understand that the man is hospitalized, and as we speak, he is being interviewed by the Police. He is in possession of information, and has perhaps kept records of certain things which if they became known, especially to the Police, could jeopardize certain business dealings the family are currently involved in. The family intended to punish him for milking the system, but you have now moved things on to a point where the family did not want to go."

"He owed us money," said Gunner, "We couldn't let him get away with that, could we."

The man said, "The family want this matter resolved. Your financial dealings with this man are of no consequence to them. They want this matter sorted. They have asked me to tell you two things. They want you to search his flat, and I am to accompany you. We will be looking for certain documents which, if found, I will remove. You can take any money or goods to make it look like an ordinary burglary, after which the family wish you to eliminate the risk. Circumstances you have created have forced this course of action. Finish what you started, for good."

He then looked hard at both brothers, until they realized the import of what he was saying, and they nodded their agreement. The man continued, "The problem of how we get into his flat is yours to solve."

Gunner said, "We have his key and fob. We were going there anyway and take the money he owes us, if we can find anything."

"I will meet you at the flat in one hour. Be there. After that, the family are willing to cut their losses so we leave you to solve the problem permanently. Once that is done the family will continue your supply as normal. Fail and they will cut you off."

One hour later, the brothers were standing on the corner of Harley Street, having parked their car in a neighbouring street. A taxi pulled up on the far side of the road and the man from the pub got out to join them.

He said, "Go and open the door, and I will walk down on my own."

The two brothers went to the front entrance of the building. The key worked. They went in the entrance lobby and held the door open, and the man walked past them. They went up the stairs and a key opened the door to the apartment. The search began. The brothers found a small amount of cash which they took. The man searched the desk, and looked through the address book and a notepad. There was nothing of significance in them. Nothing which would compromise the family. The search revealed nothing of interest elsewhere in the flat.

The man said, "We should leave separately. Please carry out the second part of the request from the family. Immediately would be good," and he stared pointedly at the brothers, then turned and left. The Nolan's continued searching and finding nothing more of interest, left a short time later.

Chapter four

Graves & Co was a bespoke tailoring business in the heart of Saville Row. It was a four story building with a shop frontage with workshops and storage facilities at the back and the floors above. Detective Inspector Joe Mozart and his companion Detective Sergeant Winston Stevens, entered the shop. Stevens was six feet two inches of power inherited from his paternal grandfather, who was part of the Windrush generation from Jamaica. He was built like a rugby forward and was Mozart's right hand man.

The assistant said, "Can I help you gentlemen."

Mozart flashed his warrant card and introduced himself and Stevens and said, "Yesterday a man was found unconscious and severely beaten, having been dumped in water. He is now in hospital, and may, hopefully, recover from his injuries. When he was found, he was dressed in a shirt and trousers, which although torn and damaged in the assault appear to have been bought from here because they bear your label. We do not yet know his name, but we wondered if you would have records of their purchase, so we might identify him and perhaps notify any relatives."

The assistant said, "Please wait I will fetch the manager."

When he arrived the Manager listened to the story again, and then said, "Can I look at the trousers." Ds Stevens produced them from the evidence bag he carried. The Manager examined the soiled and now wrinkled trousers, read the label on the inside and said, "Yes. They are definitely from here. This worsted material is one we stocked last year, and the label tells me they are bespoke and part of a suit made for a customer."

Mozart said, "Have you records that might give us a clue as to his identity."

"We don't normally reveal the identity of our customers to anyone, customer confidentiality you know," he said.

Mozart said, "I appreciate your reluctance, and in normal circumstances I would not ask. But he is severely injured, slipping in and out of consciousness, and we are keen to identify him so that we can at least tell his relatives where he is and what his situation is."

"Well under those circumstances, I am sure it would be alright," said the Manager. "Please follow me", and he took them to an office at the back of the shop, which held all the usual office paraphernalia, including a large filing cabinet. "We can tell from the label that they were purchased in September last year, and were part of a two piece suit. The material is of very good quality, top of the range. Now let me check." He then went through the files for September and said, "Ah, yes. Here we go. The suit was purchased by Mr. Mungo Ross-Harding."

Mozart said, "Have you got his address."

"Yes" said the Manager, "Flat 3b, 16 Harley Street. He comes from a very well to do family. I'm sorry to hear that he has been injured. He is something in the city you know."

Mozart said, "Thank you for your help. I am sure his relatives will be anxious to know of his predicament. By the way, how much would a suit like this cost."

The Manager smiled an enigmatic smile, knowing Mozart would never be able to afford one of his suits, and said,

"Four thousand pounds, or thereabouts. Every stitch is hand done, and we only have the finest of materials."

Mozart managed "Many thanks for your help, Mr?" "Dounne, with two n's and you're welcome."

Mozart and Stevens left the shop, returning to their car. Stevens said, "I thought he wasn't going to tell us who the man is. I thought we might have to get a warrant because of the Data Protection Act. We were lucky." Mozart said, "You win some, you lose some. Let's go to Harley Street."

Harley Street revealed that number sixteen was the offices of an eye surgeon, and Flat 3b was on the first floor. The door had an electronic lock and they couldn't get in. Mozart and Stevens went into the reception area of the Surgeons offices, and after introducing themselves to the receptionist, asked about Flat 3b. They were told that the whole of the building was owned by the Surgeon and his company, and that the flats, of which there were two on the first floor, and two on the second, were rented out to various tenants. 3b was rented by Ross-Harding, who was a single man living on his own. Mozart asked if there was a master key to the premises, which would let them into the flat, and the receptionist said, "We have, but I will have to get my boss to authorize that. He is with a patient at the moment, after which he has to go to the clinic, to carry out an operation. As soon as the client comes out, I will see if he has time to see you."

Mozart and Stevens waited, and after a short time, a lady came out of the consulting room and walked out of the building. "Hang on a minute" said the receptionist, and, with a swish of expensive hose encasing perfectly shaped legs, and a waft of expensive perfume, she disappeared through the leather padded consulting room door, which closed behind her with a whisper. A short time later, she appeared, held the door open and said, "Come in Gentlemen, Mr. Patel will see you. He hasn't got long though, he is operating soon."

Mozart shook hands with the surgeon, introduced Stevens, and related the story of Ross- Harding.

He said, "Miss Cole will look after you. I've told her to let you in. I must go."

Miss Cole let the two officers into flat 3b. It was a single mans' home. The furniture was modern, expensive, and functional. There was one bedroom, a bathroom with the usual offices installed, a large sitting room, with a modern settee, and expensive carpet on the floor. There was an antique desk, a Bang and Olafssen sound system, and the kitchen had all the latest gadgets. There was one real problem however, the place had been thoroughly turned over. Wardrobes were open and clothes thrown on the floor. Drawers had been left open. Pictures on the wall were askew, and even the bathroom cabinet had been searched. A real professional job. Miss Cole gasped. There had been no sign of a forced entry, but the place had been professionally searched. Mozart told Stevens to search the bedroom, whilst he looked through the scattered papers and an open diary on the desk. He found an address book, which had various names and addresses in it, including the names of Ross-Harding's parents. They lived at Highclere Hall, near Grantham in Lincolnshire. The address book revealed that Ross-Harding worked for a City Merchant Bank, and a certificate in a smashed frame showed that he had graduated from UCL with a first in Economics. A high flyer indeed.

After a thorough search of the flat, Mozart and Stevens locked the door again, and told Miss Cole that they would arrange for a forensic team to visit the house, but not let anyone into the premises until they had finished. Mozart took the address book and the diary with him. He gave Miss Cole his business card and said, "If anyone turns up to go into the flat, please ring me at once, day or night."

The officers then left to return to their squad office. As he entered his office the telephone was ringing. Mozart picked it up, said, "DI Mozart" and a voice said, "Mr Mozart, my name is Anderson. You are investigating a man named Ross-Harding. I and a colleague wish to speak to you urgently. Can we meet."

Mozart said, "Who are you, and why do you want to meet me."

The voice said, "Let me put it this way. We are colleagues, sort of. You have encroached onto an ongoing operation we have going, and we are very anxious to brief you on what you are getting into, and we ask for your complete discretion and cooperation."

Mozart was intrigued,more than intrigued. "I don't go meeting people I don't know, at the drop of a hat.

Especially as it could interfere with an ongoing investigation of mine."

The voice said, "That's exactly why we need to talk. It is not necessarily your investigation." "What's that supposed to mean," said Mozart.

"All will be revealed" said the voice, "We need to meet urgently. If you doubt my authenticity, please stand by the phone and shortly you will receive a call which will verify what I say."

Mozart sat at his desk, going through Ross-Harding's address book and diary, when the phone rang. He picked the receiver up, "DI Mozart" he said,

"Mr. Mozart. This is the Commissioner." "Yes Sir," "I want you to go to the Grenadier Public House, in Whitehall at one o'clock. A Mr. Brocklehurst will introduce himself to you. Please listen to what he has to say, cooperate fully with him, and then come and see me at CO."

This is getting stranger and more mysterious thought Mozart. Who are these people, what do they know about Ross-Harding. What have I got into. " DS Stevens" he shouted," we're going out, I'll explain on the way."

The two officers sat in the bar of the Grenadier. It was a typical London Pub, with a copper covered bar top and copper covered tables. It served good regular pub grub, and good beer. Each had a pint of bitter in front of them as they sat at a table to await events. When they were halfway through their drinks, a man approached. He was middle aged, medium build, wearing a dark blue suit with a fawn coloured raincoat, a plain non- descript man who would not stand out in a London crowd. He wore a thin brimmed trilby hat and carried an umbrella. He looked down on them, "Mr. Mozart. My name is Brocklehurst. I would like to talk to you, but not here. I presume your companion is Mr.Stevens. Finish your drinks and let us go for a walk. When we are outside, my colleague Mr. Anderson will join us. But before we go, there are some forms I wish you to sign."

He produced two pre-printed papers marked at the top OFFICIAL SECRETS ACT. "I want you both to read the contents, discreetly of course, and then sign them. Then bring them out to me."

Mozart said, "What's this all about."

Brocklehurst said, "All in good time, but only after you have signed your life away on those forms." He then left the pub. Mozart and Stevens looked at one another, "This is a bit over the top, how did he know who I was" Stevens exclaimed. "We better read what he's given us, sign it and find out what we have got into.

" If I can get phone calls from the Commissioner, then these guys have a lot of pull, and I for

one intend to see what's going on, and what tiger we have got by the tail," said Mozart. They both read the documents, signed and dated them, then went outside.

Brocklehurst was waiting outside, and with him was a man he introduced as Anderson, the man who had phoned him earlier.

"Shall we walk," smiled Brocklehurst, "But first, have you signed the documents, and can I have them." The documents were handed over and he checked that each was signed and dated. He then put them both in his inside pocket, and said, "Shall we go."

“Where to,” said Mozart, curiosity etched on his face and skepticism in his voice. He thought, where is this going, what have we got into. Why all the secrecy.

“It’s a short walk past the Houses of Parliament, you will see. We are going somewhere where we can talk without being overheard,” smiled Brocklehurst.

They walked on to a landmark building familiar to Mozart, but a building he had never previously entered. It was Millbank House, known throughout the world as MI5. They entered through a side door, off one of the side streets, and once inside had to surrender their mobile phones, undergo a thorough body search, including inspection of wallets and documents, before passing through an airlock entry, to be met on the other side by Brocklehurst and Anderson. “Follow me” said Brocklehurst, and they followed through a maze of corridors painted government grey, past numerous non - descript doors, some badly in need of painting, until they reached a door, which when opened revealed a small conference room. There were no windows, and the only communication appeared to be a conference telephone in the centre of a twelve seater table. There was a steaming coffee pot on a stand and cups on a side table and Brocklehurst offered coffee, which they gratefully accepted. Mozart looked around at what he saw as a bland functional room rather than decorous.

"Please sit" said Brocklehurst, I have to make a call and we will be joined by our Director." He then dialed a number and said, "They're here" The voice said, "I will join you in a minute".

A few minutes later the door opened, and in walked a man, smartly dressed in a dark suit, white shirt and maroon silk tie. He had a maroon handkerchief in his top pocket. Mozart assessed him as about forty five, with sharp features, blue piercing eyes, and dark smoothed down hair. He emanated energy and intelligence.

He said, "Let me introduce myself. My name is Peter Simpson. I am a director, in other words head of department, within our organization, which I am sure you know of as MI5. I presume you have signed the official secrets act, otherwise you would not be here." He looked at Brocklehurst who nodded his assent. "Let me explain why we wanted to see you, and what you have unwittingly got yourselves into by being involved in the assault on Mungo Ross-Harding."

"As you now know, Ross-Harding is in high powered banking and private finance in the City of London. What you may not know is that he comes from a family of landed gentry, his father was the director of a Merchant Bank in the City until he retired to the country, and is now established in the squirarchy of rural Lincolnshire. Mungo had a private education, is now in his late twenties and is single, although he has had various Chelsea set girlfriends. You know he has a flat in Harley Street, because you have been there according to our watchers, but what you don't know, yet, is that he is also a drug addict. He started going to the usual parties, where he was introduced to heroin, and it appears to have got a hold on him that he cannot shake. This has led to him being introduced through drug lines, further up the ladder to some very unsavory people. People who maim and are prepared to kill. They are major importers and suppliers of all kinds of drugs to various drug dealers in and around London and the home counties and we know them as The Family. Drugs would not normally be part of our remit, but the Nolan brothers, known as the Whitechapel Cartel, from whom Ross-Harding obtains his drugs, passed him higher up the chain to this crime family. They obviously spotted his potential and blackmailed him into laundering their ill gotten gains. Using him because of his unique position and knowledge of the worldwide banking and the investment system. Mungo is very well paid by his bank, which is just as well, because he has a very expensive drug habit. He was sucked into the periphery of their organization for just this purpose. We have someone looking into these financial dealings at the moment, but it is very complicated, and taking a long time to get to the bottom of what he has been doing and where the money is located. Again you will say, that is of no particular interest to MI5, it's more a matter for the Police. And you would be quite right. The family, by the way, is run by a father, George Armstrong, now in his sixties, and two sons, John and Graham, both in their late twenties, early thirties. They have of course, acolytes who work with them and who front their so called legitimate enterprises. This family supply drugs to dealers and the family sometimes get those lower down the scale to carry out their bidding, particularly the nasty stuff. The Whitehall Cartel has Ross-Harding as a client and they are supplied by the family. The Whitechapel cartel, is a fanciful name for two middle order criminals named John and James "Gunner" Nolan, who make a living supplying drugs which they get from The Family. Ross-Harding owes them a lot of money, which he hasn't paid, and as a result they have taken it upon themselves, without the knowledge of the family, to him beat up to enforce payment. Their unauthorized actions have really upset the family, because what the Whitechapel boys don't know is that Ross-Harding works for them and has a vast working knowledge of where their money is hidden. They obviously wanted to protect their boy and did not want him dealt with in this way, especially as there was a danger it might bring their activities to the notice of the Police. In their view the Whitechapel cartel's unauthorized actions spell danger to the family, especially if Ross-Harding talks. The family, are, on the surface a perfectly respectable family, very wealthy, and run what seem to be respectable businesses. They own several enterprises and their empire is growing. They own a plant hire company which supplies major road and building projects with heavy equipment, and as a sideline they do up and sell second hand plant in African countries at the end of its useful life in the UK. They have found a ready and profitable market especially in countries which have a trade embargo on them, like Zimbabwe. They also have contacts in Somalia . We suspect that they supplement the exports of plant with a supply of stolen JCB's , bulldozers, trucks, forklifts, and dumper trucks and other heavy equipment and information just in tells us that there is a yard somewhere in the Barking area, where these things are stored prior to shipment, and where some of the stolen trucks are broken down into component parts before shipping abroad. They also own a garage or two selling new and used cars and some of their vehicles get shipped abroad with the plant equipment, all at vast profit. Plus they have just started a private plane charter company running out of Manston Airport with two ten seater aircraft. In addition they own a small transport company, and are currently negotiating to buy a golf course in Kent. We know George Armstrong has a very large share portfolio which Ross-Harding takes care of in private banking, and they are getting to the stage where they do not really have to resort to crime to live a very comfortable lifestyle. But it appears that old habits are hard to break, and they would find it hard to step off the bandwagon at this time, as they now have the need for an awful lot of money to furnish another, far more dangerous and perhaps far more lucrative enterprise, which we will come to later. They live on a family farm in rural Kent, and George and his two sons, John and Graham, split their time between their legitimate enterprises and the not so legitimate. The most lucrative part of their business is the drug dealing. They are very particular about distancing themselves from the day to day running of their drug empire. They appear clean in all respects, for instance all their business interests are in other people's names, apparently unconnected with the family, but the truth is that the father is a long time London villain with several convictions for robbery and violence in his youth. However he is now a very successful criminal, untouched for years, and he has brought up his two sons in the same mold. Again you might think, what has this got to do with MI5, this seems more a National Crime Agency or Police matter, and it was up to this point. It's because of the NCA's inquiries that we know so much about the Armstrong family. However, they have started to diversify so the NCA brought it to us. The family have started to move toward the supply of arms, particularly to the criminal element, but more worryingly to terrorist organizations. The family have now made contact with several arms manufacturers. They have been rebuffed but they now know of two Russian Arms dealers who operate with the clandestine authority of their own government. The Armstrong's have travelled extensively throughout the Middle East to drum up business, and even made contact with rebel organizations in Somalia, in particular one very nasty individual in Mogadishu by the name of Mohammed Ubedi Hassan, who is not only the head of a pirate enclave, but is a full blown terrorist affiliated to middle eastern terrorist groups, and a so called friend of the President of his country, who for certain heavy payments allows Hassan and his organization to shelter and flourish in his country. By violence and intimidation Hassan helps to keep the President and his political party in power."

Mozart looks at his Sergeant, raised his eyebrows and puffed out his cheeks. What have we got into. We have a tiger by the tail, he thought, and it's a man eater.

Simpson saw Mozarts' expression, smiled a sardonic smile and said, "I thoroughly agree with your sentiments Mr

Mozart. Your expression says it all. You have touched on the periphery of a very nasty organization and the situation is likely to blow up into a major international inquiry, which appears to be well above your police remit at the moment. However, we have looked into the backgrounds of you and your Sergeant. You being a graduate entry to the Police, and having served in the Royal Marines and latterly in the Special Boat Service, and your Sergeant being an ex-para, you both would appear to have the right credentials to join us in a joint enterprise to bring these people, and especially the family, to justice. We will be joined shortly by a senior officer from the National Crime Agency, who will also join our enterprise, so please be patient, and he will bring us up to speed on what his organization know about this family and their criminal activities."

As the group sipped their coffee and waited, the telephone rang. Simpson answered it and after listening to the call, said, "The NCS agent is here and will be joining us." A short time later there was a tap on the door, and in walked a medium sized man, with dark hair, dressed in a dark blue suit and a conservative blue tie. Standard dress for working in London. He shook hands will all present and introduced himself as Agent Nick Braithwaite of the National Crime Agency, carefully assessing each man present as he shook hands with them.

Simpson said, "I have been bringing Mr Mozart and Mr Stevens up to speed, so they are now fully aware of what they are involved in. Both have signed the official secrets act, and I am confident that they are both on board. I believe that the way this is going, it is going to require a multi-agency effort to bring The Family to justice. They have milked the market on the drug scene, and have now moved on to be able to distance themselves from the drug dealing, leaving most of the dirty work to others in their organization. However, with Ross-Harding being beaten up, obviously the organization and the family behind it, are worried about their cash flow and the effect that he is having on their laundering operation. Their proposal to move into the supply of arms to terrorists and pirate groups, causes HM Government a great deal of concern. Because we know that the family have already made contact with illicit arms suppliers in Russia, it is imperative that we counter their efforts, and urgently so. We need at this stage experts in investigation, and that is where Messrs. Mozart and Stevens come in. They will lead the investigation, under the supervision of the Counter Terrorist Command, led by Commander John Russell. We also at this stage need the input of asset tracing trained officers, and none are better in the country at this time than officers of the City of London Police Fraud Squad, therefore the group will be joined by Detective Inspector Steve Easterbrook. Mr. Brocklehurst and Mr. Anderson of our organization will also be appointed to the group, with myself popping in from time to time. My job will be to facilitate things for the group. I can see a time when we will need surveillance, armed responses, and even code breaking, and I am in a position, with the approval of the Home Secretary to provide these additional extras should it be necessary.

Gentlemen, this operation has the approval of the Prime Minister, that's how seriously we are taking this threat. We have been granted the use of a government owned secure suite of offices in the City of London, with underground parking facilities, which is rare for the City, and this office is being set up as we speak by the Police facilities and IT departments and I propose that we all meet again at 1400hrs tomorrow and to hit the ground running at the new office."

He then passed around a printed card with the address, and telephone number of the new office. " It is obvious to me that the family are worried about Ross-Harding and it may well be that they see him as a weak link, and want him disposed of. I have arranged for him to be moved when his injuries allow but meantime he should be guarded by armed officers, and Mr. Mozart I wish you to arrange this with your Commissioner as soon as possible. Meantime, here is my card and it shows a number on it which I will answer day or night. This operation is highly secret, and I have a secure mobile phone for both you and Sergeant Stevens, which will be handed to you on the way out. There are two things I would suggest that need to be prioritized. Firstly, we need to move Ross-Harding to a safe place, and second, we need to know what the family were searching for at his flat. I'll leave that to you to sort out Mr. Mozart, but I would suggest sooner rather than later. When you leave here, you are instructed to go to see your Commissioner at CO. Don't forget."

Chapter five

Mozart and Stevens walked into New Scotland Yard and after the usual security checks were allowed onto the Commissioner's floor. They were kept waiting in the secretary's office for a short while until the telephone rang.

The secretary said, "Mr Mozart, you can go in first. DS Stevens please wait."

Mozart was shown into the presence, and stood before the Commissioner who invited him to sit.

"Mr. Mozart" he said, "I wanted to see you before allowing Ds Stevens in, because I have something to say to you which I think would be better said on a one to one basis." Mozart raised his eyebrows, with a look of concern on his face. The Commissioner continued, "I have been reading your file, to ensure that you are the right man to progress the inquiry you are currently on, and I believe that you have the right credentials. However, because this case is going to get really complicated involving other Government agencies, it needs someone of a higher rank to effect the liaison properly. I want a more senior officer overseeing the inquiry on behalf of the Met."

At this point, Mozart's disappointment momentarily showed on his face and he quickly adopted a neutral expression. He had had many disappointments in his life and this was another he would have to face.

The Commissioner smiled and said, "Cheer up Mr. Mozart, I am merely saying that with immediate effect you will be promoted to Detective Chief Inspector. My congratulations. However it may be a poisoned challis because from what I understand, this case is likely to escalate and have very serious and international repercussions. However, we will talk about that in a minute. " He then operated the internal telephone and said to his secretary, "Send in DS Stevens."

Stevens entered the room and stood at attention in front of the Commissioners desk. A puzzled expression on his face.

The Commissioner said, "Sergeant Stevens. I have just promoted Mr Mozart to Detective Chief Inspector, you may wish to congratulate him." Stevens looked at his boss, smiled and nodded, which was his way. The Commissioner went on, "As this case is going to involve other government agencies, and is likely to go international, I wanted someone of that rank in charge of the day to day running of the inquiry, and for him to be able to hold his own with the others involved. He is well due for promotion anyway. I am taking both him and you off divisional duties. You will became part of SO15 – Counter Terrorism Command, and whilst you both will have almost a free reign to pursue your inquiries, you will at all times keep Commander John Russell, head of SO15, in the loop and he will keep me up to speed and facilitate your needs. You will continue to work with Mr Mozart, and you have my assurance that I will be keeping a close eye on you and taking an interest in your future, especially when we know the result of your recent attempt at the promotion exams. Now," said the Commissioner, "I want to have Commander Russell join us, he is waiting outside, and then you can brief us on the full circumstances of the case, and what has been achieved so far. I want to hear your suggestions on how to proceed further".

At the Commissioners command Russell entered the room. The group sat around the small conference table, coffee was served and the briefing began.

When the briefing was over the Commissioner asked, "What is your immediate need."

Mozart said, "I understand that a suite of offices has been made available in the City of London. I believe it most important we detach ourselves from any of our normal buildings. I believe at this stage we urgently need to protect our only asset at the moment and that is Mungo Ross-Harding. He obviously has much more he can tell us, if we can get him to talk. He is very reluctant to even reveal his true identity, but he doesn't know we know who he is, and that his flat has been turned over. He doesn't know we believe he was regularly laundering money for the organization through contacts at his bank. The Family behind this will see him as a danger to their operation, and probably believe he has records hidden somewhere which could be vital both to the family and important evidence for us. It's a race now, as to who gets the records first. If they don't get them, then certainly Ross-Harding's life is in great danger. He had already had a taste of what real villains are capable of, and he must be very worried what they might do to him, if they get to him again. From here, I want to see him and talk further, then have him moved to a more secure location, although he still requires medical attention and may do for a while. I am sure our friends in MI5 have safe houses, or other facilities for this sort of thing, and could quickly arrange it. However I believe the matter so urgent he should be moved today. I also believe this case has the potential to involve firearms, and I want your authority for Ds Stevens and myself, together with any other officers co opted to the inquiry, to be armed at all times."

The Commissioner said, "Agreed. Commander please arrange that at once. Is there anything else?"

Mozart said, "I am sure there is. I need time to think about it. When I know what I need, I will deal direct with Commander Russell. Off the top of my head, we will need full office equipment, secure phones, secure computers, and a full staff, fully vetted, and non-descript vehicles with secure communication. It may be we will need input from the Foreign and Commonwealth Office and the Home Office, but I am sure sir that you can easily facilitate this, and of course we will need fully funded credit cards. I can see a need for an unlimited budget". Mozart looked directly at the Commissioner with non verbal query on his face.

The Commissioner smiled and said, "As this is a joint operation the finances are assured by HM Government and us. The equipment you require is being installed as we speak. Every one on the inquiry will have a secure mobile, you will have a mixture of Detectives,MI5 and MI6 operatives, and others with the skills you require, including access to SO11 and SO 15 for surveillance and manpower. Now I propose you just get on with it and good luck. Make sure you keep me posted!"

They were then ushered from the presence, taken to the basement where they were both issued with Glock 9mm handguns with shoulder holsters. They were given a list of contact numbers, and pre-set mobile phones.

Mozart looked at Stevens, "If you can't take a joke you shouldn't have joined." "Congratulations boss," said Stevens, "Although I'm not sure that congratulations is really the right word under the circumstances. "

Chapter six

Mozart and Stevens drove to the hospital. They parked in the car park, and went in through the main entrance. They took the lift to the fourth floor. As they approached Ross-Harding's room there was no sign of a uniformed officer at the door.

Mozart shouted, "There's something wrong."

They ran down the corridor and burst into the room, Stevens tripping on and falling over the inert body of the policeman lying on the floor. A large man, of brutal features, standing over six feet tall, dressed in a white coat stretched across his enormous frame stood next to Ross-Harding's bed with one hand on the drip tube and in the other he held a an empty hypodermic syringe.

"What are you doing" shouted Mozart.

The man said "I am a Doctor, and I am just giving the patient a pain killer."

Mozart shouted, "You're no doctor, you're wearing a white coat. All the doctors here wear scrubs, you're not, and you've got no stethoscope and no ID tag. What's he doing on the floor" pointing to the policeman.

The man dropped the hypodermic and whipped out an automatic pistol from his coat pocket. He pointed it at Mozart, who ducked. The shot went over his shoulder, and the bullet shattered the glass in the door, embedding itself in the wall opposite. Stevens, from the floor drew his gun in one fluid movement and double tapped the man, putting two in his chest. The man fell backwards over the bed, and the gun slid from his hand. He was dead, and bleeding out over the patient in the bed.

Ross-Harding started to writhe in the bed, jerking back and forth, reacting to the substance the man had introduced into the drip in his arm and the weight of his body.

Mozart snatched the drip needle from Ross-Harding's arm and shouted to Stevens, "Sound the alarm. "

A Medical Crash team ran into the room .

Mozart shouted, "We are the Police. That man", pointing to the dead man, "was putting something into the drip tube. I don't know what it is but it's obviously affecting him and it's probably deadly. Do something quick."

The Doctor shouted at the nurse behind him, "Saline, now, we need to get another drip into him." He punched the crash team emergency button and checked the dead man's body for a pulse then pushed him to the floor, as members of the crash team arrived.

Stevens checked the policeman on the floor. He was unconscious and bleeding from a scalp wound, but he could feel a pulse. The crash team held Ross-Harding down as he jerked and writhed, mouthing incoherently. Mozart helped push him down on to the bed to hold him still while the doctor attempted to get another drip into his arm.

Mozart put his head close to Ross-Harding's, "Wake up man, wake up. Don't go to sleep." Ross-Harding began to mutter incoherently but Mozart could just identitfy the words, **"KEY, DESK**", before he lapsed into unconsciousness.

This allowed the doctor to get a new drip into his patient, and after a while he calmed down, but his breathing was now shallow and laboured, and he stopped breathing.

The Doctor in Charge of the Crash Team shouted, "Defibrillator. Quick." The machine was produced, the paddles placed on his chest. The Doctor shouted "Clear" at which Ross-Harding jerked. The nurse held a stethoscope to his chest, "Nothing" she shouted. The Doctor readjusted the paddles, "Clear" he shouted, and again Ross-Harding's body jerked to the charge. The nurse listened again. "We have a beat, faint but getting stronger." The Doctor shouted, "Let's get him out of here. Intensive Care."

They shoved the bodies on the floor to one side and the entire crash team moved the bed, Ross-Harding and drip stand out of the room.

Mozart looked at Stevens, "Are you okay Win," he said.

"Yes boss.

"You go with the crash team and stay with him. I will sort this lot out," said Mozart.

Stevens followed the crash team. Mozart knelt over the inert policeman, who was now regaining consciousness. He grabbed a sterile pad and held it over his head wound.

He then helped him to his feet and sat him in the chair in one corner of the room.

"Are you alright" said Mozart.

The Policeman said, "I've felt better. Who are you."

Mozart said, "Detective Chief Inspector Mozart, SO15. What's your name officer." He said, "PC Noel Griggs. " Mozart said, "Can you tell me what happened."

"I was standing outside the room. I had been told to check everything and everyone coming into the room. This bloke, that's him on the floor, said he was a Doctor and he wanted to check on the patient. I started to get on the radio to check him out and I guess he hit me. That's the last I remember until now. Is he dead"

Mozart said, " Yes, my sergeant shot him. You are lucky. He had a gun. Stay there, I will call this in."

Mozart called Commander Russell at SO15 and briefed him.

"Stay there, I will send a team," he instructed.

Mozart went through the pockets of the dead man, and found a wallet. His driving license showed him to be

James Nolan. A check with the PNC showed him to be a known career criminal born and bred in the east end of London, with a track record of robbery with violence, possession of firearms, and intelligence indicated he was one of the Nolan brother's known as the Whitechapel Cartel. He was believed to have been involved in many of the major armed robberies in the Capitol, lorry hijacks, and although never proved. A thoroughly nasty, professional and longtime criminal, with the nickname – Jimmy the Gunner, a nickname he earned because of his use of firearms. He was a feared figure around the east end.

The gun he used was a 9mm Beretta, and it appeared the serial numbers had been obliterated. This was placed in an evidence bag. The syringe, which Mozart recovered from the floor, had residue in it and Mozart placed this in another evidence bag.

Mozart took PC Griggs out of the room and sat him in a chair in the corridor. He then got a nurse to dress his wound. "Are you able to hold the fort here, while I go and see if Ross-Harding is okay, "asked Mozart. PC Griggs said, "I'll manage."

Mozart entered the room in intensive care where Ross-Harding was being attended to. The medical team were still working on him and Ross-Harding was still unconscious, but breathing. The doctor in charge said, "Well he is as stable as we can make him at the moment, and he is still alive, just. What do you think was put into him."

"Well " responded Mozart, "I have the syringe here, and it will need to be tested, but I would suspect, knowing the background of the dead man, that he put a large dose of Heroin into him, intending to kill him, but we will have to test the syringe to see exactly what he used." "We have lab facilities here," said the doctor, "we need to know what was used so we can try and counter it. Could we have a sample from the syringe." Mozart said, "Well the syringe is now evidence, but I could come and give your lab access to the remains for testing." Mozart was then taken to the hospital laboratory by the doctor, and handling the syringe carefully in its bag, managed to squeeze out small drops of its content.

The doctor said, “We will get this tested as soon as possible and let you know.” Mozart handed the doctor his card and said, “Please call me when you have a result.”

He then returned to the room which had housed Ross-Harding, to find that a full forensic and firearms team had arrived.

He introduced himself and then fully briefed them, “I’ll leave you to it. Let me know the result. Who’s in charge of the armed response team”.

A Sergeant stepped forward. “Come with me,” said Mozart and then took the team to Intensive care. “I want an armed guard on this patient, 24/7 from now on. At least two officers. No access unless proved ID, until further orders. Can you arrange that Sergeant.” “Yes sir”, said the Sergeant.

“I also want PC Griggs taken home and his station told what has happened. Can you do that please? “Yes Sir” he responded.

Chapter Seven

Mozart and Stevens went from the hospital to Bethnal Green Police Station, straight to the offices of the local intelligence officer, PC Paul Pascale.

Mozart introduced himself and said, "I would like to know if you recognize this man. " He then showed the picture of the dead man shot at the hospital, which he had taken on his mobile phone."

PC Pascale said, "That's James Nolan, known as Gunner. He was a small time villain, but we know that he has come up in the world since he got into the supply of drugs. He and his brother John run what has become known as the Whitechapel Cartel. They don't work, but they run expensive motors, and they have premises that we know about in Barking. Our CID are working on them, and have quite a lot of information on them, but so far have not had enough to arrest them. They are both nasty bits of work, and they terrorize the neighbourhood. Even the local villains, give them a wide berth. They are believed to walk around tooled up, and several of our locals have ended up in hospital after a visit from the brother's, but nobody talks."

Mozart said, "Well Gunner is no more. My sergeant here shot him dead a little while ago. He was trying to murder a man in hospital and we caught him at it. He shot at us, and my Sergeant shot back. His aim was better."

Pc Pascale said, " That's good news but it won't please our CID boss. He and his team have been working on the Nolan's for a while now, and he sees them as his personal project, but despite apparently working on them for some time, they seem to have got nowhere. They certainly haven't managed to make an arrest yet despite all the information I have passed to them. They must be slippery buggers."

Mozart said, "Who's the CID boss here." Pascale said, "Detective Superintendent McMillain. He's a hard nosed bastard, if you'll pardon my French. He won't like it, you muscling in on his patch." Mozart said, "Why do you think the local CID haven't managed to sort the Nolan's out?"

Pascale gave Mozart a blank stare and shrugged his shoulders. "As I said, our Detective Superintendent won't like you muscling in on him. Be careful what you say to our CID boss."

Mozart looked hard at Pc Pascale, who just raised his eyebrows and meaningfully shrugged his shoulders." Mozart said, "We'll see about that."

They then left Pascale's office. Mozart said to DS Stevens, in a whispered aside, "There is a strong rumour that McMillain and some of his staff might be bent and on the take. So keep your eyes and ears open when we get up there. The going could be rough. I have met the man a couple of times. He is not a nice person, but keep that to yourself at present. Let's see what happens."

They then went upstairs to the CID Department, and Mozart asked for Detective Superintendent McMillain. He was pointed to his office, he knocked and went in without the usual invitation leaving Stevens in the outer office.

The man sitting behind the desk glowered at Mozart, "Mozart, what the hell are you doing in my office, " he growled in an offensive manner, annoyance showing on his face.

Mozart said, "I am here because this morning James Nolan was shot dead in the local hospital whilst trying to murder a patient. My Sergeant shot him after he shot at us. I am dealing with it, and I want to go and arrest his brother and search their premises including any business premises they have. It's your patch so I would like a team of your officers to accompany me and want to take a firearms team with me when I do so."

"You do, do you," said McMillain. "Well let me tell you, that any nicking of the Nolan's is down to me and my blokes. I will do it. They are mine. I've been working on them and no one's going to nick them but me."

Mozart said determinedly, "Sir, I believe they badly beat up a man who owes them for drugs they supplied to him, and I was called to deal with that. However, it appears that the case has wider implications, which is why I am here."

"Well, you're not going to nick them Mozart. The Nolan's are mine. I don't give a shit who you are. I'm taking over. You're on my patch now, so step aside."

Mozart said, "I came here for your cooperation, not to argue with you sir. As I said this goes much higher than just the Nolan's. I would like your cooperation."

"Well you're not going to get it. Anything to do with the Nolan's is mine and mine alone, I have an ongoing operation on them and I'm not going to tolerate anyone coming in from another nick and spoil my case. Leave my office. I have work to do."

Mozart left McMillain's office. He was obviously not getting anywhere with McMillain, and certainly no cooperation. Outside in the main office he made a telephone call to Commander John Russell SO15, who being a suspicious old style detective said, "Look at his office. Is he on the phone."

Mozart said, "I can see him through the glass, he looks worried, and he's got a mobile in his hand."

Russell said, "He may be on the take and trying to warn them off. Get in there and stop him, and tell him to wait for a phone call from me."

Mozart called Stevens over and they went uninvited back into McMillain's office. When he saw the two officers he stopped dialing and said, " I thought I told you to get out. I'm busy."

Two things then happened. The office phone rang. McMillain answered it, ignoring Mozart. He started to look worried. He kept saying "Yes sir. Of course sir. Right away sir." He looked at Mozart with a startled expression on his face, especially when through the door of the main CID office burst local district Commander Bertram Whalley in full uniform. A large bull of a man with a commanding presence.

He walked straight into McMIllain's office, ignoring Mozart and Stevens and said to McMillain, "Give me your mobile." McMillain dropped his phone on the floor and as he bent down to retrieve it, he clumsily attempted to slip another phone from his pocket, which he handed to Whalley. He had tried to switch phones.

Whalley said, "Give me both phones."

McMillain said, "That's my private phone. I use that for private calls."

Whalley said, "Who were you phoning just now." He then opened the phone and said, "Whose number is this,"pointing to the number shown on the screen.

McMillain said, "A friend."

"Which friend," said Whalley. "Just a friend" said McMillain.

Whalley turned to Mozart and said, "Has he been cooperating with you Mr Mozart."

Mozart said, "Well not really. I came here to ask for local help to search the premises of a man we shot at the hospital this morning, who was trying to murder a patient. He turns out to be James Nolan known as "Gunner" who according to your intelligence officer, is one of the Nolan brothers known as the Whitechapel Cartel, who are local drug dealers, and who have apparently been operating freely on your patch. But they seem to bear a charmed life. Everyone knows about them, but nothing has been done. "He," pointing to McMillain, "has been nothing but obstructive since I got here. I wanted help from him and his team, to find and arrest the other brother , John Nolan and to search his home and business premises and he has refused to help. He threw me out of his office."

Whalley said, "I have been wondering for some time why the Nolan's have been untouched by my local CID. Sit down gentlemen. We will wait for reinforcements."

McMillain sat down at his desk. He was pale, and sweating and his hands started to tremble. He was not a happy man. Conversations were buzzing in the outer office, as the CID officers present there sat at their desks obviously curious as to what was taking place in their boss's office. Whalley went to the office door, opened it and commanded all the staff to hand their mobile phones to Sergeant Stevens. He instructed Stevens to look into their clothing lockers and desks and to search each officer, and to seize any additional mobile phones he found. He found three pay as you go phones, and handed them to Commander Whalley. Whalley switched them on and found that all three had some identical numbers on them to those shown on McMillain's phone and he showed them to Mozart without saying anything. The officers present sat, waiting, in worried silence.

A short time later a uniformed Inspector from the Met Firearms Team walked through the door with ten men. At Whalley's orders he stationed the men around the room. Then Whalley announced that no one was to leave the CID office, The presence of the firearms team produced an even more worried silence.

A short time later the door opened again and in walked another man in plain clothes, followed by a team of ten plain clothed officers. The man obviously in charge of this group joined Commander Whalley and the others in McMillain's office.

He said, "I am Detective Chief Superintendent Alfred Beare, Directorate of Professional Standards Office at the Yard. You have a problem I understand.

Whalley said, "Please have two of your men sit in Mr McMillain's office with him, whilst I brief you with Mr Mozart here" indicating Mozart by a nod of his head.

Whalley then took both officers to his own office and said, "Mr Mozart is now a DCI. He was until recently one of the officers under my district command. He has now been attached to SO15 on a very special project which has governmental implications. He is not at liberty to disclose any details, but he recently had dealings with a man who had been viciously assaulted and left tied up and unconscious at Barking Creek. He has now established the identity of this man. It appears the man who was beaten up owed money to the Nolan Brothers who are known round here as the Whitehall Cartel. Whilst in hospital James Nolan, known as Gunner, made an attempt to kill him. However he is still alive. Then he shot at Mr Mozart. Fortunately he missed. Nolan was shot dead by Detective Sergeant Stevens , who is Mr Mozart's sergeant, and the two of them have come here, asking the cooperation of the local CID to arrest the surviving brother and to search their houses and business premises, but all they got was obstructive behavior from our local Detective

Superintendent. He was stopped by these officers and me from making a telephone call on a pay as you go mobile phone to this number," and he showed McMillain's mobile phone display," and when I asked him to hand it over, he tried to palm me off with his official phone. We now know that three other pay as you go phones have been found in the CID office which show some of the numbers we found on McMillain's phone, including this number, and of course there may be more similar phones with some of the staff who are off duty, which raises my suspicions about McMillain and his staff. The Nolan's have had a good run in this district. They are well known drug dealers and although we are supposed to be investigating them, they always seem to be one jump ahead. I have my suspicions that McMillain is bent as are some of his staff. I believe this is a corrupt unit, and we need to have a clear out, but what is more important, Mr Mozart here has good reason to arrest John Nolan and search their premises in relation to the GBH and attempted murder of the man in hospital. John doesn't know his brother is dead yet and they need to get to him fast before does know. You know the situation now Mr. Beare. I want the whole CID office locked down, I want my suspicions confirmed and with a bit more work I think you will find those on McMillain's staff I suspect are on the take, and I want them all held incommunicado to give Mr Mozart a chance to complete his inquiries and arrest John Nolan. Will you now take over here, arrest where necessary, it's up to you. But don't let any of them get to a phone until I give the word. Clear?"

Beare said, "Crystal. Leave it to me. Me, and my team will sort it."

The firearms team were called from the CID office, to join Mozart and Stevens downstairs. This left Chief Superintendent Beare and his staff to hold the CID staff in their offices.

In the Commander's office, Mozart, Stevens and the Inspector in charge of the firearms unit, planned a search and arrest operation for John Nolan, and then left with hastily arranged search warrants for their houses, and business premises.

The front door of John Nolan's house crashed in at the first blow. The Firearms team, with Inspector Steve

Williams leading rushed into the house shouting, "Police. Stay where you are."

A woman appeared at the head of the stairs and started screaming. A man came out of a downstairs room, shouting "What's going on. This is my house, get out." He was pinned against the wall by two burly officers.

Mozart walked in with DS Stevens, he said, "Are you John Nolan." "What of it" said the man. Mozart said," I am arresting you for causing grievous bodily harm to Mungo Ross-Harding, and for his attempted murder at the hospital." He then cautioned him.

Nolan said, "Who. I don't know a Ross-Harding. What do you mean, attempted murder." Mozart said, "Your brother James tried to murder this man in hospital by injecting him with what we suspect is heroin. He was stopped, but he drew a gun and tried to shoot me. He was shot and killed."

"What" said Nolan, "Me brother was killed."

Mozart said, "That's right, and there is evidence which leads us to believe that you were involved." We are going to search your house, your cars , and your brother's house and cars, and your business premises in Barking. You will be coming with us."

The house was then searched by the firearms team £27,000 in cash was found in the main bedroom. Mozart arranged for a forensic team to carry out a more detailed search of the premises. Nolan in handcuffs was led away in a Police car, and two officers stayed at the house. Nolan's mobile phone was seized, and a pay as you go phone was found. When activated this showed calls made over the last week to a number familiar to Mozart. It was the number of the pay as you go phone owned by Detective Superintendent McMillain. Mozart relayed this information to Commander Whalley.

The team crashed through the front door of James Nolan's house. It was a similar scene. A woman screamed hysterical abuse at them, but started sobbing when told that her husband had been killed whilst trying to carry out a murder in a hospital. The team searched the house, and found £30,000 in cash in a box in a kitchen cupboard. The cash was seized. A pay phone was found and handed to Mozart. When it was activated, it showed contact in the last few days with a number now familiar to him. He made Commander Whalley aware of this find.

The team went to the business premises owned by the Nolan Brothers, in Ripple Road, Barking. It stood alone in a street which had demolition sites along it, and further along the road were car breakers yards and scrap yards. It was a dead end, and isolated. Mozart had the keys, and opened the street door. An alarm buzzed on the wall, and a short time later the burglar alarm activated, sending a strident clamouring klaxon sound both inside and outside the property. There was no one local to take notice. A search began. There was a ground floor office, and two desks, both of which had to be forced. There was a safe, and the safe key was on the bundle in Mozart's hand. He opened the safe and on an inside drawer was a cash box, which contained £45,000 in cash and a ledger. The ledger showed a number of names and initials, with amounts of cash shown against each name. One interesting entry was a series of amounts and date, marked RH. The figures totalled over a 4 month period to £12,000. This was obviously what Ross-Harding owed the Nolan's for his drug supply. On another page with the initial M, there were entries over the period of a year in sums between £1000 and £5000, totaling £43000, and there were similar entries, but for smaller amounts, made on the same dates with other initials against the entries.

In the main part of the safe Mozart found a Biretta 9mm pistol with a full clip, and some spare 9mm ammunition. The number on the gun had been filed off. Nothing was found of other interest, until they found the house had a cellar.

Mozart and Stevens entered the cellar. The walls were painted white over unplastered brick. The floor was plain cement. There were no windows and the door was a thick plain wooden one, with a substantial lock. There was a single light in the centre of the ceiling, and an anglepoise lamp on a waist high cupboard against one wall. Under the centre light was a single wooden chair, and there were traces of blood, and water stains on the chair and the floor around it. In one corner, there was a length of rope. Mozart looked at the rope. It appeared identical to the rope he had recovered at Barking Creek, which had been used to tie up Ross- Harding. Also on the floor around the chair were lengths of rubber hose, which had obviously been cut from a length of hose found in one corner. This was a forensic treasure trove. In one corner of the cellar they found two loose floorboards, under which were several large packets of white powder. These were seized as evidence. Ds Stevens took many pictures on his mobile phone and arranged for a forensic team to come to the premises.

Mozart heard a commotion at the front door. One of the Uniformed Officers was talking to two men in security uniforms. They had responded to the alarm. They managed, after contacting their head office, to turn the alarm off. The team were grateful for the silence.

Mozart arranged for John Nolan to be transferred to Paddington Green Police Station, which was the Metropolitan Police Station which specialized in holding terrorist suspects. It had a specialist custody team and a high security cell complex. Mozart telephoned Commander Russell at SO15, and related the results of the arrest and searches.

"I will arrange to have Nolan questioned by my specialized officers, meantime tell the forensic teams to do a thorough job and to prioritize a report to me at the yard.

Use my name, that should get them moving, " said Russell. "Well done, keep up the good work."

Mozart said, "I am sending DS Stevens home and I will go home too. It's been a long day. First thing in the morning, I will check in at the hospital to see that Ross-Harding is alright and then come to the office."

Chapter Eight

The following morning Mozart was picked up at home by DS Stevens and they went to the hospital. Ross-Harding was in a coma but still alive, and two officers from SO19 were present and alert. There had been no further problems after James Nolan had been shot.

Mozart and Stevens left the hospital, and on the way to the office Mozart said, "I've an idea, yesterday when we searched Ross-Harding's flat we found his diary and an address book. There's nothing apparently incriminating in either, but when I was holding him down, I heard him say "**key, desk**". We searched his desk at home, but found nothing significant. We know that he worked in the Private Banking department of The T G Grindley Corporation Bank, in the City. He must have a desk or locker there, and he might have been trying to tell me that we would find something there. It's likely we are a looking for a key, which has got some significance to the case. Let's go to his work place."

The offices of T G Grindley Corporation Bank was in Bishopsgate, in the city. Mozart and Stevens were shown up to the 17th floor, which housed the private banking department. The head of private banking was Paul Lanscombe. They were taken to an opulent private room.

Mozart introduced them both to Mr Lanscombe. "I believe one of your staff in the Private Banking Sector of this bank is Mungo Ross-Harding. He is currently in hospital, having been beaten up. He is unconscious at the moment."

Lanscombe said, "I wondered why he hadn't come to work for the last two day. He has not answered either his home phone or his mobile, and we were really worried about him."

"Well, we don't know at this time what is going on, but we do know that today an attempt has been made on his life, and his life is in danger. Whilst he was at the hospital he was able to say just two words," key and desk". We have been to his home, which has been burgled, and searched, but there is no key in his desk there. So we don't know if the burglars were searching for the key. We would like to look at his desk here, to see if we can find the key he was referring to."

"Under the circumstances, of course" said Lanscombe. "He has a private office in the corner there. As we deal with private clients, all our staff have their own offices where we can remain completely confidential. We are a very small department you know, with a small but very exclusive client portfolio . Of course our clients are all very wealthy and rely on us to invest their wealth for safety, security and of course to increase their assets. What we do is highly confidential, and that is the watchword of our department. Complete trust and complete client confidentiality. You understand of course?"

Mozart said, "We are this stage are only looking for a key. Not details of your clients. Could we look at his desk."

"Sure" said Lanscombe. He led them to Ross-Hardings office. It was well furnished with solid furniture, leather armchairs, original paintings on the wall, well decorated with a coffee table in one corner with decanters and a selection of spirits, and an antique leather topped desk. There was also a tall antique carved locker in one corner and an antique umbrella stand, which held several umbrellas showing the bank's logo. The whole area exuded wealth and taste. "Our clients are used to the best" said Lanscombe when he saw the raised eyebrows. The desk was locked. The locker was not.

Mozart said, "Is there a key."

Lanscombe said, "I don't think so. The only key would be with Ross-Harding."

"May we look" said Mozart.

"Of course, anything to help."

Mozart looked into the unlocked locker, it was a valuable antique. The locker contained a raincoat, but a search of the pockets found nothing. There was a small metal box on a shelf inside, but this contained small change and some keys. None of which fitted the desk, and they did not look to be of any real significance.

Mozart said, "We need to look in the desk drawers. It will mean forcing them I'm afraid."

Lanscombe said, "This is most unusual."

"Well" said Mozart, "We are talking about a very serious assault upon your colleague, who is in hospital and we don't know whether he will live or not. We could get a warrant, but that would waste time, and we are anxious to get to the bottom of the matter."

Lanscome nodded his agreement. Mozart nodded his head to Stevens, who produced a substantial clasp knife from his pocket, and soon the drawers were open for inspection. None of the drawers produced anything of note, certainly not a key.

"That's strange, " said Mozart, "he said, Key and Desk to me. We must have missed something." They looked again, but this time pulled the drawers out fully. The bottom drawer snagged as he pulled it. Taped under the bottom drawer in the desk was a key, with a round tag bearing the number 46.

"This must be the key he told me about" said Mozart, "We will take this with us."

Lanscombe said, "I don't know why it was there, but it's certainly not one of ours. Take it."

"Mr Lanscombe" said Mozart, "We are only just at the start of our inquiries. We don't yet know where this is going, but Ross-Harding has been beaten very badly, and a second attempt made on his life. This key must have some serious significance. What I have told you so far is of a highly confidential nature. Could we rely on your complete discretion. "

Lanscombe said, "Certainly."

"It may well be that we will want access to his client list at some time in the future, but I want you to also keep that to yourself."

Lanscombe said, "You can rely on me, but if you want access to his client list, it will require a court order. Confidentiality is, and always will be our watchword. It is our ethos."

"Rest assured, that if we want that access we will get a court order. Meantime, please keep what I have told you to yourself. We don't know whether he will live or die, and we haven't told his relatives yet. But thank you for your cooperation."

Outside the bank Stevens said, "I didn't realize banks had private clients. It's a different world."

Mozart responded "Well it's outside our pay grade that's for sure. Now this key. Let's try my hunch."

They went to the Liverpool Street Railway Station left luggage facility, it being the nearest locker facility. They saw the man in charge, showed him the key with the tag 46 and said, "Is this one of yours." "It looks like it," said the man. He then took them to the bank of lockers. The key fitted No.46. Inside was a notebook. It contained what looked to be coded information. Letters, figures and sets of numbers. Indecipherable to Mozart and Stevens.

It also contained small caches of white powder in small plastic pouches, and a hypodermic syringe still in its packaging. They took all the items and placed them in evidence bags.

On his way to the office Mozart received a telephone call. It was the doctor from the hospital which housed Ross-Harding.

He said, "We have had the contents of the drip and the hypodermic analyzed by our lab. It was pure Heroin. Had he had enough of the stuff, it would certainly have killed him. As it is, he is now in a coma, and because his vital signs give us great cause for concern, we will keep him in a coma. He may still die, only time will tell. He has not yet regained consciousness."

"We will keep an armed guard on him until further notice. Thank you for letting me know Doctor. Please, if there is any change, contact me. Meantime I will have his relatives informed. Thank you again doctor," said Mozart.

Mozart walked into his new offices situated off London Wall in the heart of the City of London. The front and back entrances were guarded by officers of the Ministry of

Defence Police, and they carried hidden loaded weapons, with access to more firepower in secure lockers. The building was guarded 24/7 with a Sergeant in charge on each shift. They looked as if they could handle trouble if the need arose. They used a machine to scan their faces followed by fingerprints, and then issued Mozart and Stevens with passes. An officer then conducted them to the fourth floor, where they were shown into a conference room. Anderson, Brocklehurst and Simpson the MI5 officers they had met the previous day, set down their coffee cups and shook hands with the two police officers officers. As they were doing so, the door opened again, and in walked NCA Agent Nick Braithwaite. Further introductions were made.

Commander John Russell arrived. He said, "Relax gentlemen. At 1400hrs others of the team will arrive and we will start the briefing. Meantime Mr Mozart, you will be sharing a side office on this floor with Mr Stevens. I.T. is already installed. It is the familiar Police system. The offices are all fitted with a secure telephone system. Encrypted mobile telephones will be issued to all seconded staff, and each phone has all of our numbers pre-installed on speed dial, so we can communicate with one another. A fleet of special vehicles will be arriving, fully equipped with secure communication, and there will be enough body sets to ensure continued communication even when leaving your vehicles. SO11 will provide surveillance teams, backed up by operatives from MI5, who will also provide telephone taps, bugging devices and any other necessary equipment. It is urgent we get the whole operation up and running immediately, time is short, if our information is correct, and Mr Simpson and I will tell you more at 2p.m. Meantime familiarize yourself with your surroundings, and make yourselves at home. In here for two."

Just before 1400hrs the conference room was full, Mozart and Stevens knew some of those present, but others he would have to get to know. At two on the dot, Peter Simpson, John Russell and Nick Braithwaite entered the room, and sat at the head of the table. A high powered triumvirate of national security guardians.

Peter Simpson took the chair, "Be seated gentlemen" he said. "Before you is a numbered folder, which must not leave this room. Inside that folder, the first page or two relates to the Official Secrets Act. If you have not already done so, I would ask that you sign this document now, because what we have to tell you is top secret, and if we are to achieve a result, then it will require inter-departmental cooperation on a scale not seen before in this country, and it will require some very detailed, dedicated and painstaking investigation, with all of us working as one team, towards one goal. The goal is the bringing to justice of one of the most prolific, and now one of the most deadly criminal organizations this country has managed to produce, so much so, that they have moved from small time to the big time. They now have semi legitimate businesses, which give them international contacts, most of them very unsavory, and they are making an awful lot of money. I'm talking millions. It is suspected at this time, that they have got to the top by violence, intimidation, and murder, although this is unproven at present. There are several missing persons among the criminal and drug fraternity which we believe is down to them, but nothing so far has been discovered that would lead to a conviction. No one, so far, has talked against them and those that might have talked have disappeared. They have managed to distance themselves from general drug dealings, and even the large scale importations they are suspected of organizing, they manage through intermediaries. So far they have been untouchable, but we have a breakthrough. Mungo Ross-Harding, a private banker was beaten up, we suspect because he has been employed by them for money laundering purposes. He is a drug user himself, and was being supplied by the Nolan brothers, who call themselves the Whitechapel Cartel. He owed money to the Nolan's and they took it upon themselves to punish him, putting him in hospital. The following day one of the Nolan Brothers went to the hospital and made an attempt on Ross-Harding's life, we suspect at the behest of the Armstrong family. DCI Mozart and DS Stevens interrupted him and shots were fired. James Nolan is dead, and Ross-Harding is now under armed guard but in a coma. We suspect that the Armstrong's ordered the Nolan's to kill Ross-Harding because they saw him as a danger to their anonymity. We intend to move Ross-Harding to a private clinic under an assumed name and place an armed guard on him. Hopefully he will recover enough to provide us with a guide to the Armstrong's assets. The attempt on his life shows us the Armstrong's are willing to write him off to protect themselves, despite Ross –Harding having knowledge and control of a large swathe of their assets."

After a short pause and a quick sip of his drink, Simpson continued, "We have here representatives from SO15, SO11, SO19 from the Met Police. The National Crime Agency, MI5 – my own organization, and GCHQ. We also have present a representative from our sister organization MI6, Mike Hornsby," indicating a man sitting at the far end of the table, who raised his hand in greeting. This raised a few eyebrows around the table. "We are here to brief you on what has transpired thus far, but first I want everyone at this table to introduce themselves. I will start." The introductions went clockwise round the table. "Now you can put the faces to the organizations, and can guess their purpose. Agent Nick Braithwaite will open the briefing."

Braithwaite stood and said, "Lady and gentlemen. For some time the NCA have been making inquiries about a drug group in the east end of London, which is known as the Whitechapel Cartel. A grandiose name for a bunch of east end villains, who have set up a supply chain across southern England using the usual methods of county lines. The Whitechapel cartel is run by two brothers, both well known thugs, who have done their apprenticeship starting with minor crime and working upward. John and James "Gunner" Nolan, are both the organizers and the muscle behind their so called cartel. In fact when we hear from DCI Mozart we will hear that James Nolan was shot dead yesterday at a hospital here in this city. Their drug operation has grown over the years and has attracted the attention of the NCA, but of course we are more interested in going after the bigger fish. Those big fish are a family called Armstrong, living on a large estate in Kent, near Maidstone. They have the international drug connections with Amsterdam, Afghanistan and even Columbia. They are now very wealthy and own several supposedly legitimate businesses, including a transport company, a heavy plant hire company and two private jet aircraft which they hire out, based at Manston airport. George Armstrong is the head of the family, born in the East End, and then known as "Custer" although no one has had the nerve to call him that for some time. He is now in his sixties, and did his apprenticeship as a criminal in his early years. His last conviction was for armed robbery many years ago, when he was sentenced to five years imprisonment. He hasn't appeared on our radar since, except to say we have information that he has moved into big time drug importation. He regularly goes abroad, mostly in his own jet to meet with the representatives of these various cartels. He is the source of supply to the Whitechapel Cartel and many others in the south, and east of England and continues to expand. He is now an apparently wealthy man, with the business interests I have outlined. He has a wife, Sharon, of a similar age, who also came from the East End, and is certainly aware of her husband's activities. They have two sons, the eldest is John Armstrong, known as Little John, and his brother Graham, known as Bull. Both are in their thirties. They are both married, with small children, and live in cottages on the estate, and they are both heavily involved in the family business interests. John runs the transport company. Graham runs the private jet hire, and the heavy machinery hire company, hiring out cranes, diggers, JCB's etc. We have found out they have employed the services of a Private Banker, Mungo Ross-Harding, to take care of their cash. He is also a drug user, and with some persuasion and threats, he has taken on the duties of their personal banker, and has now moved on to take on laundering their cash from the drug importations. We have reason to believe that recently the family have discovered that Ross-Harding has been syphoning off cash into his own coffers. Ross-Harding has been getting his drug supply from the Nolan Brothers, who in turn get theirs from the Armstrong's. Ross-Harding owes the Nolan's money and they decided to teach him a lesson, putting him in hospital. What they didn't know was that Ross-Harding was the Armstrong's banker, and knew a great deal about their illicit and illegal financial dealings. When the Armstrong family found out about the Nolan's punishing Ross-Harding they were less than pleased. They see that as a danger to their organization, and were prepared to write Ross-Harding off, rather than allow him to reveal what he knows to the Police. We believe the Armstrong's told the Nolan's to complete the job and do away with Ross-Harding. I will let DCI Mozart brief you on this part of the operation. To continue, we have been watching Ross-Harding's flat and carrying out a surveillance operation on him, and we have seen the Nolan Brothers visit Ross-Harding's flat, and we now know they searched it. Again I will leave DCI Mozart to tell you why. However, we have also learned from our source that the Armstrong family are not content with making large amounts of money from their drug importation and distribution network, but they wish to get into another lucrative enterprise, namely the illegal supply of arms, and I will now hand you over to Peter Simpson, a Director from MI5."

Peter Simpson stood and said, "Lady and Gentlemen. Mr Braithwaite came to us, because of the threat to national security, but it now appears the threat is moving toward an international threat, so I have invited Mr. Mike Hornsby from our sister service, MI6 to be present. His organization has more to do with foreign problems, and I can tell you that it already has international implications. As a result of Mr. Braithwaite's intelligence, we have asked the Met. Police for the use of their surveillance capabilities. DI Dave Harley from SO 11 is present, and has already started work on this with his team. They will now dedicate themselves to this task until completion, together with ourselves and our sister service taking their lead from DCI Mozart who has been appointed the coordinator of this operation. We have already installed and intend to install more electronic surveillance measures. There are moves to monitor their telephone calls, both from their mobile phones and house phones. We are also monitoring their use of computers, and wherever they go they are will be followed. We know that George Armstrong and his son Graham have used one of their jets to fly to Harare, supposedly to set up a heavy machinery hire company there, where he was given VIP treatment by one of their businessmen and government officials. Unofficially we believe that members of the Mugabe regime have met with the Armstrong's to do an arms deal. As a result of this meeting, we know the sum of two million dollars was paid to George's bank account, as a deposit for the supply of heavy machinery, but in reality was a down payment to secure a consignment of arms and ammunition. As you will know, the United Nations have placed a weapons embargo on the Mugabe regime, as he operates using violence and intimidation to remain in power. Mugabe has been unable to obtain arms and ammunition in the normal way, and has to rely on unofficial sources to arm his Police and Security Forces, which keeps him in power. There is a shortage of arms at present in Zimbabwe, and when Mugabe's Government officials heard that not only could Armstrong supply heavy plant, but had contacts to supply arms, they jumped at the chance. Gave him a plant hire contract, hence the two million payout, but the real deal was that he could supply them with an array of suitable arms and ammunition through his unofficial sources. We know, from our surveillance, Armstrong Senior and his son John, flew in one of their private jets to the City of Odessa in the Ukraine, landing at Odessa International Airport (ODS). I will let our friend from MI6 take up the story from here."

Mike Hornsby then stood and said, "Thank you Lady and Gentlemen. Having heard from our colleagues in our sister service, the NCA, we were able to carry out some covert surveillance on the Armstrongs. They booked themselves into the Hotel De Brusselles, off Ekaterininskya Square, in Odessa, on the night of the fourteenth of this month. Two single rooms and stayed for two nights. During that time two Russians booked into the same hotel, and the four of them, met. The Russians were booked in under the names Alexsei Komarov and Dmitry Sidorov. They took the rooms directly opposite the two Englishmen, and also booked in for two days. We know that Komarov and Sidorov are both ex or may be current GRU, connected to a Russian, Moscow based, criminal organization. This organization without doubt operates with the full knowledge of the Russian authorities, a knowledge and approval of which goes all the way to the very top. We assume that the Zimbabwean businessman who deals with the Armstrong's has brokered a connection between them and the Russians. We also know that the four men had meetings in nearby restaurants in Odessa, and in the hotel bar, and the meetings seemed very amicable. After two days the Russians flew back to Moscow, and the Armstrong's flew back to Manston. We now know, from telephone taps, and other means, that the purpose of the meeting was to discuss the supply of Kalashniokovs, automatic pistols, grenade launchers, hand grenades, mortars and anti-tank weapons, plus ammunition, to the Armstrong's. We also know that George Armstrong has arranged to withdraw four million dollars from one of his foreign bank accounts in the Caymans to be ready the first of next month. We assume this is to pay for an arms shipment. We also assume because of their connection to Zimbabwe that the arms are intended for them, thus breaking the embargo. We also assume a two million wire transaction deposit to the Armstrong's account in the Caymans has been made to them by the Zimbabwean's as a deposit for the shipment. So we can take it that the Armstrong's intend to move into the big league. They are dealing with some very nasty people and some nasty regimes. We also know that the Armstrong's flew to Mogadishu in Somalia recently where they booked into the City Plaza Hotel. They stayed for three days and during that time they met with Mohammed Umbedi Hassan. He is the leader of a well known pirate group operating out of the Mudug province of northern Somalia. It is known the Armstrong's have previously supplied second hand plant to a businessman in Somalia, but it now appears he has put them in touch with Hassan, whom we know has political ambitions, and is in league with some of the military and government officials. We have yet to know precisely why the Armstrong's are now speaking to Hassan, who is a particularly nasty individual, but as his group are well known as a Somali pirate group, and Hassan has political ambitions, and they are now cash rich from their piracy, we believe they may be using them as a go-between to effect an arms shipment. We have yet to confirm that however. It is at present only our best guess. Because of international embargoes, Hassan would find it very difficult to obtain arms legitimately at this time, especially if the in situ government were to know of their intentions.

Chapter Nine

The Armstrong's property consisted of a large isolated farmhouse, near Maidstone, in Kent. It was surrounded by two hundred acres of farmland, with barns, and cottages. The Armstrong's ran their businesses from home, and they used the barn and various outbuildings, and a fenced off yard to house their plant machinery and equipment. There was constant movement of medium size lorries, low loaders and heavy goods vehicles to and from the farm, where plant machinery moved on a regular basis. The Armstrong's employed staff to service their business interests, and some of these employees were associates from George Armstrong's past.

Detective Inspector Dave Harley and his SO11 team had been detailed to carry out external surveillance of the property and monitor the movements taking place. They positioned themselves in the entrance to a field, shielded by a high hedge, about half a mile from the target property. Harley watched a screen as one of his staff manipulated the controls of a drone, fitted with a high grade camera. He related what he could see on the screen to an ordnance survey map of the area he had laid out across the bonnet of his car.

He said, "Run the drone across the property and back, at high level, so we can get an idea of what we might be dealing with. We can then replay the recording, and plan how we can approach the problem."

The drone ran quickly across the property at a thousand feet, and revealed the spread of the acreage, the location of buildings, a number of vehicles, and movement of people. It seemed to be a busy property. It soon became obvious that any surveillance in and around the property would have to be at night, and that the use of zoom lenses would form a large part of his team's efforts. Harley was confident, with his years of experience, they could carry out successful surveillance on the move, but movement inside the property, whilst highly desirable would be more difficult.

Harley said, "Right, I've seen enough for now. Let's get back to the office and do some planning."

Later at the office, Harley sought out DCI Mozart. "We have had a look by drone and driving past the property, and getting close is going to be a problem. Following will be easier to achieve, but in my view we need electronic means to be able to do a proper job."

Mozart thought for a moment, "Let's talk to Peter Simpson of MI5. He might have some thought on the matter."

The two officers went to Simpson in a side office, and Harley explained situation. Simpson had his colleagues, Brocklehurst and Anderson join the discussion.

Simpson said, "We have been working on this problem for some time, and we already have telephone taps on their home phones, and their known mobiles. They are known to use one off, pay as you go, burn phones for their business deals. They use their ordinary phones for their legitimate business, but we need to track their vehicles, to overhear their conversations and we're working on that. We know George Armstrong has ordered a new computer, which is to be delivered within the next few days. We have got to his supplier, and the computer is currently with our technical people, after which we will deliver it. From this we will be able to monitor its use, but more importantly, we will be able to hack the camera and sound system, which might give us more information from the inside. I have had a team working on this for some time, and between us and SO11 we have managed to place trackers on about half of his vehicles, and this is an ongoing operation and we hope to complete the job for the rest of his fleet within days. We should also be able to hear what they are talking about inside the vehicles using voice activated recording devices which are to be fitted to the vehicles. We know that the house and some of the outbuildings are alarmed and they have extensive cctv coverage. We are now able to hack the system and Annie Forbes from GCHQ can tell you more about this. So we are well on the way to a comprehensive surveillance package, and between us and your SO11 team we should very quickly get a picture of their activities. It is, however, manpower intensive, and it will mean pulling out all the stops. We must not let them gain a toe hold into the supply of illicit arms, especially to the regimes they are in contact with."

Harley said, "We are prepared for foot and vehicle surveillance, and if we combine this with the electronic stuff your department have and are continuing to install, then we stand a chance of success. I will put a man, 24/7 watching the main entrance. There is a convenient field, with a thick hedge right opposite the main entrance which gives a view down the farm track to the house. You can leave that to me. I can also put a drone over the property, but I would suggest that we confine this to very infrequent passes especially during daylight hours, but we can slightly increase this at night because one of our drones is fitted with infra-red and heat seeking capability. If they go abroad to meet people to arrange arms shipments, our remit will not allow this. We are constricted to domestic activity only"

"I know," said Simpson, "We have arranged with our sister service and with our military, to cover. We know the Armstrong's have been to Harare, and Odessa. MI6 will take care of monitoring this. The Prime Minister and the Home Secretary have been apprised of the situation and we have been authorized to do whatever is necessary to prevent any arms shipment getting into the hands of either the Zimbabweans or the Somalis. GCHQ will also be heavily involved, as will the military. This is an unprecedented operation. We have never put together so many agencies for a common purpose before, and we need to work together toward a common goal, which is the disruption of any arms supply, and the arrest and conviction of those responsible."

DI Harley contacted the local policeman. He explained the situation to him and briefed him about the Armstrong's and their suspected drug activities, and then had him sign Official Secrets Act papers.

"I want to find a large detached house with outbuildings in the area, close to the Armstrong's farm, with an occupant who can be trusted completely, to use as a forward base for my surveillance team. Have you any suggestion?."

P.C. Robert Cook said, "There is one about a mile away on the same road. Major Angus McKay and his wife Margaret. He is ex-Army Intelligence Corps, and I know him because I have to inspect his firearms certificate and his shotguns every now and again. I would trust him completely."

DI Harley said, "Can you take me to him."

They drove to Major McKay's house. He gave them full use of his driveway and a barn on the property. "You can come and go as you please," he said, "I would be delighted to help. It takes me back to the old days. My son is now a Major in the SBS and he does covert things like this. It's quite exciting. Please feel free to make use of our barn and drive for as long as you want." Harley's team moved in that day.

Detective Constable Don Ambrose a specialist officer of SO11 wormed his way into the deep hawthorn hedge opposite the entrance to Armstrong's farm. It was 8p.m. and a moonless night. He was protected from the thorns by the hooded sniper suit he wore. He looked like a grassy hump. He was equipped with a night vision camera with a long lens, and he could see the house and yard clearly. He began photographing every movement and passing the information to his backup team.

That night three men of SO11, moved stealthily into the grounds of the Armstrong farm. All was quiet. They were dressed in dark clothing with balaclava hoods, and soft soled shoes. They spread out among the trees on the farm estate. They were able to get within a short distance of the house and farm buildings, but outside the range of the CCTV cameras. Each had two automatic cameras, which were camouflaged and mainly used for the tracking of animals in the wild. These they strapped to trees, hiding them in the foliage, but with a clear view of the property. They would recover the sim cards from the cameras later. They left the estate as quietly as they had arrived, and returned to their forward base. "All in place boss," said one to Harley.

The following morning, the barn at the McKay house had been fitted out as forward control for the SO11 surveillance team. A base station radio had been set up, to monitor the radio traffic of each of the team. DC Ambrose had been relieved from the previous night, by DC "Dick" Barton. The radio came to life. He reported vehicle movement coming from the farm estate. A black Range Rover, was leaving the property and had turned in the general direction of Maidstone. It was driven by Graham Armstrong, he would be driving past the McKay property. DI Harley and his team swung into action. They allowed the car to pass the house, and then drove in pursuit. Using their well practiced methods of vehicle surveillance they followed him into the residential area of Maidstone, where he was seen to park his car in a side street. Armstrong then walked a short distance to a small detached house, where he entered, having been greeted on the doorstep by a good looking woman of about thirty, with dark hair and curvaceous figure. He went inside. The team plotted up the area and Harley asked for a PNC check on the vehicle, which showed that Graham Armstrong owned it. He then had a check done on the occupants of the house to find that one occupant was registered to the address. A Mrs. Valerie Reynolds. She was registered as the sole occupant, except the team saw children's bikes in the front garden. She was obviously a divorcee or widow. The team waited for developments. Three hours later Armstrong was seen to leave the house, and return to his car, and he then drove back to the farm. Harley had this logged as a potential extra-marital liaison, and regarded it with some potential.

That same afternoon, a silver Mercedes 4 x 4, registered to George Armstrong left the farm. There were two occupants. George himself and his son, John. Harley and his team followed using their usual surveillance techniques. They followed them to Manston Airport, to the offices of their private hire business, ArmAir, where they stayed for some time. They were followed into the airport lounge where they met with a man in a pilot's uniform. They were seen to shake hands, and they had an hour long discussion over coffee with the pilot. They then returned to the farm, followed by part of the team, whilst the other part followed the pilot. He went from the meeting into the airport offices and was in there for over an hour.

DI Harley returned to the McKay's house. He made telephone calls and was put in touch through airport Police contacts, with the Senior Customs officer covering Manston Airport. He was Greg Murrison, based at Dover. DI Harley phoned Murrison and made arrangements to meet him at his offices in the port of Dover.

When they met, DI Harley introduced himself and said, "I am involved in a large scale operation relating to a family living on a farm near Maidstone, who are strongly suspected of importing drugs."

Murrison said, "You mean the Armstrong's, don't you."

Harley raised his eyebrows at this information, at which Murrison said, "Very confidentially, we have been watching them for quite a long period of time. They have a Private Hire company at Manston Airport, and they keep flying abroad to some unusual destinations. Our Investigation Branch have a dossier on them, but so far we have not been able to pin anything on them. We have intercepted the occasional consignment of drugs, mostly in container traffic coming into various ports like Felixstowe and Dover but we have never been able to pin them down to this family. You need to talk to Richard Woodgate, from our Investigation Branch. He knows a lot more about them."

DI Harley introduced himself to Richard Woodgate, in his office at Dover Port. "I understand you have a working knowledge of a family named Armstrong, who live on a farm estate near Maidstone, and who have a private hire company with two ten seater jets, based at Manston."

Woodgate said guardedly, "Yes, why do you want to know."

DI Harley said, "May I make a phone call." Woodgate looked puzzled, but nodded his head." Harley phoned the squad offices in the City of London, and asked for DCI Mozart. "I am with Richard Woodgate a Senior Investigator with HM Customs. I understand he has been working on the Armstrong's." Woodgate raised his eyebrows but remained silent.

"I believe that Mr Woodgate should be brought in, because he holds valuable information, and he appears to be paralleling us." Harley said,

"Have Mr Woodgate stand by. He will receive a telephone call within the hour."

DI Harley requested that Woodgate wait for the call. A while later Woodgate answered the office phone.

"Mr Woodgate," said the voice, "This is Charles Bishop, Head of HM Customs and Excise." Woodgate knew his voice. "You have DI Harley with you from SO11. You have an ongoing file open on the Armstrong family. You will report to an office in the City of London at ten a.m. tomorrow, together with your files. You can get the address from Mr Harley. You will ask for a Detective Chief Inspector Mozart of SO15, and cooperate fully with him. You will be seconded to his squad forthwith and until further notice, meanwhile please assist Mr Harley in any way you can."

Woodgate looked amazed at the speed of communication, and could only guess at its implications. He said, "You have some powerful friends." With a shrug of his shoulders. "How can I help."

"Well we would like to know what flight plans the Armstrong's have lodged. The where and when they are going. We would also like access, covertly, to their aircraft. But first, I understand that you are to report to our office in the City in the morning. I will see you there. But I must emphasize the confidentiality. So please tell no one. I will see you in the morning, but if you could bring the information I have asked for I would be very grateful." They shook hands and Harley left a puzzled and concerned Woodgate.

At 10am the following day, Woodgate reported at the front entrance of the offices in the City of London as instructed. He was asked to wait. A short time later DI Harley appeared, and took him to a side office where he was identified, had his photograph and fingerprints taken, and a pass issued.

"This will give you access to this building and our offices. It will also let you into our underground car park should you need to bring a vehicle with you," said Harley.

He then took his charge to the 17th floor offices, where he was introduced to DCI Mozart and DS Stevens. In the conference room there was a small group of people.

Peter Simpson approached and introduced himself and said, "This is Commander John Russell SO15. I am a Director from MI5. You are to be coopted onto our squad because of the work you already have done on the Armstrong's. What you may or may not know is that the National Crime Agency have been paralleling your work. They too have been interested in the Armstrong's. I know both organizations suspect them of running drugs into the country, but so far have been unable to pin them down. We, however have bigger fish to fry with them. Before you is a briefing folder, and inside the top document is an Official Secrets Act declaration. I want you to read that, and sign it before we proceed. This document will supersede any other Secrets Act documents you may have signed in the past." Woodgate, his curiosity turned up to high power, signed the document and handed it over to Simpson.

Mozart said, “I suggest you read the documents in the folder asap, but first we will tell you, as you are now part of the squad, what is going on.”

Mozart, Simpson and Russell in turn, briefed Woodgate, on the details of purpose of the squad. When he heard about the arms procurement, he gasped in amazement.

Simpson said, “Perhaps now you can see why we have put together a multi-agency squad. To catch them will take a joint effort using all the talents we can assemble. If these arms get into the wrong hands then several countries in Europe and the Middle East might see an increase in very nasty terrorist activity.”

“We thought they were just clever drug importers, but we had hopes of catching them soon. I can now see why you have such a high powered effort being made to bring them to justice, I will help all I can,” said Woodgate, with fervour.

Later that night, DCI Mozart, DS Stevens, DI Harley and Richard Woodgate met at Manston airport car park, together with two anonymous technical officers from MI5. Woodgate, with his security passes, got them through to airside. He then took the two technical officers to where the two ArmAir jets were parked. Harley had checked with his forward headquarters. "Where are the Armstrong's, " he said over the radio.

"All at home, no movement," replied the controller.

"Go ahead," said Harley over the radio, and the two technicians opened the aircraft with tools they had with them. Each went into an aircraft and after half an hour, they came out, locked the aircraft up again, and left as quietly as they had arrived, with the epithet, "We will now hear what they say when on board." Woodgate thought to himself, these guys don't mess about. I could have done with this sort of power from the start. He said, "I'm impressed. Where do we go from here." Mozart said, "You are now part of the team. You will be working with us from now on."

Chapter Ten

DCI Mozart received a telephone call from the Sergeant in charge of the firearms team guarding Ross-Harding in the hospital. “He is awake, and wants to know what is going on,” said the officer.

“I will make some arrangements and then be right over to talk to him,” said Mozart.

DCI Mozart and DS Stevens entered the side ward in intensive care which housed Ross-Harding.

"We have met before Mr Ross-Harding, " said Mozart. "This is Detective Sergeant Stevens. We saw you the night you were brought in, unconscious and quite severely beaten. At the time you told us your name was Green and refused to say how you got injured, but things have moved on since then. We now know who you are, and why you were beaten up and dumped in a puddle at Barking Creek. We now know you to be Mungo Ross-Harding, you work in the private banking department of Grindey's Bank in the City. You live in a flat in Harley Street. So will you tell us now what happened to you and why."

Ross-Harding said, "I am saying nothing. I got in a fight, that's all."

Mozart said, "Well what you may not know, is while you were unconscious, an attempt was made on your life. We found a man, we now know to be James Nolan, injecting morphine into the drip in your arm. Fortunately we arrived just in time to stop him. He pulled a gun on us, and we shot him dead. Thanks to the swift action of the doctors at this hospital your life was saved. Why did he want to kill you."

Ross-Harding looked startled, refused to look Mozart in the eye and lamely said, "I don't know."

Mozart looked hard at Ross-Harding and said, "My Sergeant and I know you are lying. The man we shot was a well known drug dealer. We know you are a drug user, and we surmise you owed him money. What you may not know, is that Nolan has a brother who we have arrested as part of the conspiracy to kill you, he is a very nasty individual, who is even more upset now he has lost his brother thanks to you. We believe very strongly your life remains in great danger, because if he gets bail he might well try to finish the job himself or get one of his associates to do it for him. We believe he was doing it on behalf of the Armstrong's, who have even more resources at their disposal." With that Ross Harding went pale, looked agitated and appeared very very nervous. "Therefore we have made arrangements for you to be moved to a more secure location. A private hospital, where you will be kept under armed guard until we get to the bottom of this. We cannot guarantee your safety if you remain here, it's too public. Tomorrow morning you will be moved."

Ross-Harding said, "And if I object."

"Then I have no doubt they will make another attempt on your life, and this time, we might not be there to prevent it."

At this news Ross-Harding's mouth began to twitch, and he stared at the ceiling in deep thought.

Mozart said, "I want you to think very seriously about what you have got yourself into and how you might extract yourself from the situation you are in. When you are ready to talk, then ask the officers we assign to protect you to contact me. You will be moved in the morning." Mozart and Stevens left a very worried Ross-Harding.

The following morning Ross-Harding was taken by ambulance from the hospital to the Easton Clinic in Northampton, with two armed officers sitting in the ambulance beside him. What he and his escort didn't see was a black Jaguar saloon pulling out of the hospital car park, and following the ambulance at a discreet distance. As the ambulance entered the clinic grounds the Jaguar drove past the entrance. The driver pulled into a layby further along the road, speed dialed a number on his mobile phone and said, "Easton Clinic, Northampton."

Mozart and Stevens pulled up at the front gate of GCHQ, known locally as "The Doughnut". The gate guard asked their business. Mozart introduced them both to the guard and said, "We have an appointment to see Ms Annie Forbes."

"Please wait" instructed the guard. He then went back into his security hut, and made a telephone call. He returned a short time later, "Please drive into the visitor's car park to your right at the end of the drive. The reception desk is just inside the main entrance. Please display this in your dashboard," and he then gave them a printed ticket of authorization.

At the reception they were made to wait, whilst they had visitors badges issued. After a short interlude Annie Forbes appeared, looking like she had just been to a photo shoot of Vogue magazine. She was tall, slender, with luscious long dark hair to her shoulders, and piercing blue intelligent eyes. Her smile radiated self assurance, as she approached the two men. Mozart had been impressed the first time he met her, feeling an instant attraction, and was even more impressed this second time, when the attraction was confirmed. She moved towards them, gliding across the floor to the rustle of her pencil skirted suit, and shook hands with the officers. Her grip was firm but gentle, and Mozart noticed her long, well kept, violinist fingers and perfect nails. Mozart felt an uplift of hormones as she caressed his hand.

"Good morning gentlemen," she said in her low sultry voice, "Welcome to GCHQ. Please follow me."

Mozart looked at Stevens, lifted his eyebrows in unwritten body language, giving a half smile. Stevens raised his eyebrows in reply. You're smitten, boss, he thought. She took them to a small conference room. "Please sit," she said, "Coffee".

Once the niceties had been done, she said, "What can I do for you."

Mozart produced the notebook which belonged to Ross-Harding, and said, "We found this in a luggage locker at Liverpool Street Station, after we found the key which fitted the locker taped under one of the drawers in Ross-Harding's office at his bank. It appears to be coded, and we wondered if your expert code breakers could translate it for us. We suspect that Ross-Harding has been money laundering for the Armstrong family, and they have been looking for this because we know they searched his flat, but couldn't get to his office like we did."

She took the book and glanced at the hieroglyphs written on its pages.

Mozart continued, "We suspect that not only has Ross-Harding been money laundering for them, but he has been syphoning off some of the cash for his own use. Knowing him, there will be details of numbered accounts and perhaps safe deposit boxes in this book, and we want to know what, how much, and where." He paused and said, "It must be important, because they were worried enough to write off the cash by silencing him for good. He must know all their financial dealings, and they can't afford for him to talk. The Nolan's have not done the Armstrong's any favours by punishing him, because it brought him to our attention, and we expect they were not best pleased. We think the attempt on his life in the hospital was on the orders of the Armstrong's who were intent on cutting their losses because they feared he might talk. He is now under guard and we have moved him up country to a private clinic. If you can interpret his codes, we would be in a position to trace the cash and recover it."

Forbes said, "Leave it with me. I will have it worked on and be in touch."

Mozart said, "Steve Easterbrook of the City of London Fraud Squad is a specialist in asset tracing. He has developed contacts throughout the financial world, and once the codes are broken, he would be the best man to work on following the financial trail."

"I will be in touch as soon as possible, but there is something pressing that you ought to know right now. Our monitoring system has picked up a call made to one of the Armstrong's phone we have just started monitoring. We have pinged it and that call was made from Northampton. It lasted only 25 seconds. Could that have any significance."

Mozart raised his eyebrows again, "I'll deal with it," he said.

Forbes said, " I will see you at the update tomorrow at the office. Until then." She then shook their hands and again Mozart felt the thrill of her touch, brief as it was.

Outside, and in the car Mozart telephoned Commander Russell on his encrypted phone.

"I have just left GCHQ who are going to translate the notebook found in the locker at Liverpool Street Station, but more importantly GCHQ have picked up a call to the Armstrong's which was made from the Northampton area. It was only 25 seconds long. I believe they know we have moved Ross-Harding. May I suggest two things governor, first, let's get a covert firearms team to the clinic, because I believe that they will make another attempt to silence Ross-Harding, and second, can we get someone to look at the Hospital CCTV, to see if we can spot anyone on foot or in a vehicle following the ambulance away from the building."

Russell said, "By the time you get back I will have actioned your suggestions. Good thinking."

Mozart and Stevens pulled into the car park of their City of London Offices. On the 17th floor they saw a hive of activity. Commander Russell was in his office and gestured for them to enter.

He said, "A firearms team has been installed at the clinic, and they will be covering 24/7 until further notice. They have been fully briefed, and know there is a chance of an imminent attack. I have a small team monitoring the cctv from the hospital and they have already identified a black Jaguar saloon car, which came out of the car park and followed the ambulance. They are now checking the route cameras, especially the motorway monitors, and if we get a hit on the same car, we will know we have to worry about another attempt on him. The PNC shows the Jaguar is registered to an employee of the Armstrong's, so I believe you were absolutely right in your assessment. Time will tell, but we are ready for them."

Chapter Eleven

At 10am the following day, all the representatives of the various agencies involved were assembled in the conference room. At the head of the table were the triumvirate of Commander John Russell SO15, Peter Simpson MI5 and Mike Hornsby of MI6.

Russell opened the meeting, "Good morning lady and gentlemen. This is a progress meeting to discover where we are now, and what we need to do to progress. Before we proceed, I need to tell you that Ross-Harding has been moved, but we believe the move has been compromised, so we have taken measures to negate the threat. We have moved Ross-Harding to another more isolated room at the clinic with armed guards in civilian clothes. We have replaced him in the room first allocated to him with one of our own, and kept the uniformed armed guard on to give the impression that he remains in situ. We know the ambulance was followed by one of the Armstrong's employees, we have seen him following the ambulance away from the hospital and we have now identified the car following on motorway cameras. We are now setting up additional cctv at the clinic, and its approaches, and this system is being monitored by the protection team there. DI Harley. Its your turn."

David Harley said, "We have the front entrance to the Armstrong's property under 24/7 surveillance and we have placed cameras in the grounds. We now know that John Armstrong regularly visits a divorcee with two small children in Maidstone. There is no doubt he is over the side with her. We intend placing a tracker on his vehicle, together with a voice activated recorder which will reveal any conversations held in the vehicle. We have set up a forward Operations Point about a mile from the farm having found an ex-army intelligence Major who has allowed us to use his barn as an HQ and his driveway for our vehicles. The advantage is that all is well back and hidden from the road and gives us the opportunity to follow whenever we need to. We have bugged their airplanes. I would like to introduce Richard Woodgate at this point. He is a Senior Investigating Officer from HM Customs and got us access to the planes. He also knows of the Armstrong's and had in fact started a parallel investigation on them. We are monitoring them on the ground from our forward HQ, but when they use the planes that will take more powerful equipment and an input from Air Traffic Control. We can easily obtain any future flight plans they have so we should know in advance where and when they might be going by air. We have also sent a drone over the Armstrong's property, and have printouts showing the layout of the property. We intend to bug all the vehicles we can gain access to. "

Russell then called upon Richard Woodgate to introduce himself.

"I had started an inquiry into the activities of the Armstrong's because they are frequent travelers both by air from Manston mostly in their own aircraft, and through Dover to the Continent. We, in HM Customs suspected they were heavily involved in drug importation on a large scale, through various ports around the UK, and I believe that this family have been supplying heroin and crack cocaine to the Nolan's who call themselves the Whitechapel Cartel, and to other county lines organizations in London and the home counties. I had started a file on them, when DI Harley came to see me. I can facilitate access to Manston, particularly airside, and can easily obtain details of flight plans without raising suspicion. I can also have them monitored through any port in the country again without raising their suspicions."

Commander Russell said, "Would you please work with DI Harley, and keep DCI Mozart in the loop. Please assist where you can. I have spoken to your chief, and he has agreed to your attachment to us for as long as it takes. You are now part of this team for the duration."

"Now, let us hear from Ms Forbes from GCHQ", said Russell.

Forbes glanced at her notes and said, "Gentlemen. GCHQ can offer a monitoring service. We are in a position to hack their computers, listen by means of any bugs that are placed on or in the property, and even to view the inside of the property through their computer cameras. In addition we are working on decoding a notebook kept by Ross-Harding which we suspect is a record of the financial dealings he has carried out on behalf of the family. We suspect he has been helping himself by creaming off a percentage. We should have more soon."

Commander Russell said, "Thank you Ms Forbes. Once you have made progress with the coded notebook, I will get DI Steve Easterbrook from the City of London Fraud Squad to liaise with you, and he can crack on to trace the assets as it is his expertise, but please keep DCI Mozart apprised as he is our coordinator."

Annie Forbes nodded her agreement at Steve Easterbrook and said, "Perhaps we can talk afterwards."

As Commander Russell saw the surprised look that passed over Mozart's face at his suggestion that Mozart would be coordinating the whole inquiry, he said, "Yes Mr Mozart. I feel that it is necessary for someone on the ground to have all the information as it progresses. We at this end of the table will come and go from this office, but you will be the lynchpin which holds the whole thing together and gives it direction. It is a great responsibility, because you will be fed information from below, and have to brief those above. The decisions on the ground will be yours because you may have to make decisions at speed. If you want or need authority for anything which you cannot solve yourself then come to me, I will back you up. What you should all be aware of is the Home Secretary is fully aware of what is going on, and he is keeping the Prime Minister up to speed. We have full authority to use whatever means we feel are necessary to bring these criminals to justice, not just for the importation of drugs and other domestic criminal activities, but for the suspected procurement of arms intended for terrorist or insurrection purposes in another country. We do not know for certain which country that may be, but we already know that the family have had preliminary meetings in Zimbabwe and Somalia.

DI Harley's phone rang. He said, "Excuse me, I must take this call," and he left the room. He returned a short time later and said, "My team followed John Armstrong again, to Maidstone, where he went to see his girlfriend."

Russell interrupted, "I thought he was married with children."

Harley said, "Yes, but he visits a woman named Valerie Reynolds, a divorcee in Maidstone. Last time he was there for three hours. This time we have struck lucky, he visited her in the evening when it was dark. He parked his car in the next street, so my team put a watch on the address, and whilst he was inside, they managed to place a tracker on his car, and to insert a voice activated recorder in the vehicle. We should now be able to track the vehicle electronically and to hear what might be said inside the vehicle. We are working on getting all the vehicles the family use fitted in the same way. We have also managed to do the same with George Armstrong's wife's car. She went shopping, and we carried out the same operation on her. We are making good progress on that front."

"Thank you Mr Harley, said Commander Russell. "Now, Mr Woodgate. We would like you to monitor any flight plans the family submit, but we cannot rule out they may use scheduled airlines from other airports. I am sure if they move in any direction, then Mr Harley's team will be on it and let us know. Meantime, please continue your efforts to trace their drug importations, because we cannot ignore the fact this family have accrued their wealth mainly by importation of large quantities of drugs, and by the use of violence and intimidation have become, in their eyes, almost untouchable. We are here to change that view. Now Detective Chief Inspector Mozart, in your role as coordinator and lead investigating officer, have you anything to add."

Mozart thought for a few seconds and said, "I believe the family are prepared to eliminate Ross-Harding for two reasons. One he has been syphoning off investment funds for himself, and two he had been laundering their money and sending it to secret bank accounts. He knows too much and might tell us. They broke into his flat looking for records of the transactions, but they didn't find anything. They don't know we had more success and have found coded records. That they are prepared to eliminate Ross-Harding, even though he has some of their money in his own name, must mean they see him as a threat, and are prepared to write that sum off, to guard their future operations and ensure they are not in danger of discovery. That the ambulance has been followed to Ross-Harding's new location only confirms what a threat they perceive him to be. They don't know we know, and we have now made full preparations should another attempt be made on his life. He would be an important witness if we can turn him. We also believe the Armstrong's will need to access their funds to pay for future drug and arms consignments. We need to ensure we know their movements in advance and where the money is. To this end I will liaise with Ms Forbes and DI Easterbrook. There is a still a long way to go, and it will require a concerted effort from all departments represented here to bring this to a successful conclusion."

He smiled and said, "It seems I have been handed the poisoned chalice. Let's hope I don't have to drink from it."

The meeting then broke up, and everyone returned to their allotted roles.

A short time later Mozart's phone rang.

The voice said, "Mr Mozart, this is Michael Carrington from the Forensic Science Laboratory at Lambeth. We have news for you about the Ross-Harding case. We will start with the cellar at the Nolan's office. There was blood on the floor, on the chair, on the pieces of hose and the rope pieces found at Barking Creek. They all matched Ross-Harding's blood. To be sure we are doing DNA testing and this should prove conclusive. We have liaised with the hospital. The syringe definitely contained heroin, and it had James Nolan's fingerprints on it. Again a DNA test should back this up. The bullet taken from the hospital wall was definitely fired from Nolan's gun, and tests on the other gun found in John Nolan's house showed it has been used in two shootings in London, both drug related incidents. One man was killed and the other wounded and still lives. A test on the Nolan's truck shows that Ross-Harding was transported in it. His blood was found in the back of the cab, and no doubt the DNA testing will confirm this. In summary we can tie the Nolan's to the attempted murder of Ross-Harding, and to one other unsolved murder and a serious wounding in the city. The rope you found in the cellar is the same rope used to tie Ross-Harding up, so forensically speaking you have a very strong case against the remaining Nolan."

Mozart said, "Thank you very much for this timely information, it will help to keep John Nolan locked up on remand, and out of the way. I will await your report and the DNA results in due course."

Mozart then rang DI Harley of SO11. "Hi Dave, how's it going."

"Hallo Joe, " said Harley. "Going well at the moment. We have one car to go, that's Mrs Armstrong's second car. We managed to fit trackers on all the other vehicles. Old man Armstrong went for a haircut yesterday, and we managed to fit up his car with a tracker and voice activated recorder. We've also seen the black Jaguar which was mentioned as following the ambulance. It was at the farm yesterday. It belongs to Donald Baxter who lives in Maidstone. He works for the Armstrong's in their plant hire business. He's got form for GBH, and armed Robbery, and he's done time. Nothing recent. We managed to tool up his car as well with a tracker."

"Good job" said Mozart, "Keep it up."

"Always" Harley responded with a chuckle, and rang off.

Mozart's phone rang again. It was Annie Forbes. Her low sexy voice stirred Mozart. She said, "I have some good news for you Mr Mozart." Call me Joe, please." said Mozart. "Well Joe, I'm Annie. We have been studying the codes in the book you gave us, and it looks like Ross-Harding has syphoned off £2.5 million from the Armstrong's and has stashed it in a bank in Luxemburg. It is a numbered account, and can be accessed electronically, so we should be able to recover the cash. We are now working on the rest of the book, but it looks promising. I will need to come to the city tomorrow to see Steve Easterbrook at the City of London Fraud Squad to confer with him, and then I'll come on to your office and update you."

He said, " That would be good, well done. I'll buy you lunch."

She said, “It’s a deal. See you tomorrow.”

Chapter Twelve

A t 8.30am DC Alan Smith of SO11 reported to his control from his positioned at the front of the Armstrong's property. "Graham Armstrong has just left the farm, turning right out of the drive, west."

DI Harley and his team sprang into action. A motor cycle left the house where they were all assembled. After a short while the rider reported he was behind Graham's Land Rover Discovery, heading towards the A2. The rest of the team caught up. The motor cycle pulled back allowing cars from the team to continue to follow. The tracking device fitted to the car, enabled them to drop back out of sight. They continued the follow to the Dartford Tunnel, and then on to the A13, where the car turned off towards Grays. The car was seen to pull into a transport company yard, which contained several lorries and a wooden building which was obviously the office. As Graham Armstrong's vehicle stopped outside the office, a man came out and he was seen to shake Graham's hand. They then went into the office together. The company board at the entrance showed the logo PTC Transport. The SO11 team positioned themselves away from the yard, leaving one vehicle hidden with a view of the yard. Graham remained in the office in the yard for most of the morning.

It was 10am Mozart's phone rang. "Joe," said the voice, "Dick Woodgate here. Things are moving. Our team Customs Search team at Felixstowe have searched a container and found a large quantity of heroin under a false floor and in false walls. It's street value would be about £15 million. It came in on a ship from Rotterdam. Under normal circumstances we would have allowed it to get collected, but unfortunately the drugs were found before collection, and the container was still being searched with goods stacked around it, when a lorry turned up to collect the load and the security let him in. The driver had papers on him showing a collection order for a company in the Grays area of Essex. Purfleet Transport Company – PTC Transport - is written on the lorry. He has been detained, but all he is saying is that his company had orders to collect the container, which the documents show as loaded with electrical goods. Our investigations show the PTC Transport is owned by Trevor and Michael Burns. Both have previous for GBH and Robbery. Nothing recent, but your intelligence system shows that they are both from the East End of London and Trevor Burns went to school with Graham Armstrong. They set the company up a few years ago, and bought two lorries for cash. They now own ten and appear to be doing very well indeed. They have a yard at Grays, with a repair shop and outbuildings. Our Dutch colleagues have been informed and are making inquiries for us at their end. I'm sorry about this, it was just a routine stop search. Normally having found the drugs, we would put it all back together and put a follow on when it was collected, then make the arrests. It was unfortunate timing, the guy turning up to collect it, as we were searching it and he saw all the customs activity and what we were doing. I will let you know if we manage to hold the driver and charge him, but with what he is telling our team at Felixstowe, it's probable that we will eventually have to let him go or he will be bailed."

Mozart said, "Funny you should say that but our surveillance team followed Graham Armstrong this morning and he is currently at the PTC Yard at Grays. I bet he's waiting for the load to arrive. I presume that your team would normally go to the yard at Grays as a follow up. Any chance you can delay that until this afternoon, so Graham has gone. We have bigger fish to fry with him, because we have just learned from your colleague Greg Murrison that the Armstrong's have had a flight plan submitted, for a flight tomorrow to Harare, via Cyprus and we don't want to put them off."

At the PTC Yard at Grays, after a time lapse of three hours, Graham Armstrong was seen to come out of the office, gesticulating furiously and shouting at two men. He jumped into his car and roared off in an obvious temper. He was followed and seen to be talking on his mobile phone, and he drove straight to the farm.

DI Harley phoned Mozart. He related what his team and seen and details of the follow to Grays.

Mozart said, "Can you make arrangements to recover the recorders from his car at the earliest opportunity. It will be very interesting to hear what he was saying on the journey back home." "Will do, " said Harley.

As soon as Graham Armstrong left the yard, a team from HM Customs and Excise based at Felixstowe, but joined by Richard Woodgate, descended upon the PTC yard and made arrests relating to the drug importation through their port. The Customs were left to get on with their usual role, with Woodgate keeping a watch in brief on proceedings for anything which could connect the Armstrong's to the drug haul. He would be looking for evidence of a distribution network, and into the finances to see if the cash flow could be traced to the Armstrong's. Initial indications however, showed that the financial route was convoluted and complicated, and would take time to unravel. What was important at this time, was that the drugs had been taken off the market, and The Family had taken a huge financial hit, at a time when they wanted cash for their other illegal activities.

DC Alan Smith, wearing his sniper suit, and lying under the hawthorn hedge opposite the front gate of the Armstrong's farm, activated his radio.

He said, "A Black Jaguar", and he gave the number, "Has just turned up at the farm I saw three men get in the car, and they put some things in the boot. They have driven out of the farm again, four up, heading west towards the A2."

The remainder of Harley's team sprang into action. They caught up with the vehicle, quickly, and following their usual surveillance practices followed the Jaguar around the M25, and up the M11 North to the A14 and on to the M1 North. Mozart received another telephone call, where the Jaguar's movement was reported to him.

"Keep following. I think they might be heading to Northampton. I will warn the team at the clinic where Ross-Harding is."

He then telephoned the Inspector in charge of the firearms team in Northampton, and brought him up to date.

He said, "I will tell you when they get close and what they are doing. You might want to beef your team up. I'll keep you posted."

The surveillance team followed the Jaguar on the M1 to the junction with the A45. They saw it pull in to the Burgoyne Hotel, just off the motorway. The men went in, and were seen registering by an officer of the team, who entered the hotel, and went to the bar. They had two double rooms and went to them. The surveillance team scattered around the hotel, and the leader, Detective Sergeant Sue Barnes contacted DI Harley and told him what the team had discovered.

"Stay there, if necessary book into the hotel. We must know when they make their move. Meanwhile I'll pass it on to Mr Mozart."

The surveillance stayed in place until it was dark, when all the men came out of the hotel, dressed in dark clothing. They got into the Jaguar car, and drove off, discretely followed by the Police Team. The armed police team at the clinic were warned, their numbers boosted since they first received the information, and they deployed inside and outside the clinic. The jaguar went past the clinic, driving slowly and was spotted by the police team, it then turned round and drove slowly back past the clinic entrance, to the entrance to a track running alongside the grounds of the building. The men were seen to leave the car, and they entered the gardens of the clinic by climbing over a low wire fence. They split up, and went towards the main building. They crossed against the lighted windows and were seen to be carrying guns which looked like automatic machine guns, but it was difficult to be certain in the dark, and they could only go by silhouetted images.

The men got up to the outer wall and were approaching an unlit window when they heard "Attack! Attack! Attack!. Armed Police, Stand Still" to find themselves bathed in high powered torchlight.

Two raised their guns, and one of the attackers got off two shots, before four rapid shots rang out from the Police team. Two of the attackers dropped to the ground screaming and the other two dropped their weapons. One tried to run and was brought down with a blow to the head and quickly cuffed. The one man remaining standing, dropped his weapon, and stood still, blinking in the torchlight. Other armed police officers came round the corner of the building to discover the Police Inspector in charge of the firearms team on the ground groaning.

He had been shot twice in the chest but his Kevlar and ceramic plated vest had stopped the bullets. He cursed, "I think the buggers have broken a couple of ribs."

One of the attackers was dead, another wounded in the chest. One was unconscious, laid out on the ground. The man left standing was handcuffed and held by two officers. The semi automatic machine pistols were sophisticated and the latest model of Ceska Zbrojovka Scorpion machine pistols, manufactured in the Czech Republic , and four Berretta 9mm automatic pistols. The machine pistols had full clips and the handguns were fully loaded. All of the identifying serial numbers had been filed off. The men, including the dead man were thoroughly searched. The unconscious man recovered enough to stand, and he was handcuffed. The police team recovered the Jaguar Car.

Mozart phone rang, "Mozart," he said, "Hello sir, this is Inspector Ron Stovell, Northampton Police Firearms team. Thanks to your surveillance team we were able to ambush the guys coming for Ross-Harding. They were well tooled up, they had Scorpion Machine Pistols and handguns. We've got one dead, one wounded, and two others in custody. All under escort and on their way to our main police station. We have recovered their car, and we have a forensic team going to their hotel rooms at the Burgoyne Hotel. We will do a full forensic search and let you know the result in due course."

Mozart said, "Well done. Are you alright, you sound out of breath. "

He replied, "They shot me. My vest stopped the bullets, but I think I have two broken ribs. I should have ducked."

Mozart said, "Can you hold them incommunicado. This will come as a nasty surprise to the persons who sent them, but I don't want them to know just yet. If they have mobiles on them a list of the numbers would be useful. Please send them to my office," giving Stovell the telephone number, and then added, "I would like to thank you and all your officers for their help. I will make sure that goes up the line to your Chief in due course. Many thanks and well done. Please pass that on to your men and get yourself some treatment. Can you tell our surveillance team they can stay overnight, and come back in the morning."

Mozart rang Peter Simpson at MI5. He related what had happened at the Clinic in Northampton and said, "This is the second attempt on Ross-Harding's life. Both have failed. Before they try again, can we move him. Surely you have a safe house somewhere remote to hide him."

Simpson said, "We have a place in Norfolk. But what treatment is he needing."

Mozart said, "He has recovered from the drug infusion, but he is still recovering from the beating they gave him. Nursing and a visit occasionally by a Doctor should suffice. Annie Forbes at GCHQ and DI Steve Easterbrook of the City of London Fraud office are working to decode Ross-Harding's note book, and to trace both his and the Armstrong's assets, and when I have most of the stuff I need from them, I will need to talk to Ross-Harding. He must know that his life is in danger, and we are his only way out of the mess he's in. I see him as a potential witness, but that is a bit down the line. The main priority now is to get him well out of circulation, to be held incommunicado until we can make him see it our way."

"I agree. I will send a team to move him and I'll let you know when and where once I have finalized the arrangements."

Four hours later a small convoy of 4 x 4's turned up at the clinic. They held a 6 man team of armed men, all looking like ex-military, with a nurse. Ross-Harding was removed from the clinic and driven to Norfolk, where he was made comfortable in a large country house, surrounded by 10 acres of fields. The party was met by a man and a woman who were the resident caretakers, and he was taken to a large comfortable bedroom. The armed team remained at the house, and took over residency. Meals were prepared by a resident chef, and men, looking to be agricultural workers and gamekeepers, patrolled the grounds day and night. There was a control room, and an extensive alarm on the building with an internal and external cctv system which was monitored by the staff 24/7. People in the district were fed the information that the house belonged to a multi millionaire Arab Sheikh , who only occasionally visited, but he had the house permanently manned by a resident staff, to cater for his occasional visits. They had seen the occasional limousine, and the odd landing of a helicopter in the grounds, which merely added to the truth of the rumour.

Chapter Thirteen

"Mr Mozart" said Commander Russell, "George Armstrong has had his pilot submit a flight plan for tomorrow, to fly to Harare via Cyprus with his son John. His flight leaves at ten a.m. tomorrow, landing in Larnaca about 1p.m. The plan shows an overnight stay in Larnaca, and then an onward flight to Harare the next day. We need your Detective Sergeant Stevens to be on a direct flight to Harare tomorrow morning leaving from Heathrow at eleven. He will be met by someone from the British Embassy when he lands who will look after him. He is on flight BA 672 which goes via Johannesburg, to Harare. It will take about 15 hours and we have booked him out business class, so he can get some sleep. He may be busy when he gets there. According to our friends from Millbank House, George Armstrong first went there to sell second hand plant, and he has a regular contact who arranges the purchase of the machinery, but our friends' say, the man he deals with in Harare, is a friend of the regime, more especially the head of the Police and some cabinet members. The regime have somehow become aware that the Armstrong's have contacts for the supply of arms. That the team arrested in Northampton had the latest version of the Scorpion machine gun only confirms this, and from what our friends have learned, a meeting has been set up not only to do a deal on the sale of plant machinery and farm machinery, but arrangements have been made for Armstrong to meet a government official to discuss the supply of arms. The Zimbabweans cannot get the arms legitimately themselves because of the embargo, so they are very anxious to get them by any means. So please brief Sergeant Stevens so he knows what he's getting into. Assure him that he will be looked after by our embassy staff, and we are signing him on temporarily to the diplomatic immunity register."

Mozart called DS Stevens to his office and gave him the news.

"What's it all about boss," said Stevens.

"I have told you all I know. You will be met and fully apprised when you get there, but basically the Armstrong's are going there via Cyprus, tomorrow, and you will be able to get there ahead of them and be met at the airport and briefed there." "Right boss, " said Stevens. "The good news is that you will be flying business class, so draw some expense money. Dollars would be good, because the currency in Zimbabwe is worthless. You have to take barrow loads just to buy a cup of coffee." "Okay Boss, No problem," said Stevens.

"Keep me posted, and don't hang about I need you back here soonest" said Mozart.

Sergeant Stevens walked out to the concourse of Harare International Airport after a 15 hour overnight flight. He had slept during the flight sufficiently to make him alert to his new surroundings. His passage through immigration had been short, but he had the feeling from the start that Zimbabwe was a country where every outsider was scrutinized closely, especially if they were British, and the Immigration Officer at entry had left him with the impression that he would be watched. When Stevens reached the barrier separating the concourse from the Immigration and Customs Hall, he saw a man bearing a placard with his name written on it. This man was about 40, medium height, with light brown hair, and a moustache. He wore grey slacks, a white shirt with a club tie, and a navy blue blazer.

Stevens approached, and stood in front of the man, who said with a soft Scottish accent, "Mr Stevens. My name is Duncan McKenzie, I am the Military Attache at the British Embassy. Welcome to Zimbabwe. I have a car outside and I will take you to the embassy where we can talk. I have arranged a room for you at the Continental Hotel, in Samora Michel Avenue, in Harare. It is the same hotel that George Armstrong is booked into. The idea is that you and I cover his meetings while he is here, and hopefully we will get to know some of his plans."

Stevens was then driven to the embassy. On the way McKenzie said, "We are being followed. Don't look round. It is normal. They are a very suspicious lot the Zimbabweans and it is routine. I expect whilst you are here, they will assign a team to watch you. You will see them because they aren't very good at surveillance."

They drove through the embassy gates having stopped at the entrance to identify themselves to the security officer there. Stevens was then taken to McKenzie's office on the third floor of the imposing colonial style building, and briefed over coffee.

After an hours conversation McKenzie said, " I will now take you to your hotel, where you can freshen up, and I will come by this afternoon. We will act naturally. Two colleagues socializing. The Armstrong's should be arriving this afternoon, and it would be useful if we could see who they are meeting, and perhaps get a smattering of what they might talk about. When we get to the hotel, please assume your room will be bugged. If you make any calls they will be monitored, and the same applies to your mobile phone. I will leave you with my mobile number and office number. The Zimbabweans are already aware of these details, and no doubt by now they will have included your details in their files. If you go out, expect to be followed. Other than that, enjoy yourself."

Stevens gave him a look which conveyed the irony of the situation at which McKenzie smiled. "I know" said Stevens, "If you can't take a joke you shouldn't have joined."

McKenzie's smile broadened, and he laughed aloud. "You and I will get on Mr. Stevens." "My name is Winston," said Stevens, "Win to my friends." McKenzie stretched out his hand and said "Duncan."

At the hotel Stevens found he had been allocated a large room, with en suite and balcony, on the second floor. There was a large double bed, and a mini bar, with tea and coffee on a tray on the sideboard. The bed was comfortable. The room tastefully furnished with a coffee table and armchairs, the towels were fluffy and the shower produced a powerful jet of water. He did not look for electronic bugs, he expected them to be there.

Stevens set the alarm on his mobile phone for two hours hence, and slept the sleep of a weary traveller. He woke at 1p.m. local time. Showered and dressed. The phone rang.

McKenzie said, "I am downstairs. It's lunch time. Come down and we will eat."

They made a show of greeting each other as friends, and went together into the restaurant where McKenzie selected the table. They each ordered drinks and a light meal. McKenzie made small talk about life in Zimbabwe, Stevens discovering he was a married man, and his wife was with him. He had an embassy house on the outskirts of Harare. While they were waiting for the lunch to arrive McKenzie dropped his napkin on the floor. It went slightly under the next table. He bent down to retrieve it, and then carried on talking small talk. They had a pleasant lunch and McKenzie suggested they walk to digest their meal, and for him to show Stevens the sights. They left the hotel and were able to talk freely despite the two men following him. One about 50 yards behind and one on the other side of the street.

McKenzie said, "We sat next to the table which has been reserved for the Armstrong meeting later tonight. I have planted a high powered bug under the table. We will have covert ear pieces this evening, and should be able to hear them from across the restaurant, it will record as well and we can retrieve it later. I will reserve a table well away from them, but their conversation should prove informative. I have also been to the room Armstrong reserved and bugged it, so we should get more from there. It should be an interesting evening."

At 7.30p.m. that evening Stevens and McKenzie were seated at their table in the restaurant, and had started their meal, when George and John Armstrong walked in with two men. One McKenzie knew, Milton Ombegwe a government official whom he had seen at various diplomatic functions around Harare, and the other a man he did not know.

McKenzie excused himself for a moment between courses, and when he returned he said, "The man I didn't know is Horatio Womadie, he is a local business man, and buys second hand tractors, plant machinery and vehicles. He runs his business here in Harare. I believe he is a regular customer of the Armstrong's, and he has important government connections and Ombegwe is one of them. The head waiter is a mine of information, and he knows his tip at the end of our meal will be in dollars and more than the usual ten percent. If Womandie operates in the usual way, he is making payment to some government officials, which allows him to trade. Every government minister and official appears to have at least one income other than their official pay, and trading with foreigners, whilst officially frowned upon, is encouraged, particularly when they pay in dollars. Ombegwe is high up the chain in The Zimbabwe Defence and War Veterans Department. He lives very well, and is well connected. If there is to be an arms deal, he will be the one brokering it."

McKenzie asked the Head waiter to take a picture of him and Stevens as a memento of Steven's visit and he handed him his mobile phone. They pushed their chairs close together and smiled. When they viewed the picture, there was a clear view of the four men sat around the

Armstrong's table in the background. It would enhance well.

Stevens and McKenzie watched whilst they ate their meal, and listened intently to what was being said at the other table. At the end of their meal, the two went to the bar, having paid a hefty tip to the head waiter, and they listened to a very interesting conversation, which later continued in the Armstrong suite. Stevens and McKenzie did not hear everything said by the group, but they heard enough to know that Armstrong had boasted of connections in Russia to obtain a large variety of arms such as anti-tank weapons, grenades, Kalashnikov rifles, machine pistols, mortars, explosives and ammunition. A large consignment was being talked about, at least one large container full, perhaps more, with a value of $12.5 million. Armstrong asked for a deposit from the government official and after a haggling session, the sum of $2 million was agreed, as a deposit. The port of Odessa in the Crimea was mentioned as the port of departure.

Leaving Stevens to sleep, McKenzie said, "I will see you in the morning. I will join you for breakfast, say 8.30am.

McKenzie went back to the now closed restaurant. It was in darkness, but the door was unlocked and he recovered the voice transmitted and recorder from under the Armstrong's table. He would listen to it in full and have a transcription wired to London. Things were getting interesting.

At breakfast McKenzie said, "I have arranged for you to return to London later this evening. I believe we have done all we can here at present. I have spoken to my colleagues in London and it is imperative we find out who Armstrong's contacts are in Russia, where and when he might meet them, and where the shipment of arms will depart from and on what ship."

Steven said, "We should know when and who he is meeting, because we are having all his calls monitored. If he goes to meet them, it is probable he will fly, and probably in one of his own jets. We should get his departure date and destination when he puts in a flight plan. If he goes by scheduled airline, then we should be in a position to know the where and when."

"That's good," said McKenzie "My colleagues in London will keep me in the loop and if I find out any more, I will pass it on. Meantime, maybe we will have some fun with our shadows. I have booked us onto a half day tour of the Thetford Game Reserve. Its only 40 minutes away on the Mazowe Road, and it should give our escort palpitations, because to do their job properly, they will have to book the tour too. There is plenty of time to do the tour and get back to the airport for your flight. Let's go and enjoy ourselves."

Chapter fourteen

Annie Forbes entered the office in the city and went into Mozart's office. Mozart looked up from his work and he greeted her with a lopsided grin.

"Hallo Ms. Forbes", he said, "Things are moving quite fast."

She said, "I wanted to give you a progress report on what we at GCHQ and DI Steve Easterbrook from the Fraud Squad have found so far in Ross-Harding's notebook. We have cracked the code he was using. Simple really, Ross-Harding's certainly no code expert. You were right he has been syphoning off cash from the Armstrong's. He has salted away $2.5million and we can get it back electronically because we have cracked all his passwords, and account numbers. It's all in the book. We are still working on the Armstrong investments and accounts. We already know that there is $56 million salted away in the Cayman Islands Investment Banking Corporation. (CIIBC). This is invested in the name of a Cayman Registered company called the British Cayman Property Investment Company (BCPIC) the directors of which are two local businessmen of dubious character. The Chairman of the Company is George Armstrong, and on the board are his two sons, John and Graham. They are supposed to be a property investment company, but so far we have no records of what they are investing in, and the money is just sitting there. Again we have the codes and could access their cash. However, the Armstrong's don't seem to have the codes yet. We don't think Ross-Harding has had time to pass them on.

Mozart asked, "How easy is it to set up a bank account in the Caymans then."

Forbes said, "I'm no expert but from what DI Easterbrook tells me, you simply have to choose a bank, create an identity, open an offshore account, move money into it, then invest and spend the money. I'm sure it's not that simple, but that's what he says." She continued, "We have also traced a numbered account in Panama which the Armstrong's have been using. It is their oldest account, and they have been using it presumably for their drug deals, because Steve has traced records of large sums going out on a regular basis to other numbered accounts. This account only contains $15 million, and we are assuming, because of the transactions we have traced and the past usage, this will be the account from which they will draw money to pay for the arms. We believe there is also an account in Mexico City, which contains a substantial amount of money, but we are still working on that. The Armstrong's also have business and personal accounts in various UK banks in the names of their business interests, and from time to time these accounts get boosted by transfers from abroad. All in all, their legitimate businesses seem to be run well and are profitable, all except their Private Hire Company based at Manston. This has yet to make a profit and seems to be more private airplanes for family use, rather than a viable business. The directors of all these businesses are George Armstrong and various members of his family. From small beginnings he has quite a business portfolio and he could afford to retire. But I feel it is us who will force his retirement."

Mozart said, "That's all good. It's coming together very nicely. Armstrong is in Zimbabwe at the moment supposedly doing a deal to sell another batch of second hand plant, and other vehicles, but we know he has met a government official and they are going to pay him a deposit for an arms shipment. DS Stevens is out there at the moment, but he should be back tomorrow and we will know more then. To update you, a hit team sent by the Armstrong's, went to the clinic in Northampton where we were holding Ross-Harding. They were tooled up with some heavy artillery. We were waiting for them thanks to Dave Harley's team. Two of the four man team got shot, one dead the other wounded, and the others were arrested. The Inspector in charge was shot in the chest, but he had a vest on, and now he's got broken ribs. They had some of the latest artillery on them, and if that is a sign of what the Armstrong's can get, then we have got real trouble, and we really must stop them. " Mozart looked at his watch and said, "It's lunchtime. Would you like to come to lunch."

Annie Forbes smiled and said, "I'm famished. I thought you would never ask."

Mozart rang the Vertigo Restaurant in Tower 42, Old Broad Street, and booked a table. He and Ms Forbes left the building and walked around the corner to Tower 42. It was an imposing building and the restaurant gave panoramic views across the city of London.

Mozart and Forbes sat in the bar, over pre-lunch drinks.

Annie Forbes said, "My name is Annie I can't keep calling you Mozart. What's your first name."

Mozart said, "Joseph, call me Joe." She said, "If you don't mind me asking. Mozart. That's a hell of a name for an Englishman!"

He laughed and said, "That's because it isn't English. I am, but my grandfather was Austrian."

"There's obviously a story there, but I won't press you. I was just curious, she said."

He looked into her deep brown eyes and made a decision, because he felt an empathy between them. "My grandfather Joseph Eckart Mozart, was born in Vienna and was conscripted into the Germany Airforce during World War Two. He became a fighter pilot and flew ME 109's. He was shot down over Holland in 1944, during Operation Market Garden, and taken prisoner. He was 22. He was shipped to England as a prisoner of war. He and some of his fellow prisoners were allowed to work on a farm as trustees. I don't know how he did it, but he met a local girl, my grandmother Margaret Judd, and as a result my father was born. Prisoners could not marry of course, and when the authorities found out, he was shipped off to another camp in Scotland, and after the war he was sent home to Vienna. My grandmother brought my father up alone. She named him Manfred Joseph Judd, she assumed my grandfather's name of Mozart eventually and then changed both her name and my father's, after the war was long gone by deed poll. I don't know if my grandmother expected my grandfather to marry her after the war, but he probably had no choice other than to have the authorities return him to Germany. She never married, and went through particularly tough times as a single parent, mostly supported by her parents. My father grew up and became an architect. He would have designed buildings like this one. He met my mother Joan in the late sixties. She was a nurse, and they had me a year after they married. I was named Joseph after my grandfather. He got in touch with me a few years ago. He met another girl in Vienna after the war and married. They had a child, a boy and named him Eckart Wolfgang, but he was killed in his late teens in a road accident. They had no other children. His wife died in her sixties of ovarian cancer, and he was alone. He traced and re-united with my father some years ago, and then got to know me. He started sending me birthday and Christmas presents, and he came over once or twice to see my father and me, and I have been over to see him in Vienna. I liked him at once. He was a kindly man, big in business in Vienna and dabbled in fine art. He lived in a big house and was quite wealthy. I found out he died about three months ago. We weren't told at the time. I would have liked to have seen him again, before he went."

Annie Forbes looked deep into Mozart's eyes, her own eyes moist from the telling of the tale, and instinctively she placed her hand over his on the table between them. Mozart looked at her with a faint smile on his face, and from that moment an understanding started to grow between them.

She said, "What about since then."

Mozart said, "When I finished school I went to University and got a 2.1 in law, originally intending to become a lawyer . Then, I suppose I was bored, so I joined the Royal Marines and volunteered for the SBS. I did 8 years and came out to join the Police."

She said, "Never married?"

He said, "No, I've had some chances, but I need to find the right one." He then looked deep into her eyes, a look of hunger, of longing, a look that scoured her soul and betrayed his feelings. Annie had never been so moved, she responded by having the courtesy to blush, but she squeezed the hand she was still holding and held his gaze with her own. The waiter broke the moment, "Your table is ready," he said. Mozart blinked. The moment had passed, but the longing hadn't.

Over lunch Mozart asked, "What about you. I've told you my story, what's yours."

She said, "I have been married. I met him at university when I was studying. It was a college romance, but it never worked out. After 5 years we went our separate ways, and divorced. I started out working for an accountancy firm in the city. It was a well paid job, but I got bored. One day I was at a party with some friends, and I got talking to a woman I was introduced to and she told me about GCHQ, and how they were recruiting. I applied, got the job and the rest is history. I have an elder sister who is married with children and she lives in Oxford, married to a university lecturer. My father is now retired, and he and mum live in the village of Eynsham just outside Oxford. He was a university lecturer and taught English. The poets and all that. I have a flat in Cheltenham near where I work. I am now a senior analyst, hence working to decode Ross-Harding's notebook."

Lunch passed too quickly. Mozart was attracted by this beautiful and clever woman. It was all he could do to tear himself away and return to the job in hand. In her presence he found himself forgetting everything except he was with the most attractive woman he had ever seen. It was not just her beauty, it was her aura of sensuality, the way she penetrated his soul, the timbre of her voice, her ironic sense of humour. His attraction emboldened him.

"Annie" he stuttered hesitantly, "Could we do this again. I can't remember when I have enjoyed a lunch so much."

She looked at him with an appraising stare, hesitated, when Mozart thought, I have gone too far too soon, and she smiled and simply said, "I would love to." His heart lifted with joy, and as they walked back to the office, they talked small talk and took delight in finding out about one another.

Chapter Fifteen

In Harare, Duncan McKenzie was in the foyer of the Continental Hotel, drinking coffee having said goodbye to Winston Stevens, who had a flight to catch, when he saw George Armstrong check out of the hotel. He was with Horatio Womadei. They shook hands, and both left by the front entrance. Armstrong took a taxi obviously heading for the airport, and Womadei walked to the car park towards his car. McKenzie went to the second floor, to the room that Armstrong had just vacated. The door was open and the chamber maid was stripping the bed.

McKenzie said, "I'm sorry, Mr Armstrong sent me back. He's dropped something. I'll get it." As she went into the bathroom, McKenzie went to the coffee table and recovered the voice activated recorder from under the table top. He shouted, "Thanks. I've found it. " He then gave the chambermaid a $10 tip. He would play the tape back at the embassy and send a transcript to his alma mater in London.

Back in his office at the embassy, the tape revealed a conversation between Armstrong and Milton Obegwe the

Zimbabwean government official. They discussed a shipment of arms, and Armstrong gave details of the arms he could obtain. It was heavy artillery indeed. They were heard to discuss how long it would take to obtain the arms, and details of when and how it would be sent, and to whom it would be addressed. He then overheard a conversation that Armstrong had on the telephone with two contacts in Russia, one by the name of Alexsei and mention of the port of Odessa in the Ukraine. McKenzie had a secretary transcribe the tape and he sent this to his office in London. It was received by Mike Hornsby in his office at the MI6 building in London and after he had read it he telephone DCI Mozart and apprised him of its content.

The following morning DS Stevens arrived back at the office fresh from his flight from Harare, he had again slept well on the plane. He added to the information Mozart had already about the meetings. Mozart then called for a meeting with the various agencies, where DS Stevens briefed them on events in Harare and he played the tape removed from under the restaurant table in Harare.

He said, "The tapes from the recordings in Armstrong's bedroom will follow by diplomatic bag." He told the meeting of being met by Duncan McKenzie the Military Attache at the British Embassy in Harare, and of Armstrong's meeting with Horatio Womadei who was to purchase the Armstrong's latest shipment of second hand plant and other machinery, and he told of Armstrong being introduced to Milton Obegwe from the Ministry of Defence and War Veterans, where a shipment of arms had been discussed and arrangements made for a deposit of $2 million to be paid to the Armstrong's account . This deal would break the United Nations embargo should it go ahead.

The following morning Richard Woodgate rang Mozart.

He said, "George and John Armstrong flew into Manston a short while ago from Cyprus and they have left, presumably for home. "

Mozart said, "I will get DI Dave Harley to meet you at Manston this evening to recover the recording device from the aircraft. I'll get him to phone you. It would be good to know what was said on the plane."

Annie Forbes rang Mozart. "Thank you for lunch" she said. "We must do it again," said Mozart with a catch in his voice. She had that effect on him, an effect he had not experienced before.

Annie said, " I would love to, but that's not why I rang you. From our intercepts we have discovered that the Armstrong's intend to fly to Moscow, we don't know when yet. He has been speaking to a Russian called Alexei Komorov, about supplying arms. George Armstrong is going to Moscow with his son John to meet him soon."

"Thanks Annie. I will ask our friends at 5 and 6 what they know of him. Keep me posted if you will."

Mozart then rang Peter Simpson at MI5. He told him what he had been told about Komorov. "We know of him. He is ex KGB and now an entrepreneur approved by the government. He has quite an organization. He has a partner, Dmitry Sidorov. They are Moscow based. They have high powered contacts in the Russian Government, and they have been known to supply arms and ammunition to anyone with the money to pay, but especially if it suits Russian foreign policy. If Armstrong is dealing with Komorov and Siderov, then the Armstrong's intention to supply arms to Zimbabwe is likely to be with the tacit approval of the Russian government. I will get our man in Moscow to see what he can dig up. I'll come back to you."

Later that evening DI Dave Harley rang, "Hi Joe, we've been doing a lot of listening to what was recorded on the plane. We will get the tape to you, but I thought you ought to know. Armstrong knows about the failed attempt on Ross-Harding in Northampton. He is more than anxious about it, because with Ross-Harding still out there and in our custody, he is extremely worried that he might be talking to us. I would think that the two failed attempts at silencing him have made Ross-Harding very worried about his future prospects of staying alive too. Now might be a good time to talk him into telling us what he knows. He knows he's in it up to his neck, but I doubt that he realized until now, just what he had got himself into. These are killers he's dealing with, and I now think he understands. Secondly, he talked about the government official he met in Harare. There is no doubt they are very keen to use Armstrong and his organization to get illicit arms into the country because they have told him if he can get arms to them, then his path would be greased to lucrative business deals in the future. They paid him $2 million as a deposit, which is most unusual. He thinks this shows how desperate they are to get a shipment into the country. "

Mozart said, "They know that Armstrong is a heavy duty drug importer into the UK. They know he has been operating very successfully for years and has not been caught. They know that half the stuff he exports to Zimbabwe is genuine and the other half is probably stolen property because Horatio Womadie, whom Armstrong does business with is a crook, but they don't care because Womadie pays his dues up the line keeping the right people sweet. According to our sources in Harare, it is Milton Obegwe, who is a high up official in their Ministry of Defence and War Veterans, who gave Armstrong the names of two Russian Ex KGB Mafia figures, and who can arrange the supply of illicit arms. So they are wanting to use the Armstrong organizational skills to obtain a shipment. As to the unusual way they readily parted with $2 million. I have been thinking about that. I suppose if all goes wrong the Zimbabweans' have a guarantor for the cash in Obegwe. They would probably just recover their losses from him. They are on a win win."

Mozart and Stevens drove to Norfolk. They were stopped at the entrance to the drive by a man in a tweed jacket and matching trousers. The ensemble finished off with a tweed cap and brown boots. He looked a typical gamekeeper. He had a 12 bore shotgun under one arm.

He said, "This is private property."

Mozart produced his warrant card and introduced himself and Stevens. The man went to one of the gate pillars, and picked up a telephone handset inserted on the inside of the pillar.

He spoke to someone and then said, "Please drive straight down the drive and at the end park to the left. You will be met."

They drove down the drive, their wheels crunching on the loose gravel of the driveway. The house was a large country house, surrounded by manicured lawns, and flower beds. Discreet cameras were fixed to the building, and there were floodlights fixed both to the building and in trees. A middle aged woman stood at the top of the steps leading to the front door, and she waited for them to approach her.

"Mr. Mozart, Mr. Stevens."

Mozart confirmed his identity, again showing his warrant card, and she said, "Please do come in. You are expected."

Mozart said, "How is the patient."

She said, "He is bruised and stiff, and in fear of his life, and he is expecting someone to talk to him. He has started eating normally again since he has got the drugs out of his system. I think you will find him amenable."

Mozart said, "Is he having any medical treatment. "

She said, "Painkillers, in moderation, but he shows improvement every day. I will fetch my husband, and get him to take you to him."

"Mr. Mozart," said the man as he approached. "My name is Parsons. My wife and I look after the house and its guests. Mr. Ross-Harding is much recovered and I believe ready to talk to you."

Mozart said, "Thank you. I don't see much security around. You know that two attempted have been made on his life."

Parson said, "We are well aware sir, what you don't see is men out in the grounds, and some inside. They are all trained to a high degree, but discretion is our watchword. We are confident we can handle most situations, and we are well armed." He then took Mozart and Stevens to a room on the first floor. Sitting outside the room was a man who had the look of a soldier. He looked fit and alert. They were taken inside Ross-Harding's room. He still had a drip fixed to his arm, and sitting at his bedside was a nurse in uniform. At a nod from Parsons she quietly left the room.

"Mr. Ross-Harding" said Mozart, "Let me introduce myself, because last time we met, I don't believe you were compos mentis. I am Detective Chief Inspector Mozart and my companion is Detective Sergeant Stevens. I was the officer who first received a call because you were found injured and tied up and dumped in a puddle at Barking Creek, with WE'LL BE BACK written on your chest. It was me and my Sergeant again at the hospital when we stopped a man from pumping heroin into your drip, in an attempt to kill you. He had a gun and we shot him dead. We learned afterwards that his name was James Nolan, nicknamed Gunner. We also learned that he and his brother John were drug dealers, calling themselves the Whitechapel Cartel. We also know that you use drugs and they were your suppliers, and you owe them a considerable amount of money, which is why you were beaten up. However, when we investigated further we found your true name, although at the time you called yourself Green, we know you are Mungo Ross-Harding. You live in a flat in Harley Street and you work in Private Banking for a City based bank. We also know that among your clients you have a family from Kent, George Armstrong and his sons John and Graham, apparently very wealthy clients, who came to you, for you to invest money for them. What you may not have realized at first, was that the Armstrong's are known to us as criminals and large scale drug importers, which is how they started accumulating their wealth, and the Nolan brothers get their drugs from the Armstrong's. This is how the Armstrong's first came to know about you, and how they realized your potential in assisting them to launder their cash. However, they found out you have been syphoning off some of their cash for yourself whilst laundering their money. We know you have stashed away $2.5 million in a bank in Luxemburg. You have, however, laundered many millions for the Armstrong's, secreting their funds in offshore accounts in the Caymans, Panama and other places. What you also may not know is the Nolan's, on behalf of the Armstrong family, searched your flat in Harley Street. They were looking for records of the financial dealings you have made for the Armstrong's. They didn't find anything significant, but we did. When I first saw you in the hospital, you were only just conscious. After the attack on you, you were semi comatose but I did hear you say, KEY and DESK. We went to your bank and searched your desk. Taped under one of the drawers we found a key. That key fitted a locker at Liverpool Street Station and in it we found a small number of packets of white powder, which contained heroin. But most importantly we found a notebook. It was obviously written by you, and was coded. We have been working on the codes and find you have been a very naughty boy, and have been laundering money for the Armstrong's on an industrial scale. The Armstrong's now fear you are going to talk, and they appear to want to cut their losses. You are expendable to them, and as a consequence they have now twice tried to have you killed. We have stopped them both times, and after the last attempt we had you removed to this house, where you will remain until it is safe to move you. It isn't safe for you out there at the moment, and we fear another attempt on your life. You are in mortal danger and as far as I can see, your only chance is with us, the police. We are gathering evidence against the Armstrong's as we speak, and learning more each day about their shady deals. If you want to get out of this alive, I would suggest that you cooperate with us. You are in a deal of trouble."

Ross-Harding said, "You say they have tried twice. I was told about the first time, what about the second."

Mozart said, "The Armstrong's sent a four man team, armed with machine guns to kill you at the clinic in Northampton. That is why we moved you again. We stopped them, killed one, wounded another and arrested the others. They are not talking of course, but we know who they were working for. It could happen again."

Ross-Harding said, "If I tell you what I know, what will happen to me."

Mozart said, "Well for a start we will protect you. Secondly if you are prepared to tell us what you know, and lead us to all the cash, I have the authority to say that we will use you as a witness. Any decision as to prosecuting you is out of my hands, and will be a decision the Director of Public Prosecutions will have to take, but he will take note of your cooperation."

Ross-Harding said, "Let me think about it."

Mozart said, "Well don't take too long. The people here know how to contact me. I would make it soon if I were you. The other thing you might want to consider is the safety of your parents. Do the Armstrong's know of them and where they live. Could they be in danger because of you. Meantime, do not try to leave here. You will be stopped and arrested, and Police cells are not nearly so comfortable."

On the way out Steven's said, "Do you think he will talk."

Mozart replied, "He'd be a fool not to. The Armstrong's have a long reach and without us, I wouldn't give much for his chances. Thinking about his parents. They could be in danger. If the Armstrong's know about them and where they are, they could use the parents to get to Mungo. When we get back to the office, perhaps you can arrange some discreet protection for them without them knowing of course. I don't want to involve them unless it becomes absolutely necessary."

On the way back to the office, Mozart's phone rang. It was Annie Forbes again. She said, "Joseph" just hearing her voice stirring his emotions, "We have been monitoring the Armstrong's phones and computers. They have booked a flight for two to Moscow in two days time. Flying Flight BA 773 to Moscow Sheremetyevo Airport. They have also booked a double suite at the Napka Metropol Hotel on Teatralnyy Prayezd. The flight takes off at 1030hrs and the flight is about 4hrs 30 minutes. The airport is about 20 miles from the hotel, but there is a good connecting train service, unless they are met at the airport. I should have more later. If I do, then I will bring it to the city office tomorrow."

Thanks Annie" said Mozart, "It will be good to see you again. If you come in the middle of the afternoon I will arrange for an update meeting with everybody then I would love to take you to dinner." She said, "It's a date."

Mozart rang Peter Simpson at his office In MI5. "I have heard from Annie Forbes. It appears that George Armstrong, and probably one of his sons are flying to Moscow in two days time. I believe that they are going to meet Komarov and Siderov to set up the arms deal."

"Russia is more tricky than Zimbabwe. The authorities there are well practiced and professional. You can't go, they would pick you out in a heartbeat. I have a team I will send to cover their meeting, but it will take a team who know all the tricks of the trade. They will need to speak Russian, and they will need to be unknowns from out of the country. I don't suppose any of your staff speak Russian."

"You are probably right, they won't," said Mozart.

"Leave it to me, I will come back to you. Give me the details you have," said Simpson. Mozart then passed on the information about the flight, and hotel. "I will make the arrangements and let you know soonest." He then rang off.

Mozart called for Detective Sergeant Stevens. "Win" he said, "we need to have a heads up meeting with the various members of the team. I would like to keep up to speed on all that is happening. Can I leave you to organize a meeting tomorrow afternoon with SO15, SO11, MI5 and MI6. Annie Forbes just rang a while ago and she is coming up to see us with some intercept information, and it would be good for everyone to know what's going on all round, so we all keep our focus."

Winston said, "Leave it with me. Shall we say about three in the afternoon."

Chapter Sixteen

Mozart rang the Forensic Laboratory at Lambeth, and spoke to the head scientific officer, Doctor Michael Carrington, who was coordinating the forensic evidence relating to the case . "Can you up date me on how the forensic examinations are going. I have a meeting this afternoon and would like to be able to give an update."

Carrington said, "Well we have proved scientifically that Ross-Harding was beaten up in the cellar of the Nolan's place in Barking. The blood matches both in type and DNA profiling. The rope ends match with the rope found at the premises, and there is a blood match with Ross-Harding on the clothes taken from both Nolan's. So that's pretty well tied up. We have matched the bullet found in the hospital wall, with the gun found on Nolan at the hospital, and we have matched the two bullets taken from the chest of James Nolan with the gun used by DS Stevens, plus the gun shot residue (GSR) found on both the body of James Nolan and Sergeant Stevens shows they both discharged firearms. We have confirmed the syringe recovered at the hospital was used by James Nolan. His DNA was found on it, and it did contain heroin. We also found heroin in the drip and a trace in the blood sample taken from Ross-Harding. We have also blood and DNA in Nolan's vehicle which proves that they transported Ross-Harding in the vehicle. So that pretty well ties up the incidents at the Nolan's office and the hospital. The gun used by James Nolan is a little trickier. The serial numbers and batch numbers had been filed off. We will be able to bring them up eventually but it will take time. The other news is that this particular gun has been matched to two other drug related shootings in the East End of London. I will send you the details so you can follow these up in due time. Another gun was found at Barking, and this too has been matched to a drug related shooting in Essex, again the numbers have been filed off, and again we are hopeful of bringing that up too."

"We have the same type of proof at the clinic shooting in Northampton. Matching the shots to the guns used, and proved by GSR who discharged firearms. We have also examined the Jaguar car, and apart from knowing who owned it, we have matched all four assailants to the vehicle by fingerprints and DNA."

After you told us about the drugs find at Felixstowe Docks, we were able to liaise with the customs, and we examined the load. We proved it was 95% pure heroin, which originated in Afghanistan, but was imported through Rotterdam. We found some unidentified fingerprints, and DNA traces on the packaging, and that included the driver of the lorry who must have helped load the stuff in the lorry. Through HM Customs again, we are liaising with the Dutch authorities on this aspect to try and get a match. I believe we might get some success on that because both the Koninklijke Marechausee and the

Amsterdam drug squad have some names they can put forward, so we are hopeful. The Dutch seem to know of the gang who might be the one's used by the Armstrong's, and we have offered our findings to the Dutch and hopefully they will reciprocate."

Mozart said," I believe that we should let the Customs run with this drug find, and we ask Richard Woodgate, and Nick Braithwaite of the National Crime Agency, to keep a watch in brief and if necessary direct the Customs inquiry. They can come to you direct for forensic assistance, and keep us up to speed on their results, which we can dovetail into the whole case if necessary later. If you get any difficulty on that score please let me know. "

"Great," he said, "That's about it for now." "Thanks Mike," said, Mozart. "Keep in touch" and rang off.

At 3p.m. the various agencies arrived at the city office. They met in the conference room, and for the next few hours, they each contributed to the update meeting.

Mozart said, "We have appointed an exhibits officer to keep track of the various items recovered. When and where they were found and by whom. He will liaise directly with the Forensic team. So please make him and me aware of any and all exhibits found."

Annie Forbes was able to tell the meeting of her progress with Ross-Harding's coded notebook, the tracing of the laundered money, and of the details of the various intercept GCHQ had organized.

Detective Sergeant Stevens updated the meeting with details of the meeting George Armstrong had in Harare and the proposed arms deal.

Mozart updated them on the intended journey by the Armstrong's to Russia to meet two known ex-KGB arms dealers.

When the meeting was over Mozart was talking to Annie Forbes in his office when the telephone rang. "Mozart" he said.

"Mr. Mozart. This is Parsons. You remember from the house in Norfolk."

"Oh yes Mr. Parsons. What can I do for you."

"It's our patient. He's a very worried man. He asked me to get hold of you. He wants to tell you all."

"Tell him I shall come up in the morning. And many thanks Mr. Parsons. See you tomorrow late morning," said Mozart. He opened the door and shouted across the room to DS Stevens, "Win, tomorrow morning we're going back to Norfolk. RH wants to see us." Winston Stevens grinned and nodded.

Mozart turned to Annie Forbes and said, "Now I promised you dinner. Have you a preference. English, Turkish, Chinese, Thai."

She said, "Something exotic I think would suit my mood."

He said, "I know a nice French Restaurant in Canada Wharf. It's near where I live, and it has great views over the water. The atmosphere is great and the chef is very good. Does French cuisine suit your mood." She said, "Perfect." "I will book a table" said Mozart.

Two hours later, with Annie Forbes on his arm, Mozart entered the restaurant. He felt the sensuality of her presence, her perfume working on his pheromones. He was on a high. He was with his perfect woman, and taking her to one of his favourite restaurants. It did not get better than that. They were greeted by the head waiter.

He said, "I can take you to your table, but if you wish, you could start in the bar. "The bar, I think" said Mozart, and he steered Annie to a booth which overlooked the water. There was soft music playing in the background, an unobtrusive orchestral melody which suited the occasion. They sat opposite each other gazing over the water with the lights of the buildings dancing on the rippled water, and sipped aperitifs whilst making small talk. They were happy in each other's company, their body language was in sync, and both felt the vibrations of a growing relationship. They were so conscious of each other that they failed to notice the head waiter hovering over them. He coughed discreetly, bringing them temporarily back to normality, and with a knowing look he said, "Your table is ready". The meal passed in a haze. They hardly noticed what they ate. They took their time and lingered over each course. Annie had a good appetite, but Mozart seemed to pick at his food, he seemed there but far away at times. Time flew, with the last cognac and coffee reluctantly it was time to go. They now knew more about each other, and what they learned, dragged them deeper toward a relationship. She was his perfect woman. He was her most attractive man. She admired his strength of character, his work ethic. He exuded masculinity which over whelmed her senses, she was drawn to him like steel to a magnet. He admired her obvious but concealed intelligence. Her ability to talk with authority and conviction on a multitude of subjects, her dress sense. She was perfect. Neither wanted the evening to end. Coming back down to earth, Mozart as he passed over a generous tip to the head waiter, asked him to call a taxi.

Outside the restaurant as the taxi drew up Mozart said, "It's been a wonderful memorable evening for me." He looked deep into her eyes and said, "I want, no I need, to see you again." "Me too," she said.

"Let's get you home. How did you get to London."

She replied, "I came by train."

She snuggled into his arms in the back of the black cab. He kissed her lightly, and she responded by stopping him with her hand in front of his face. She looked deep into his eyes, her voice lowering to a husky whisper. "Take me to your home." His heart leaped, he started to palpitate. He was short of breath. He had never felt like this before. He was a lost soul. He could feel her heart pounding against his chest. He couldn't speak. He hugged her tight and she responded in kind.

He opened the door to his flat. She looked round as the discreet lighting produced soft pools of light. He switched the fire on, and its glow added to the twilight atmosphere. He took her coat and she sat on the sofa with the fire glow dancing in her lustrous hair. He poured drinks and joined her. They looked deep into each other's eyes and kissed, sipped their cognac and kissed again. It was the most deeply moving experience of his life . Totally absorbing. Mozart had never experienced such longing and passion. They were lost in each other. It was meant to be. It was kismet, despite knowing each other for but a short time, they both knew it was right. It spoke of permanency. Not a word was said, but somehow they were in bed together. Her aura engulfed and consumed him. His masculinity powered over her. There was no one else, nothing would ever come close. They were one. He moved, she responded. She moved, he responded, until shooting stars shot across the heavens, and peace descended like a soft blanket to wrap them in its warmth.

Mozart woke as the dawn light was illuminating the window. There was no noise, apart from a faint rasping of breath next to him. He rubbed his eyes, and lifted his head off the pillow. He moved his arm from around her shoulders and gently stroked her skin. It was velvet. She stirred and opened her eyes. Mozart smelled her musk, he was in love. Deeply, passionately, permanently.

She looked deep into his eyes, "Is this really happening, " she whispered. "I love you. I know we have only met a little while ago, but I know I am lost to you. I know, even now, I have never been really in love with anyone else. I have only now discovered what real love is. "

He said softly. "I feel it too. Wow. It's like riding the storm. Something beyond control."

"I don't understand it yet, but I want more of you. I love you Joseph Mozart," she said.

In the dawn light they felt for one another again. This time it was not frantic. It was a slow absorption, deeply passionate, it carried them slowly to another place far away, where they climaxed with a melding of their inner beings, an indescribable ethereal experience which gave them the most peace and tranquility that either of them had ever known. They were utterly spent but now knew that love was not just physical, but an exchange of souls, a melding of minds, true, all -encompassing and complete.

Chapter Seventeen

Mozart and Stevens returned to the safe house in Norfolk. They were greeted by Mr Parsons, who was expecting them.

He said, "Miss Forbes and Detective Inspector Steve Easterbrook are already here. They are in the drawing room." He led them to the room, and Mrs. Parsons brought coffee. Annie smiled at Mozart, which brought back vivid memories of an unforgettable evening and night.

He said, "I understand Ross-Harding now wants to talk to us. DS Stevens and I will go and see if he is now prepared to cooperate. If he will, then I want to ask you both to go and see him, where he can translate the rest of the notebook to you Annie and Steve. Then you will have firsthand knowledge of the money trail. Are you happy with that." They both said, "Yes.".

Mozart and Stevens went to Ross-Harding's room. He was now sitting up in bed. Still showing bruises, and was very stiff from his beating.

Mozart said, "I understand that you want to tell us what happened to you, and what your involvement with the Armstrong's has been. He then cautioned him.

Ross-Harding said, "I have been thinking about what you said. I realize I have been a fool .I am way out of my depth. It all started when I went to a nightclub with a girlfriend. I was foolish enough to take heroin, and from there I gradually got sucked into the drug scene. I only started for recreational purposes. Then I started buying it. I was introduced to the Nolan brothers' Whitechapel cartel, who supplied me with the drug and from there, I built up a debt which I was paying off over time, but the habit got to me. I built up more and more debt. In the end I owed the Nolan's quite a lot of money. Along the way they introduced me to the Armstrong's. I didn't realize at first that they were the ones supplying the Nolan's. Old man Armstrong had found out I was in the Banking business, more importantly, Private Banking. At first he blackmailed me into laundering cash for him. It was fairly easy for me because I knew all the wrinkles of the system. It started gradually, and I got in deeper and deeper. I started keeping a record. The notebook you found. The sums were getting bigger and bigger, and George Armstrong wanted to know the details from time to time. I laundered an enormous amount of cash for them, and placed it in numbered accounts around the world. They are now very rich. While I was doing it, I was still using and getting my supplies from the Nolan's. I thought then, with so much money flowing in, I could syphon off a small percentage for myself and clear my debts. I ignored several warnings about payment, and when I was trying to get drugs from their courier, I had a sack put over my head, I was knocked out and I ended up in this cellar, being beaten by them with rubber hoses. All the while they kept demanding payment, but I couldn't get at the cash. I couldn't let on to the Nolan's that I had cash stashed away. I was really frightened. They beat me for a long time, and then I was dumped, tied up at Barking Creek. They dumped me in water and I thought I was going to drown because I thought I was in the Thames and they'd put me there to let me drown when the tide came in. They didn't know I was working for the Armstrong's. If they had realized, I don't think they would have touched me. They are frightened of the Armstrong's. I know that, but so am I. They are evil. Since I got into Police hands it appears the Armstrong's want rid of me because I know too much. You tell me that they have tried twice to murder me, and knowing the Armstrong's as I do, I believe they will try again. I am terrified."

Mozart said, "We have your notebook. We have translated some of your code, and are working on decoding the rest. We have traced the location of some of the funds you have laundered, but not all of it as yet. We have tracked your secret account and know you have syphoned of $2.5 million. I would now suggest your only way out is to cooperate with us, tell us everything, and we will protect you. We are after far bigger fish than you.

We've got the Nolan's out of circulation, and we want to do the same to the Armstrong's. We can do it with your help, but you have to be open with us and tell the complete truth."

He said, "I will."

Mozart said, "We have two people downstairs. One has a copy of your notes and the other is an expert in asset tracing. I will get them up here, so now's your chance to tell all you know. I will have them brought in, and leave you with them. Remember, full details and the truth."

DS Stevens brought Annie Forbes and Steve Easterbrook into the room. He introduced them to Ross-Harding. Mozart said to the two, "I will see you back at the office. Please come and brief me when you have finished." As he left he winked at Annie Forbes and whispered, "Squeeze him dry for me."

Mozart and Stevens walked into the office, to find Peter Simpson of MI5, Mike Hornsby of MI6 and Commander John Russell SO 15 waiting for him. Once in Mozart's office Simpson said, "This meeting in Moscow the Armstrong's have set up. Mike here has been doing some ground work. We need to know what is going on, and we need to do something similar to what we did in Harare, except this time we cannot use either you, Sergeant Stevens or anyone from the Embassy. The Russian's are too cute for that to work again. It will have to be a team from MI6. Preferably Russian speakers, but complete unknowns to the Russians. All strangers are carefully scrutinized on entry and followed and reported on for most of their stay. Mike", said Simpson," Tell them what the plan is."

Mike Hornsby said, "We can move a six person team in from other countries. We have a man and woman team from Germany, another pair from Norway, and one man from Estonia, and another from the Czech Republic. They are all fluent in Russian. We need this team to cover the hotel where the Armstrong's are staying to carry out a similar operation to the one in Harare. We also have another one from the UK who will be on the same flight as the Armstrong's. We can't use the military Attache he is too well known, however he will provide the technical surveillance equipment the team might need . We need the where, when, why and how the arms are to be obtained, what port they will be shipped from, the ship they will be carried on and its port or ports of destination. We know the political situation for Russians is difficult in the Ukraine because of the annexation of the Crimea. Since then Russians have become persona non grata, but Komarov and Siderov must have found a way around these barriers. We also know an intercept mentioned the port of Odessa, so it is probable that the two Russians will purchase arms in Russia the Czech Republic and possibly the Ukraine, and ship them to their various customers out of Odessa. We need that knowledge, and the team we send in to get the information has got to be fast on their feet, get the information, and get it out to us. We have some help, because we know that we have the Armstrong's mobile phones bugged, and their laptops hacked, but we need to know what the deal is. We haven't yet full monitoring of the Russians in place, although we're working on it. We have booked the couple from Norway into the same hotel as the Armstrong's. They are in situ already acting as tourists. We have another team on standby in the Czech Republic, and another in the Ukraine, and I would suggest that you Mr. Mozart put yourself on standby to fly to the Ukraine, should the Russians intend to ship the arms out through that route."

Peter Simpson said, "Komarov and Siderov are the directors of an Import/Export business known as KS International. They have an office in Presnenskaya Embankment, Moscow, not far from the Moskva River, on the second floor of a tower block building. The company have a web site and GCHQ are taking steps to hack into their communications. This is difficult because the Russians are very good at hacking themselves, and good at counter measures. However GCHQ seem confident they can do what is required without showing out. Komarov and Siderov are both known killers who were full time KGB agents and maybe are still involved. They operate their business with the full approval and backing of high placed government ministers and departments and very often their sales will come from contacts government ministers have made. Because of their business, with their world wide contacts and travel they are often used on clandestine and even kill operations against opponents of their mother regime. Their arms procurement business is carried out with the full knowledge and approval of the regime, especially when arms shipments are delivered to organizations and dodgy regimes their own government has interests in and approve of. It is all part of their government's destabilization policy directed toward areas of the world where the west have interests, or which have the disapproval of western governments. In other words they are a deniable tool of their own government for nefarious and clandestine activities. This is why they find it easier than most to procure the sort of arms from government factories other dealers would find difficult to obtain. There is even a thought the company was set up by the government and they have a stake in it, finance it, and even direct its activities. Komarov and Siderov are both very nasty individuals and would see dealing with a major drug importer from the UK, who wants to turn to arms dealing, as an ideal opportunity to further their master's destabilization policies. It is believed that doing business with KS International is very dangerous. The trail of bodies, all non proven of course, only confirms this. The Armstrong's don't really know who they are dealing with and what they are getting into. They may have bitten off more than they can chew.

Later that evening Annie Forbes and Steven Easterbrook returned to the office. "We have got everything on tape, and he has translated all his codes for us. We now know where the Armstrong's funds are hidden. The family have salted away many millions and on paper are very wealthy indeed," said Annie.

Steve Easterbrook said, "With the information I have I can prepare a case to get court orders to firstly freeze the accounts and then recover them, but we will have to wait until they are arrested on a criminal charge. Having looked into their company accounts, were they to pack up the drug importation business tomorrow, they would still be rich from legitimate sources. Except those legitimate businesses were started with illicit funding in the first place."

"Well Steve, if you can prepare a case to recover their assets, and Annie, if you can translate the codes into a document we can follow, then we will have documentary evidence to prove part of our case against the family, " said Mozart. Steve Easterbrook then left. Mozart looked at Annie. He saw a softening of her features. He raised his eyebrows and said, "Dinner? This evening." She nodded eagerly. “Let me cook for you,” she said, with a twinkle in her eye, and an enigmatic smile.

The following day DI Harley and his team followed George Armstrong and his son Graham to Heathrow Airport. They went to the BA checkout destined for a flight to Moscow. This, Harley reported up the line, and the team in Moscow were alerted. Seven hours later both Armstrong’s were seen to arrive in a taxi at the Hotel Napka Metro, Teatralnyy Prayezd. This was a hotel in central Russia close to the Lubyanka and KGB HQ. They had booked a suite with two separate bedrooms. The MI6 team had identified the room. They were able to affect entry prior to the arrival of the Armstrong’s, and conceal specialized electronic devices which would not over-bleed to other Russian devices already installed.

When the Armstrong’s got to their room the telephone rang. It was Alexsei Komarov. He arranged a meeting that same evening at a nearby popular restaurant, the Restaurante Rosario, off Kiedrinskaya Square, at 8p.m. local time. The MI6 team followed the Armstrong’s as they left the hotel. They were heard by one of the surveillance team who followed them out to give the name of the restaurant to a taxi driver. This information was passed on to the German MI6 team of a man and a woman, who followed a short time later , having booked a table at the same restaurant. When they entered the restaurant, they saw the Armstrong's were sitting in a booth with two men. They recognized them to be Alexei Komarov and Dmitry Siderov. They saw the party looking at photographs and talking but they couldn't hear what was said. The meal and discussions went on for three hours.

The MI6 agents finished their meal, and both went to the adjacent bar, where they could still see the Armstrong's. Once they had finally finished their meal, the party came into the bar, and were seen to seal their deal with vodka, after which the Russians drove the Armstrong's back to their hotel.

Annie Forbe's mobile telephone rang. She fumbled for it from under the duvet. "Forbes" she said sleepily. It was one of her work colleagues at GCHQ. She put it on speaker.

He said, "We monitored a telephone call from George Armstrong to his home. He talked of a $10million shipment being arranged by his contacts. He mentioned that it would be shipped in a container from Russia via Czechoslovakia and the Ukraine. It was a consignment of AK 47's, Scorpions, mortars, hand grenades, hand guns, ammunition, anti tank weapons and explosives. He said that the Russians would fix the paperwork for the consignment to travel from Russia through the Czech Republic in a sealed container, then through the Ukraine, which apparently is quite difficult because the Russians are apparently not popular in the Ukraine at the moment, and they would be put on a ship in Odessa. He named the ship as the MV Santa Cruz. He expected the consignment to be on board the ship in a fortnight to three weeks time depending upon the ship's schedule. He wanted his son to arrange a $5millon deposit payable to the Russian's at the Moskva BepNTb Bank, Movocheremushkinskaya, Moscow. He had to spell this out, and give account numbers, and the payee as KS International. He said the balance would be paid on delivery to the ship. The consignment will be labelled on the paperwork as plant and machinery. We've had some success in hacking into the KS International computer system and will be monitoring the order if we can. I will send you a transcript of what was said. Shall I send it to you at the office in London? "

Annie said, "Yes, do that I will be there later." She turned over, and said, "Did you hear all that?"

Mozart said, "Yes. It's good news," as he rolled closer to her in his large bed. He then kissed her lightly on the lips, which led to a harder more passionate kiss, which led to gentle caressing which lead to each being lost in one another and unconscious of time.

Mozart and Annie Forbes walked into the office two hours later, and the transcript of Armstrong's conversation in Russia was waiting on his desk. He called Peter Simpson and apprised him of its content. Things were moving apace.

Chapter Eighteen

George and Graham Armstrong returned to their home two days later. Almost immediately the telephone intercept picked up George Armstrong telephoning his second hand plant dealer contact in Mogadishu, Somalia.

He was heard to make arrangements to see him in three days time at his hotel. He booked into the Palm Beerta Palace Hotel, Madina Gate, a suite with two bedrooms for himself and his son John. The number he dialed belonged to Abdirahim Halimo Mohamed, who owned a company known as Halimo Road Plant (HRP) on Jaziira Road, in Mogadishu.

The following day Mozart answered the phone from Richard Woodgate, HM Customs Investigations Department.

He said, "George Armstrong has registered a flight plan for tomorrow. He is using one of his own jets from Manston and flying to Cyprus, and then on the following day to Mogadishu. He and his son John are the registered passengers.

Mozart said, "Thanks Richard. This ties in with information that we have that Armstrong is meeting his regular contact who buys second hand plant and vehicles from him. He appears to be trying to raise a lot of money for the purchase of arms. When I know more, we will have an update meeting."

Mozart then telephoned Peter Simpson and updated him on the latest development. Simpson said, "We need to cover the meeting. I will get our friends at MI6 to help. Have you anyone you can send."

"I could get Winston Stevens to go. He is fully briefed, but he has already been in the same hotel as the Armstrong's in Harare and if they see him again, it might be risky. Is there someone else we could send."

Simpson said, "I will send Adam Brocklehurst, and have him met at the airport. Please arrange his flight and text me the details."

Simpson called Brocklehurst to his office. He said, "I need you to go to Mogadishu. We have booked a flight from Heathrow, Qatar Airways, business class. Leaving this afternoon at 4p.m. You will be met at the airport. It's a thirteen and a half hour flight, overnight, but as its business class you should get some sleep. You are booked into the Palm Beerta Palace Hotel for up to 3 nights. Please phone DCI Mozart and he will brief you"

When Brocklehurst rang, Mozart briefed him on what had happened and what was wanted in Mogadishu. He warned Brocklehurst about Somalia being a hotbed of spies and intrigue. The Russian held a lot of sway in the country and did a lot of business there. They were not averse to using third parties as conduits to supply questionable goods to the country, There was no doubt the authorities would know the Armstrong's business deals with Halimo were borderline illegal, and if they knew so would the Russians.

Adam Brocklehurst walked through the exit doors leading to the main concourse of Mogadishu's Aden Adde International Airport, having travelled business class on Qatar Airways Flight QA 157. He had slept overnight and was feeling refreshed. An upright man of about 45, with light brown hair, wearing grey slacks and a white shirt was holding a placard bearing his name. The man introduced himself as Major Jonathan Barwood, Military Attache at the British Embassy. The embassy itself was unusually situated within the boundaries of the main airport, and was heavily guarded by the Somalian army on its outer perimeter, and by Royal Marines inside. Adam, as he walked through the embassy compound with his host, thought this a most unusual arrangement and an early indicator of the security situation in the country. This was quickly confirmed by his host Jonathan Barwood, who advised him never to go out alone, and to always go armed. Once inside the embassy Barwood briefed Brocklehurst as to the do's and don'ts in the country, and he issued a Glock handgun with shoulder holster to him to back up his advice.

The embassy placed a 4 x 4 vehicle at Brocklehurst's disposal, with a driver and armed escort. If he had to leave the hotel he should only do so with Jonathan Barwood or in an embassy vehicle with an armed driver. Barwood and the escort took Brocklehurst to his hotel, the same one the Armstrong's were registered to use, and allowed him time to settle in. On the way he was surprised to see the number of people on the streets of Mogadishu openly carrying guns, mostly AK47's. This reinforced the view that Mogadishu really was a dangerous city to be in, especially for a foreigner.

Barwood arranged to meet Brocklehurst for dinner that evening in the hotel restaurant, by which time the Armstrong's should have arrived. He warned him that his hotel room might be bugged.

Barwood turned up early and tapped on Brocklehurst's hotel door. When he answered the door, and before he could say anything, Barwood held up his hand in a signal, not to say anything, signing that he suspected the room was bugged and reminding him to be careful. He then showed Brocklehurst electronic devices he had brought with him whilst carrying out normal conversation but in the bathroom whispered that the Armstrong's had the next door suite. Both rooms had adjacent balconies, and Barwood slipped silently out of the balcony doors, climbed onto the adjacent balcony, opened the sliding doors to the Armstrong's room and disappeared. He returned after ten minutes.

He said, loudly, "Shall we go to dinner. I have reserved a table in the restaurant."

Brocklehurst said, "Yes, I'm hungry," and they left the room.

On the way down to the restaurant Barwood whispered, "I bugged the room and here's an ear piece. I will try to see which table they have booked and try to place a device there."

Once in the restaurant the two saw one table against the far wall in an isolated position, and they both sat at this table which had a small reserved sign on it. They pretended not to notice the sign and Barwood managed to place a recording device beneath the table. A short time later the head waiter came over and said, "I am sorry sir, but this table is reserved for a Mr. Armstrong and party." Barwood apologized profusely and they moved to a table across the room.

As they were on their starter course, Abdirahim Halimo Mohamed came into the room with George and John Armstrong. They sat at the reserved table and ordered drinks and food. The device beneath the table picked up most of their conversation but it proved difficult to understand Halimo's broken English. However they understood enough. A shipment of refurbished plant and second hand vehicles, including some high value vehicle parts, was due to arrive in the port of Mogadishu the following day. It was a shipment from the Armstrong's, which Halimo expected, and for which he had paid a deposit of $500,000. The balance would be paid by electronic bank transfer upon arrival and inspection of the load at his depot in the Jaziira Road.

The later part of the conversation was of the most interest to Brocklehurst and Barwood. Halimo had been approached by what he called a "very bad man" who had learned from a government source, that he had a meeting with two men from England. The source knew these men were arranging shipments of plant and machinery including suspected stolen high value vehicle parts, but he also knew they had contacts who could provide arms and ammunition. This obviously meant this man knew someone in government with serious Russian contacts. Halimo was talking about Mohammed Umbedi Hassan. Halimo described him as the leader of a group of pirates and hijackers, who had political ambitions, and who was, to his face, a friend of the current President of Somalia. He often did dirty work for the Somali government. Although his main purpose appeared to be piracy and insurrection. His hidden agenda was political power. Hassan and his group had made millions of dollars from the pirating and hijacking of ships transiting Somali waters in the past. Some of these dollars had found their way into the pockets of his political contacts. Hassan held sway over his followers by proclaiming himself the reincarnation of Mohammed Abdullah Hassan, known as the Mad Mullah whose followers earlier in the 20th century fought the British and became known as the Dervishes. The modern day Hassan invoked the malevolent spirit of the Djinn to terrify his followers into believing his cause was holy, and as a result his following had grown into a small army of fanatics who believed in his leadership and "Holy" war. They were feared because of their devotion to revolution and terror, and were quite prepared to use extreme violence to further their aims. All this Brocklehurst learned from Barwood, as he was listening to the conversations at the other table coming through his earpiece. What became apparent was that Hassan had, through his government connections, learned that the Armstrong's were intent upon purchasing arms from the Russians, and he wanted to meet them to come to some sort of similar arrangement. It was made clear to the Armstrong's if they wanted to carry on doing business in Somalia, they had better listen to what Hassan had to say. Halimo had set up a meeting the following day at his business premises, for Hassan to meet them and discuss the supply of arms. Halimo placated the Armstrong's by saying that Hassan had many millions to spend from his piratical activities, and would be prepared to pay top dollar. This appealed to George Armstrong's mercenary instincts, particularly as one more lucrative deal would allow him to retire and perhaps go totally legitimate. He was short of funds at the moment thanks to the unexpected drug seizure at Felixstowe Docks, and the Nolan's treatment of Ross-Harding. Ross-Harding held the key to his secret accounts, and remained a danger which would have to be dealt with. Ross Harding however was beyond reach at the present time.

Back in their hotel room, George and John Armstrong were heard to discuss the situation. They were amazed that Hassan knew of their proposed arms deal. This meant that the Russian presence in Somalia had connections back in the motherland, and said much about the efficiently the Russian spy network and how it operated. It indicated to the Armstrong's, that Hassan had gained knowledge from the Russians about the proposed arms deal and that suited the Russian destabilization agenda in Somalia, using Hassan and his organization as a conduit to further Russian ends. Komarov and Siderov were certainly acting with the full blessing of their politico masters, whose intelligence system was fast, up to date and thorough. It was easier in a totalitarian state as their state intelligence network worked its way into every niche of everyday life. The Armstrong's worried they were being played as pawns in a wider Russian game but the lure of a financial killing overpowered every doubt. From the tone of the discussions in the Armstrong's room, they were concerned their supposed secret dealings were known beyond their own close knit circle and they were being directed like puppets by a much more powerful force. Realization was beginning to slowly sink in that they were not really in control of their own destiny. They had no doubt the arms deal would go through, and they would make a profit but the wider implications were, with the success of the deal, Russian influence would predominate in the country and exploitation of Somalia's natural resources would then be open to them.

Brocklehurst and Barwood were listening to the conversation between George and John Armstrong next door, when they heard George Armstrong say, " I've been thinking about what Halimo said and there may be a way to make a profit and satisfy the Somalis. They are pirates, aren't they. We have a $2 million deposit from the Zimbabwean's, so let me run this idea past you. What if we gave the details of the ship with the arms on board to Hassan and suggested to him he hijacks the ship in transit to Zimbabwe. That's what he does so it should be fairly simple for him. The ship's got to come close to Somali waters, and we can give him the route and schedule. If he raids the vessel, brings it to port in Somalia, he can take the arms off. He could then ask the owners for a ransom for the ship and its load. That way he could almost recoup what he would pay us for the arms consignment. We could claim insurance for the load, which is supposed to be plant machinery, and if we don't go back to Zimbabwe, we get paid for the arms load by the Somalis', we keep the $2 million from the Zimbabweans, the Somalis get the arms, we get the insurance money and they get their money back from the ransom money. It's a win win situation for us and them. We wanted to go legitimate, and this would be a perfect time to do it and make a lot of money into the bargain. After this, we get out of the drug business, although there is one more load on its way. I retire and you and your brother become legitimate business men. What do you think."

John said, "I would go for that. One more big payday and then go legit. I like it."

George said, " It will need refining, but we could make the suggestion at tomorrows' meeting with Hassan and see if he will go for it. He would probably jump at the chance of getting hold of an arms shipment sooner, rather than waiting for us to arrange another load. I don't feel comfortable in the arms trade. It's not what we really do, and it involves dealing with bent governments. The deeper we get in, the harder it will be to get out. Let's think about the idea overnight, and discuss it more fully in the morning, but I'm for a one off hit".

Brocklehurst and Barwood looked at one another. Brocklehurst raised his eyebrows and Barwood silenced him by hand signal, motioned for him to follow into the bathroom where behind closed doors he whispered, "These Armstrong's are devious bastards. I know they are thinking on their feet, but if Hassan goes for it, it means he will have enough armament to make a move toward destabilizing the country even sooner. Enough perhaps to bring about a revolution, and make a bid for absolute power. This country could become a haven for terrorists and a base for Jihadi's in the region. It doesn't bear thinking about. It would also appear that the Russians have a separate agenda. Destabilization will only help their cause. We know that they have long wanted port and docking facilities here and perhaps more, which would increase their overall influence in the Indian Ocean, and by allowing this arms shipment to get into Hassan's hands I can foresee that the Russian's will be able to increase their presence and influence. I will inform London and tell them of my fears."

They then went out into the main room where Barwood said, "I will see you at breakfast." He then left, leaving Brocklehurst pondering and worried about what he had heard.

The following morning Barwood met Brocklehurst for breakfast at the hotel and saw the Armstrong's leave for their appointment with Halimo and Hassan. They followed at a discreet distance, parking out of sight, but with a view of the front of the building, and as they sat they saw a cavalcade of three trucks arrive at the building and a team of armed men deploy in the yard of the building. A tall bearded man in a flowing white thobe, and wearing a Khimar on his head got out of the middle truck and with his robes flowing in the warm breeze walked with purposeful strides toward the building. He was greeted obsequiously at the front door by Halimo who almost bowed in his presence. Halimo stood to one side and the man strode into the office ahead of Halimo, dismissing him as insignificant by an imperious wave of his hand. This was obviously Mohammed Abdullah Hassan himself, but the long range picture Barwood took would later confirm his identity. Hassan was closely followed by two tough looking armed guards.

Barwood handed Brocklehurst an earpiece. “What’s this” said Brocklehurst. “Listen” said Barwood, last night I had a team plant a device inside the office. Hopefully we will hear what’s going on. It records as well.” Brocklehurst looked at Barwood with admiration. He was impressed at his clandestine efficiency.

They both listened in silence. There was no doubt who was running the meeting. They heard Hassan telling the Armstrong’s he knew about an arms shipment and he wanted it for his own purposes, and urgently. He knew the shipment would come from Russia via Odessa, and he wanted the ship diverted to Mogadishu so he, instead of the Zimbabweans could take delivery of the consignment. He dismissed the Zimbabweans and their reasons for wanting arms as insignificant. His was the greater cause. He was heard to say with fervour, "I am chosen one. I do his will. Our need greater. I pay you $12million. You take care of Zimbabwe later."

They then heard George Armstrong make the proposal he and his son had discussed in their room the previous evening. There was a long pause and Hassan said, "It is agreed. You give us name of ship, we take load. We pay you. You happy, we happy. You get message to me when all arranged. I give you half the money when I hear ship on way and other when we have ship."

Brocklehurst and Barwood saw Hassan leave the building, get into his truck and the convoy swept out onto the road and headed north. They then heard the Armstrong's, and Halimo express some relief at the way the meeting had gone and then go on to discuss the arrival of the shipment of plant, and final payment arrangements for the load.

These details were recorded by Barwood, who said, "I will give you a copy to take back with you, and send another in the diplomatic bag to my masters in London." Barwood then suggested that Brocklehurst returned to London as soon as possible, to add what he had learned in Somalia to the overall picture. The details would prove invaluable to the investigation.

Chapter Nineteen

Brocklehurst walked into the City Office and went straight to Mozart's office. DS Stevens was called into the office and Brocklehurst briefed them both on what had occurred in Somalia, showing photographs as they listened to the recording of the conversations between the Armstrong's, Hassan and Halimo.

Mozart then said, "We need to brief our friends at GCHQ and your boss Peter Simpson. I'll make a call, and arrange a meeting this afternoon." Mozart then called Simpson and briefed him on what Brocklehurst had said, and Simpson said, "I will get someone from the Foreign and Commonwealth Office (FCO) to tell us about Hassan. They keep dockets on all such characters. It would be good to know as much about him as we can. He sounds very much the zealot who would attract jihadi's from all around the middle east.

At 2p.m. that day Peter Simpson, and Adam Brocklehurst from MI5, Annie Forbes from GCHQ, Mike Hornsby from MI6, Commander John Russell SO15, and DI Dave Harley SO11, joined Mozart and Stevens at the city office. Also present was a man from the Foreign and Commonwealth Office (FCO) who held a briefing document of Hassan.

Mozart had Brocklehurst relate what had occurred in Mogadishu. He described Mohammed Umbedi Hassan and told them of the meeting held at the Halimo Road Plant offices, and they listened to the tape he brought back.

Mike Hornsy said, "I have been in touch with Jonathan Barwood our Military Attache in Mogadishu, and he is sending me a copy of the tape, but he is also including a locally gained profile of Hassan. This information seems to accord with and expand upon what the FCO know about Hassan."

The man from the FCO said, "Mohammed Umbedi Hassan, as far as we know was born in the province of Mudug, His name was Mohammed Umbedi Mohammed. He is a Sunni Muslim, and when in his teens was orphaned, and got involved with a pirate group operating in that area of Somalia. At an early age he knew how to handle firearms. He has killed in the cause of piracy, and he is known for using a machete if people get in his way. He is tall and well built, is a practitioner of Jihad, and he has risen to the head of his own group which not only carry out regular hijacking of ships, but who harbour jihahi's and further the cause of Islamic terrorism. Through his piratical endeavours, he has made himself cash rich, by stealing container loads of goods and holding ships and their crew for ransom. He has become a friend of the current President of Somalia, who no doubt sees some financial benefit from him, so allows him free reign to carry out his piratical activities. However, Hassan has moved on from mere piracy. He has political ambitions and the President might not know it but he is playing with fire associating with Hassan. He has attracted a few hundred followers, and more and more Jihadi's who have fled from Iraq have joined his movement. He is believed to be clinically insane. He has gained notoriety for his messianic belief that he is the reincarnation of Mohammed Abdullah Hassan, the Mad Mullah who fought the British in the early 1900's and has assumed his name and is now known as Mohammed Umbedi Hassan. He has taken to delivering long rousing speeches to his followers, who are devoted to him and their cause, but who are also terrified of him. He rules by fear and has been known to behead followers who have disagreed with him. If he gets sufficient arms for his followers, he could cause insurrection in his country, could attract more known terrorists to his cause, and the end result would be chaos and revolution, perhaps bringing about change and turning Somalia into another Iraq. He is a very dangerous zealot, and must be stopped from gaining that arms shipment which could pave his road to power."

Mozart turned to Annie Forbes and said, "Well now we know about Hassan, and how dangerous he could be, have you learned anything from the hacking and intercepts on the Russians, Komarov and Siderov. "

She said, "Yes. We have learned that they are putting a shipment of arms together from Czechoslovakia and the Ukraine. They seem to have a network in both countries, despite the Russians annexing of the Crimea, they appear to be able to operate there without hindrance. The factories they are dealing with can supply a variety of arms, including AK 47 semi automatic rifles, Scorpion machine guns, mortars, hand grenades, antitank weapons, explosives and ammunition. One 40 foot container could hold enough arms to equip a small army. The Armstrong's have already paid the Russians a deposit for the shipment, and we have learned that the container is to be put aboard the MV Santa Cruz in the port of Odessa on the 14th of this month, this is in two weeks time. I have made inquiries about the vessel. It is a medium sized container vessel, with a Pakistani Captain and crew and is presently in the Indian Ocean, heading north."

"Thank you Annie, keep us posted if you will."

Mike Hornsby of MI6 at this point said, "I have had our people working inside Russia. There is no doubt that Komarov and Siderov are working as contractors on behalf of their previous employers with authority and approval coming from higher up the chain. It appears they are encouraging the supply of arms to the Armstrong's because it is in their interests to cause disaffection on the African continent. The more chaos, the more the Russians can gain power in the region. They believe they are in a winning situation. If the arms go to Zimbabwe, breaking the embargo, the Russians can deny any knowledge of the supply of arms because they are allowing the sale through a deniable contractor. Although those in high office will know the truth and will reward them with other business. If the arms get hijacked and end up in Somalia, the same applies. It's a clever move on behalf of the Russians, and all deniable. The one advantage we have is knowing the movements of the ship, and we will have people watching for its departure. I will ensure that the PM is briefed, and will recommend that we use our military resources to track the vessel in transit, and use our special forces to prevent the arms being taken to Somalia. I am sure that the PM when apprised of the facts, will call a COBR meeting and give approval for military intervention."

Mozart said, "One thing is certain. The Armstrong's think they are so clever, but they are being manipulated by a far more powerful and intelligent organization, with far more resources at their disposal and a world wide reach. They are seriously outgunned. They are trying to rip off the Zimbabweans, by taking their deposit money, whilst making alternative arrangements to sell the arms elsewhere to double their profit. If we stop them delivering the arms, they are finished. We have enough evidence against them for attempted murder, drug and arms supply and perhaps a lot more, which could take them out of circulation for a long time. We also have enough evidence now to enable us to track and trace their assets so we can present a case to the courts for asset seizure after we prove they have been money laundering. I hope and believe that we are on the brink of giving them a very nasty shock. What I need to do now is have an officer chart our progress on the various aspects of this inquiry. It's a case with many tentacles and we must be sure that each one is investigated to the full, with foolproof evidence to back up each charge. Perhaps you will make a start on an evidence flow chart Win, and we will sit down and make sure our case is watertight."

"Right boss" said Stevens," I will make a start on that. We don't want any slip ups on technicalities."

Mozart said, "This could become a major part of the investigation, and I will get a small team to help you, because it's going to get complicated."

Mozart invited an update from DI Harley. "How's the plot going Dave. Has there been any movement."

Harley said, "Well the Armstrong's have come back from Somalia. There is a lot of activity at the house, and we have overheard them talking in their car coming back from the airport. They seem well pleased about the Somali deal, and are seeing this as George Armstrong's swansong. He wants to retire, and let his sons carry on with the legitimate business. Most importantly he talked in the car about their next drug consignment. It's coming in through the London Gateway on the Thames. It's coming from Rotterdam on a container ship they called the MV Castelo del Rodrigo, a Spanish ship, docking in about three weeks time. It's coming in a load of oranges. They were talking about it being picked up and taken to Grays, but because of the load of drugs found by the Custom at Felixstowe they think they will have to close down the Grays connection, so they are arranging another destination."

Mozart said, "Good work. I will pass this on to Richard Woodgate and Nick Braithwaite who are dealing with the drug side of the inquiry. If you find out any more, let me know. I believe the Armstrong's will be arranging to fly to Odessa soon to link up with the load of arms there. They have to pay for the consignment before it goes to sea."
"Will do," said Harley on his way out of the door.

The following day, DI Harley rang Mozart. He said, "We are following George and Graham Armstrong at the moment. They are heading out through Essex. From what we have heard they are going to another place out in the sticks, to arrange for the load from the London Gateway to be dropped off. I will come back to you when we have a result."

"Good work," said Mozart, "Keep in touch."

Mozart rang Annie Forbes at GCHQ, and briefed her on the latest information from DI Harley. She said, "I will check with our people and let you know what the latest is from their comms and computer. I will come back to you." Half an hour later she rang back and said, "I have checked our hack on his computer and he was looking at his bank account. He has considerable funds, and it appears he's making arrangement to purchase $6 million in bearer bonds, to be available by the 12th of this month. I presume he intends to pay for the arms using the bonds. They are as good as cash and can be used anywhere in the world."

Later that same morning, DI Harley rang Mozart, "Joe," he said, "We've followed George and Graham. They're right canny buggers. They have practiced all sorts of anti-surveillance tricks. They even went into a cul-de-sac in Cambridge. We were right behind them, when they did a three point turn and sat in the car for a minute. Our driver was quick on his feet, and drove up a blokes' driveway. His garage was open and we drove straight in. There was a bloke up a ladder, painting the house and he didn't take any notice of us. So once they had gone, we backed out, waved to him, and just drove off. He was scratching his head as we left and looked puzzled, but he didn't come down the ladder to ask us what the hell we were doing in his garage."

Mozart chuckled, and said, "Well that's a first."

"Anyway" said Harley, "We managed a follow to a plant nursery on the outskirts of a village called Balsham, north of Linton. One of our blokes went in as a customer and got their details. George and Graham went into the house on the property and have now been in there for some time. There are plenty of outbuildings, sheds, and barns, poly tunnels, plus an agricultural area. It's well isolated, and would be a perfect slaughter (A place to hide stolen or illicit goods). The place is named Springhill Nursery. We've done a check on the owner. He's a Londoner, so they say in the local pub. His name is Sam Leonard, they know him as Sam the Man. I have done a check on him and found out he is an associate of the Armstrong's from way back. He comes from Whitechapel the same as them. He has form for armed robbery and GBH, but way back. He bought the property about 15 years ago after winning a large sum of money from a dodgy property deal where he bought a cottage at auction in Suffolk and gave a demolition company instructions in a false name, to knock it down and then went along and told them he did not authorize the demolition. He sued them and won, and got enough money to build two large properties on the plot, and when he sold them he had enough money to buy the nursery. He, in effect got the properties for nothing. He also got money from a dodgy insurance claim. He bought an old high street garage in the village of Thaxted, North Essex. He had planning permission to do it up as a restaurant, but one night there was an explosion and it went up in smoke. The cause remains unknown to this day, but the fire brigade put out the theory that it was fumes from the underground petrol tanks that went up. After the insurance claim, the place was sold off and again Leonard made a lot of money on the deal. He's a con man. He lives in Balsham with his wife and he has a son, Andrew, who works with his dad, and lives in a cottage on the property. The locals think he is a jack the lad. Talks like a Londoner and they don't trust him. There are always lorries going in and out and often at strange times of the day or night. There's also a lot of people seem to visit him, mostly from London by their accents. There's no local Policeman and it's a very quiet spot. Mind you it's the sort of village where you would have to live there 50 years before they accepted you as a local. The nursery would be an ideal location to stash large amounts of drugs. I will know more later, when we have had a chance to do our research, but already I get the feeling that this is the place where the drug consignment will end up. I'll be in touch."

Mozart said," Good job Dave. Leonard sounds like a right villain from the old days. Keep at it. I love the bits about the garage in the cul de sac, and the property scams that will cause a laugh at the debrief." "Will do," said a chuckling Harley and rang off.

Mozart then rang Richard Woodgate of the HM Customs Investigations. He said, "Richard, you and Nick Braithwaite are putting your heads together about the drug consignment supposedly coming in via the London

Gateway." He said, "That's right. We are both doing our research now." "Well" said Mozart, "I've just talked to Dave Harley of SO11. He is on a follow at the moment. George Armstrong and his son Graham have been followed to a property just outside a village in Cambridgeshire. It's right out in the sticks, and would be an ideal place to run a drugs load in. It belongs to one of their associates from way back, and looks a good bet. Because of the find at Felixstowe, the Grays depot is out for future use, and anyway they are all being dealt with by your boys from Felixstowe, and are probably out of the picture. It looks like the address in Cambridgeshire could be the one for this load."

Woodgate said, "Interesting."

"Well, can I suggest you get hold of Dave Harley and get the details. He is busy at the moment. He and his team have plotted up the place and are there at the moment. So speak to him tomorrow, and keep me posted."

"Will do, and many thanks," said Woodgate.

Mozart then rang Annie Forbes at GCHQ. "Annie," he said, "SO11 have followed George and Graham Armstrong to the Springhill Nursery, in Balsham, Cambridgeshire. It is owned by an old associate of George Armstrong's, named Sam Leonard. We know that the Armstrong's have arranged an importation of drugs through London Gateway, and because their previous load was confiscated at Felixstowe, it led to their tracing its destination to a yard in Grays. The Felixstowe Customs are dealing with this find, so we believe they may be wanting to use the nursery in Cambridgeshire as an alternative distribution centre. Could your department do your thing on the nursery and see what their communications can tell us?"

"I will get our people on it right away, and let you know later what we find," said Annie. "In any event I was coming to see you later to update you on the Russian end."

"Good," said Mozart, "How about dinner tonight?" "I thought you'd never ask," she replied.

Chapter twenty

One thousand two hundred kilometers east of Moscow, near the river Izh was the Izhevsk Machine Works, known as the armoury of Russia. This was the main factory which produced the famous AK 47 Kalashnikov assault rifle, in its automatic and semi automatic variants. It was a weapon, whose manufacture was franchised in a few of the former eastern bloc countries, was very reliable even in untrained hands, and one which could take a beating from all weather conditions and temperatures. It fired the standard 7.62mm ammunition and was capable of firing 600 rounds per minute. A formidable weapon, and a favourite of terrorist organizations, and armies alike. It was to this factory that Alexsei Komarov and Dmitry Sidorov went, with the tacit approval of their former masters, to obtain the majority of arms to make up the load ordered by Armstrong.

The two Russian's were well known at the factory, having done many similar deals in the past, and knew the factory had stocks of older and unused weapons to dispose of. Deals like the ones Komarov and Siderov proposed were ideal to offload their surplus and second hand stock. The factory could also supply hand guns, mortars, and hand grenades, as well as ammunition to fit all the weapons. They especially kept the older stock of refurbished and second hand stock to fulfill certain deals, and this was one such deal which did not warrant the latest weaponry. The factory were fully aware of the destination of the load from their own sources although the relationship that Komarov and Sidedrov had with the management of the factory was on a nothing to hide basis, after all they all operated for the same masters. What it did mean, was the purchase of the weapons would cost a lot less than purchase of the latest ones, and the profit as a consequence would be greater..

A deal was done and the quantity of weapons from the factory would be ready for collection in a few days. It would be properly packaged and crated, ready for transit, as and when required. All it required was a large container.

Komerov and Siderov then contacted the sales manager of the Ceska Zbrojovka a.s. weapons and munitions factory in Svatopluka Cecha, Uhersky Brod, Czechoslovakia, a man they knew well, and placed a similar order for Scorpion automatic and semi automatic machine guns, various models of hand guns, RPG anti-tank launchers, and ammunitions. They also had a stock of older and second hand refurbished weapons which they were more than willing to dispose of. The sales Manager was well aware of the illicit nature of Komarov and Siderov's weapons deals, provided he and his other managers benefitted financially from the deal, he would give his approval. They operated almost as if they were still part of the soviet bloc and for the right price were more than willing to provided false end user documentation, which would allow the transit of such a load through their own country and would also be acceptable to the Ukrainians. The two Russian's were well aware that should they be stopped in transit, under the counter payments would facilitate the passage of the load to its destination. The trickiest part of the journey would be through the Ukraine to Odessa, because the political situation between Russia and the Ukraine was strained due to the annexation of the Crimea by the Russians. However, most of the Ukraine was Russian speaking, and the two Russian's could not foresee problems as they knew the system and the officials with whom they could do business. They had done it many times before. The load was to be described as farm machinery, and the purchase of a small amount of tractors parts and other farm equipment, packed at the rear of the load should ensure that the load passed all but a close inspection. They would drive the load themselves and make the delivery to the ship in Odessa, meeting the Armstrong's at their hotel near the port to receive payment.

Annie Forbes came to the office late that same afternoon, and sought out Mozart and Stevens. She said, "I have got the team back at my office working on the communications from the Russians. We have to be careful, because they are particularly canny at detecting hackers, and eves droppers. However, we have some of the best experts in the world and I am sure we are doing it without them knowing. What we do know is that the two Russians have booked into the London Skaya Hotel, on Prymorsky Boulevard, in Odessa. They are staying for three days. They have booked the container onto the MV Santa Cruz leaving port on the 14th, through Marine Logistics a local freight forwarding agency, and looking at their computer records the Russian's have used this company many times before.

We are checking Lloyds list for confirmation, but it is believed the ship, after leaving Odessa, is calling at Alexandria in Egypt, the west dock, where it is due to pick up more containers to complete its load. It is then due to sail through the Suez canal, into the Red Sea and Gulf of Aden into the Indian Ocean where it will pass very close to the coast of Somalia. Its next port of call should be Beira in Mozambique, which is the main port to service goods to and from land locked Zimbabwe. Beira is connected by a railway system to Harare. It would appear the ship will be partly unloaded there, including our container, and then go on to South Africa as its final destination".

"Good work" said Mozart, "and thanks. I would like to take you to dinner later, if you would like." "Yes please," said Annie, and Mozart felt a thrill of desire as he looked at her, magnetized by the effect she had on him. The world was a much better place when she was around. He shook his head to clear it of such thoughts, he must concentrate, he had work to do.

Mozart telephoned Peter Simpson, and updated him on developments.

Simpson said, "I will talk to Mike Hornsby at MI6 and get his man in Kiev to travel to Odessa and check out the ground. I should start thinking you might have to go to Odessa yourself to see the load onto the ship. If it is to be hijacked at sea, we will need to make some arrangements with our military, probably your old mob, and the navy, to ensure that the arms don't get to Hassan. He's quite mad you know. A fanatic."

Mozart said, "I will hold myself ready. Let me know when."

Mozart looked at DS Stevens and said, "It's all coming together Win. It looks like the arms will soon be on their way to Odessa, and then by sea to Harare, but it looks like the Armstrong's have arranged for Hassan to hijack the ship off the coast of Somalia. If he gets his hands on that consignment, then Somalia could be drowning in blood within a very short time. We can't let that happen, Somalia's got enough troubles as it is, with poverty rife in the country it is already attracting jihadi's exiting Iraq. Peter Simpson is going to ask the military for help, he said probably my old mob, the SBS. That should be interesting."

Richard Woodgate from HM Customs Investigation unit walked into the city office, together with Nick Braithwaite from the National Crime Agency. They went into Mozart's office.

Woodgate said, "The good news is that when we raided the yard at Grays after the drugs find at Felixstowe, we found a JCB and a tractor. They were in the process of stripping it down to its component parts. Our lads have checked and the JCB was stolen from road works in Nottingham. The tractor was stolen from a farm in the Fens. It appears this is how the Armstrong's are getting some of their machinery parts which they then export to countries like Zimbabwe. We can't yet prove a connection with the Armstrong's other than we suspect they are the finance behind the transport business in Grays. We might need Steve Easterbrook from the City of London Fraud Office, to help us on this to prove a connection with the Armstrong's through financial traces. All the people from the business in Grays are still in custody and should be out of the way for some time."

Mozart said, "That's good progress. Well done."

Woodgate said, "I have talked to Nick about the Leonard family in Cambridgeshire. What would you like us to do about it."

Mozart said, "Well to be honest, it's a side issue to our main inquiry about the arms, and from our point of view we would love to be able to leave it to you and Nick to deal with. You already have the drug find at Felixstowe which was destined for the yard at Grays, and you are dealing with that and have made a good number of arrests, and if you can, I would like you two to concentrate, with your teams, on the Felixstowe drug find, the Grays Transport company, and the next load which we believe is due in through the London Gateway, and now looks like it might be heading for Cambridgeshire. Mozart said, "If you use your own personnel, plus NCA and

SO11 you should have enough manpower to make the follow and carry out the arrests. That will leave us free here to concentrate on the arms shipment."

"Well Nick and I have talked about it, and we can put a team together as you suggest and I will talk to Dave Harley about involving him. I would suggest that we mix the teams, Customs and Police."

Mozart said, "That's great, but if you want firearms cover, and I suggest you do, we will supply that whether it be a local firearms team or we arm the SO11 lads. Please use this office to coordinate matters, and keep me posted. I have asked Annie Forbes to get GCHQ to monitor the communications at Springhill Nursery, and on the Leonard family's mobile phones."

Mozart called Annie Forbes to come back into his office, and he told her Woodgate and Braithwaite were forming a joint team to track and trace the drugs shipment from London Gateway and asked her to keep in contact with them and pass on with any details gained from monitoring the communications from the Nursery, and from the Armstrong's themselves.

She readily agreed, and said, "You know the Armstrong's have moved their drug communications to CryptoChat."

Mozart said, " What's that mean." She said, "CryptoChat is an encrypted messaging network which crime and drug syndicates are using now to communicate. They are now ordering their drugs from Cartels through the system. The good news is that we've cracked it and they don't know. That's how we confirmed the London Gateway consignment."

Mozart said, "That's good news, but let's keep that close. It's strictly a need to know basis."

"Okay." She said, "Of course."

Mozart said to Richard Woodgate, "Any difficulty with decision making, manpower or equipment, come back to me. We can soon pass difficulties up the line, and I am sure any complications can soon be sorted out. Our access to higher authority is now well established, and I don't want you to feel that you haven't got total backing or that you have a lack of resources."

Woodgate said, "No problem, my seniors and Nick's seniors are well aware of what we are doing and how much priority to give it. Leave it to us, we will keep you in the loop. They feel that we are part of your team and will not interfere, only encourage"

Mozart said, "If you would keep me posted, the only concern I have is that I don't want any branch of our inquiry to effect any other. So before we rush in, please let's talk about timing and strategy, so we can all act in concert."

Woodgate said, "Don't worry we won't make a move without telling you, and we will wait for your say so, before charging in." "I will get the SO11 team here tomorrow, so come back then and we can talk," said Mozart.

Detective Inspector Dave Harley from SO11 rang. "Joe," he said, "We have followed the Armstrong's back to their home. We will be covertly raiding the farm tonight to recover the footage from the cameras we have around the property, and if possible we will recover the tape from George Armstrong's car after he has gone to bed."

Mozart said, "Good work. Don't get caught. It's better not to push it at this time, rather than get caught out."

Harley said, "We won't push it, if there's any problems we will back off."

Mozart said, " If you come to the office in the morning, I want you to brief the Customs and the NCA on the Cambridge development in case I've missed anything, and it would be good to view the footage and hear what the Armstrong's were talking about on the way home. Be prepared to mix your team with the Customs team when the drugs arrive in the country and make sure you and your team are tooled up, just in case. Annie Forbes will be here and she can tell us the latest on the phone taps and computer hacks. See you tomorrow."

Mozart and Annie Forbes drove to Docklands. He said, "Do you like Chinese" "Love it," she said.

He took her to the Lotus Floating Chinese Restaurant in Canary Wharf near his docklands apartment. They sat at a corner table overlooking the water, and studied the exotic menu over drinks. Mozart sat opposite Annie, and looked at her as if seeing her anew. She was beautiful. He had never been so attracted to anyone in his life. She had a magical luster about her, and he was drawn in to her as a moth to a flame. It was as if the world around him existed only in the far distance. His breath laboured in her presence. She was the most desirable woman he would ever meet. She was speaking, but in his dream state he didn't hear. She nudged him and he came back to the present. She said, "Shall we order. I'm famished." Dazed, he stammered, "Yes, of course. You order for both of us."

She ordered a seafood platter to share, and when it arrived they used their fingers whilst devouring each other with their eyes. They were cocooned in their love bubble and time meant nothing. The dishes of oysters and scallops with seaweed and rice noodles, washed down with a passable Chablis followed and their three hour meal passed in what seemed a moment, each only ever conscious of the other and not their surroundings. They woke from their mutual trance as fireworks went off. Mozart felt fireworks in his head until he realized there really were fireworks exploding and they were reflecting in the water of the dock. Where had the time gone. Mozart had to thank an office party being held in the function room above their heads for the display, but it provided the perfect backdrop to the end of their meal, and accorded with the way Mozart felt about his companion and the shared experience of the most wonderful meal he could remember. He held her close and as they stood on the gangway to shore watching the fireworks and their dancing reflections in the water. He whispered "I love you." She looked at him, her expression soft and suddenly very serious, with moistened eyes, she whispered throatily, "I love you Joseph Mozart." Fireworks went off in Mozart's head again and the feeling was with him all the way to his home. On the doorstep he kissed her, softly, deeply, passionately, as the fireworks faded in the distance. This was the most important and magical day of his life.

Chapter Twenty One

Richard Woodgate entered the City office the following morning at 9am to find Mozart, DS Stevens, Annie Forbes, Nick Braithwaite from the NCA and DI Harley of SO11 already there. They went into the conference room and Woodgate said, "I have heard from our sources at Manston. The Armstrong's have submitted a flight plan to fly in their own plane from the UK on the 10th, via Cyprus to Odessa. They fly in to Odessa International Airport. This is a shared airport, both civil and military. They are obviously intent on being there to accept and pay for the arms shipment.

Annie Forbes said, " My people at GCHQ tell me they have booked a double suite on line in the London Skaya Hotel, Prymorskyi Boulevard, from 11th to 15th. "The Russian's have booked into the same hotel, so they will all be there to see the container of arms loaded onto the ship on the 14th. My guess is that the Armstrong's intend to meet the Russians', pay for the arms, stay and see the container loaded on the ship then watch it sail.

Mike Hornsby of MI6, Peter Simpson of MI5, together with Adam Brocklehurst, Commander John Russell of SO15 arrived and Mozart briefed them.

Mike Hornsby said, "I will get our man in the Ukraine to cover the meeting but may I suggest Mr Mozart that you go out there and meet him. I would suggest you get there by the 11th and book into the same hotel. Our man will meet you at the airport which is about 7km from the city centre.

Peter Simpson said, "I have had our staff check on the ship. If it leaves Odessa on 14th as scheduled, it should be in Alexandria by the 20th. Assuming the ship sails at an average of 10 knots. It's just over 1300 nautical miles. Assuming the ship takes 2 days to load more cargo in Alexandria, then the ship will have to pass through the Suez Canal, the Red Sea, The Gulf and into the Indian Ocean. The point at which the Pirates could intercept the ship, off the coast of Somalia is approximately 2800 nautical miles, at an average speed of 10 knots, the ship should be in the area in 12 or 13 days. That would make the intercept on or about the 4th or 5th of next month. We must therefore plan coverage in that area say from the 1st to the 6th of the month. Mr Mozart, at the conclusion of this briefing you and I have an appointment at the Ministry of Defence. We mustn't be late." Mozart went round the delegates who added their part of the general investigation to the meeting. Everyone was now aware how the complications of the case were coming together.

Peter Simpson, Mike Hornsby and Mozart left the building, and drove to the Ministry of Defense in Whitehall. They were expected and were ushered to a meeting room on the fourth floor of the building. They were served coffee by an orderly in army uniform, and a short time later Brigadier Athol Mckenzie, and Admiral James Vincent entered the room.

Peter Simpson introduced himself and Hornsby, and when introducing Mozart added that he had until few years ago had a military career, leaving as a Captain with the Special Boat Squadron and was now a Policeman. He updated the military men on the investigation that Mozart was undertaking. Simpson, having explained the problem, asked if the military could help.

Brigadier McKenzie said, “What kind of help do you want.”

“Well,” said Simpson, ”The ship carrying the arms is due to be intercepted at sea off the coast of Somalia by the pirates. If the arms get into the hands of the pirate chief they will be used to instigate serious insurrection in the country. Their leader is mad and is a determined Jihadist. He is gathering other jihadi's to his cause, more especially a lot are coming to him having fled from Iraq. If they get these arms, the country could be turned into a blood bath. Our government cannot allow that. Simpson continued, "We would like the ship shadowed through the Arabian Sea, Red Sea and Indian Ocean, and boarded by your special forces, and the pirates detained. I am sure deadly force would be authorized should it prove necessary. We would also like the arms shipment removed from the ship at sea."

This request raised the eyebrows of the two military men, who looked at one another, and McKenzie said, "I'm not sure we can help you without authority."

Simpson said, "May I use your phone." He used the conference phone in the middle of the table, and dialed a number. He spoke to the person at the other end and explained the situation, he was told to hold and then a voice came on the line.

"Put me on speaker" said a voice of authority.

Simpson complied, and said, "Go ahead, sir."

"Gentlemen," said the voice, "This is the Prime Minister. We have discussed this case at a COBR meeting, and you have full authority to assist these gentlemen in whatever way you can. Your Commander in Chief is fully aware, and will speak with you after your present meeting. Our intention is that you will arrange to have the ship under surveillance once it exits the Suez Canal, and have it intercepted by a Special Forces Unit after the Pirates have taken it over. The operation is of the highest priority and the assault team will have my full backing to use force of arms to achieve their purpose. It is our intention that after the pirates are detained the load of arms should be removed. We cannot allow the arms to go to Zimbabwe against UK sanctions. Your Commander in Chief will want you to cooperate with the investigation, formulate a plan of action, and dovetail with the efforts of the Police and the other agencies involved. If you have any questions, please ask them of your CIC, and come with him to the next COBR meeting tomorrow afternoon at 4p.m., with your plan. Good morning gentlemen."

The phone went dead, and the two men looked at one another, puffed out their cheeks, did a sharp exhale of breath and said, "right," In unison.

Simpson then in a softer tone, asked them to formulate a plan, and coordinate with Detective Chief Inspector Mozart. He suggested that they meet first thing in the morning at the city office, and finalize details there before presenting the plan to the COBR meeting. He also told them of the time line, to ensure urgency not only of the plan, but of events, and then thanked them for their anticipated involvement.

"If you would like we can give you a more detailed over view of the case and all that has taken place so far now."

Both men looked relieved at that suggestion.

Simpson said, "In that way, we can work out a template of a plan, which you can refine from a military point of view later, and then can refine it further in the morning, ready for the COBR meeting. Are we agreed."

Both men nodded their assent, with some relief showing on their faces. Mozart, and Simpson then detailed events so far, whilst the Admiral and Brigadier made notes.

Mozart and Annie Forbes walked into the City Office. Detective Sergeant Stevens looked up from his desk and said, "Ms. Forbes, will you ring your office urgently."

Mozart said, "Use my phone."

She went into Mozart's office and was in there for 15 minutes. When she came out she looked seriously at Mozart and said, "We need to talk. You too Winston"

Mozart and Stevens joined her in his office. She said, "There have been complications." The two officers looked at one another as she continued, "You know my people are hacking the Russian arm dealer's computers and communications?"

Mozart said, "Komorov and Sidero?"

She said, "Yes. Well we have intercepted communications from them to the two factories they are getting the Armstrong's arms from. They have now ordered another similar load, to be put in a separate container which they intend to put on the same ship. They have been contacted by the chief of a Russian private security company who are currently engaged in anti-terrorist operations in Mozambique. We have had one of our analysts do some in depth research into the situation in Mozambique. You may or may not know that Al Shabaab are operating in the north of the country around Cabo Delgado, on the borders of Tanzania. The Mozambique Defense Armed Forces (MDAF) have been fighting them for a couple of years, and getting nowhere. They are not very well led, not very well trained, and short of appropriate arms and ammunition, so much so, that they ran out of ammunition on one anti-insurgency operation, and took heavy casualties. The Mozambique government know of their shortcomings, and have employed a Russian private security company to bolster their numbers in the fight against them. The owner of the security company is a man named Pavel Shishkinski, who is a friend of the Russian President. His company is called Valkerie Security. He has a 300 strong group of mercenaries, mostly ex-Russian forces, with some ex-Spetsnaz, ex-airbourne troops and even a few disaffected South Africans. They have Mozambique government approval because the Russians have financial interests in the country which they wish to exploit such as natural gas and precious stones. However the forces the government are using are just not used to the countryside, it is hard to get around with no roads, and they have been ambushed many times and suffered as a result. Al Shabaab have attracted recruits from areas such as Iraq, and even Afghanistan, who are trained fighters, so the security forces are up against it, especially as the terrorists don't respect borders and come and go as they please. The mercenaries are urgently in need of arms and ammunition and Shishkinski has asked Komarov and Siderov to supply them. They intend putting another full load of arms and ammunition on the same ship as the first load, and off loading it in the port of Beira at the same time as Armstrong's load intended for Zimbabwe. They do not know that the Armstrong's have arranged with Mohammed Abdullah Hassan to pirate the load destined for Zimbabwe. It means, if we don't stop them, the pirates could inadvertently get twice the amount of arms and ammunition, and if we do stop them, which I believe we must, then it could upset the Russians' plans and could cause a nasty diplomatic incident. Because the shipment to Mozabique is important to the Russians', I would not put it past them to have the ship under surveillance until it reaches its destination, so if we intercept the Santa Cruz it could produce a stand-off and a very threatening situation."

Mozart puffed out his cheeks, as did Stevens, and he said, "That would put the cat amongst the pigeons. I will have to tell Peter Simpson and that will really make the upcoming COBR meeting a lively affair. We need to pass this up the line urgently, because the Prime Minister will need to know before the meeting, and he will want recommendations from us, the military, and MI5 and 6. It's a very hot potato. Winston, when Admiral Vincent and General McKenzie get here, take them into the conference room. I have urgent calls to make. Annie, can you please write up what you have just told us, and have it ready for the meeting and for me as briefing notes."

Mozart phoned Peter Simpson and him brought him up to date.

His explosion of breath could be clearly heard over the phone. "Right," he said, "I will tell Mike Hornsby and then I will pass it up the line so the Prime Minister is not taken by surprise. Delay the meeting with the military until we can get there. I can see you and Annie Forbes coming with us to the COBR meeting, so we need to have recommendations and solutions. I will leave you to brief

Commander Russell at SO15. I expect he will want to be at this mornings' meeting too."

When Admiral Vincent and General McKenzie arrived they were taken into the conference room and given coffee. Mozart came in a short time later, apologized for the delay, and explained the situation to them. At first they looked startled at the new information.

"That puts a new slant on the situation," said McKenzie. We will have to adapt our plans. What is quite clear is supplying arms to Zimbabwe is internationally illegal. They have a UN embargo on them for arms and ammunition. If it helps my brother Duncan is the present Military Attache at our embassy in Harare. He would be only too willing to assist. However, I do not believe the same applies to the supply of arms to Mozambique. They are fighting an anti-insurgent war at the moment and need all the help they can get to prevent the country becoming another Iraq or Afghanistan. If Al Shabaab take over the country the whole of that part of Africa could become a blood bath, and any success those organizations had would suck in terrorists from all over the world. We can't let that happen.

"The bottom line is that we want to prevent the pirates taking the arms. We need to stop the load intended for Zimbabwe from getting there. So we must seize them. The Police here want to arrest the Armstrong's for drug running and arms supply, and to bring them before a British Court for their crimes. This morning we must come up with a plan to intercept the ship, seize the pirates and the arms due for Zimbabwe, without upsetting the Russians' who are sending legitimate arms to Mozambique."

Admiral Vincent said, "We know that the Russians have a surveillance trawler in the Indian Ocean. It is usually in the area near Deigo Garcia monitoring the Americans', and we know that they have a Frigate from the Black Sea Fleet operating in the southern Indian Ocean. We will have to monitor their movement."

Mozart said privately to DS Stevens, "Winston, I was called to investigate a man being beaten and left tied up at Barking Creek. It had such simple beginnings for us. Now look where it has gone."

Stevens looked at his boss, "If you can't take a joke." Mozart finished, "You shouldn't have joined." They both laughed. What else could they do.

Admiral Vincent said, "Firstly we need an operational title for our actions. We propose that it be called **Operation Forsyth.** The name seemed appropriate when he explained the connection. We propose that we move HMS Bulldog, which is one of our current Royal Marines Assault ship, equipped with helicopters and fast attack boats, immediately from Valetta Harbour in Malta to HMS Juffair, which is our permanent naval base in Bahrain. We have, at present a 20 man unit of SBS, comprising a Major, a Captain both of whom speak Russian, Two Sergeants, one of whom can speak the Somali tongue that Hassan speaks, and 16 men on secondment to Oman. We can get the RAF to move them to Bahrain well in time to join the ship. We also have a Type 26 Frigate, HMS Yarmouth, presently on a goodwill visit to South Africa. We can re-deploy her to the northern Indian Ocean. We will need to keep the Santa Cruz under surveillance onward from Alexandria, and we will have to use our satellites and perhaps drones and AWAC's to monitor its progress, through the Suez canal and Arabian Sea. Once it is in radar range of our ships in the area we can more easily follow it. The idea will be to wait until the Pirates take over the ship, and then have our SBS Unit raid the ship and detain all the pirates. Probably a night or dawn operation. The container intended for Zimbabwe has to be identified, and removed from the ship before it is allowed to proceed. We will allow the other container of arms intended for Mozambique to proceed, once we have secured our load."

Mozart said, "There are one or two other essentials to the plan I believe we should consider. I am intending to go to Odessa and monitor the Armstrong's meeting with Komorov and Siderov, and see the container to obtain its markings for identification purposes, with photos if possible. I will discuss this with Mike Hornsby of MI6 to form a plan for Odessa, and I believe it will be necessary to do the same in Somalia, to monitor the pirate activity. I am open to suggestions as to how this can be achieved. The meeting discussed the general plan and modified it from suggestions round the table. It was then typed up into a working document, entitled ***OPERATION FORSYTH.***

The COBR meeting was attended by Admiral Vincent, Brigadier General McKenzie, DCI Mozart, Mike Hornsby of MI6, Peter Simpson MI6, Commander John Russell and Annie Forbes. Government officers present included the Foreign Secretary, The Home Secretary, The Minister of Defense, and it was chaired by the Prime Minister. The basic plan was approved. The Prime Minister agreed should a diplomatic incident arise out of the British Policing action, then his office would handle the diplomacy. The Prime Minister stressed that the arms shipment intended for Zimbabwe must be stopped according to international law, but the shipment from the Russians' intended for Mozambique should be allowed to proceed. The difficulty of taking a container off a ship on the high seas was discussed at length, and it was agreed that HMS Bulldog would carry a crane suitable to the purpose.

The Prime Minister gave those who would be involved in the operation carte blanche to use whatever force was necessary, including lethal force, which was a relief to those involved in the operation on the ground.

Chapter Twenty Two

Mozart flew into Odessa International Airport. As he entered the passenger hall, he saw a man holding a placard with his name written on it. He approached the man who introduced himself as Paul Sturrock, Military Attache at the British Embassy in Kiev. He was obviously a military man. He had short brown hair, was clean shaven, with a small moustache, and he moved with an athletic grace indicative of physical fitness. He spoke in short and clipped sentences, and the first impression was of a man who could handle himself, and would be an asset in any physical situation. This made Mozart comfortable that he was in the hands of a natural warrior.

Mozart said, "Joe Mozart," and shook Sturrock's hand.

Sturrock said, "I have a car outside, and we are booked into the same hotel as the Armstrongs', and the Russians, Komorov and Siderov. Once in the car he said, " We have been notified by London that they are due in tomorrow by private plane. They are coming via Cyprus. I have a team with me, because we have tasks which will involve being in more than one place at a time. Two of the team are in the same hotel as you, including me, and others at another hotel nearby. We have brought a lot a technical stuff with us and the experts to install and use them. I will take you to the hotel first to meet the team, and we can discuss a plan of action."

Sturrock pulled up outside Majestiskaya Hotel, in Pushkins'ka Street. It was an imposing hotel with a Victorian style façade.

Sturrock said, "I picked this hotel, and told them we were from an English company, supplying machine tools and were here to exploit a growing market in the Ukraine. I have booked a conference room for the length of our stay to hold supposed business meetings. Four of the team are staying here, and the booking is in the name of Alan Cockburn, one of our team. With you and me makes a team of eight. We will need to follow the load of arms from the border, to this port and identify its markings. We should be able to take photographs. I have eased our way into the port on the pretext of wanting to bring loads into the port in the future, and we need to assess its suitability. I have details of the vehicle that the Russians will be using. We have a team following it at the moment and they will let us know when it arrives and where it will be parked before going onto the ship. Our man in Moscow has sorted that out. There will be a hold up at the border, because all loads coming from Russia to the Ukraine have to satisfy strict importation rules, since the Crimea was annexed by Russia. However an amount of Rubles in the right hands always facilitates transit. The room the Armstrong's are to have is a double suite, and is unoccupied at the moment. Tonight we intend to wire it up so we can hear what they will be saying, and I will have a man listening in, so we can keep up to speed with them, we have to be careful as it is likely that the room is already bugged. We know from our intercepts that the Armstrong's are bringing bearer bonds with them to pay for the arms, and that means they will want to view the load in private surroundings. The Russians have used

Marine Logistics to facilitate the export of the load, and they have a yard inside the port where we believe the load will be inspected before payment is made."

Mozart was impressed and said so, " You seem to have thought of most things. From my point of view I will be happy to identify the container, and see it loaded on the ship, once that is done we know it is bound for Alexandria, and our plan is to monitor it on the high seas through the Suez canal, the Red Sea, the Gulf into the Indian Ocean. The Somalis intended the hijack to take place somewhere along the route and then we intend to move in with special forces. There is a complication, as there are now two loads on the Santa Cruz. One for the pirates and one the Russians have organized for Mozambique. The two loads should be addressed to the same port, Beira in Mozambique, because as you know Zimbabwe being landlocked, they use this port in Mozambique as it has the rail link to Harare and Beira is nearest port to the Zimbabwean border . The situation is that one load is illegal and the other not. The Somali's and the Armstrong's do not know of the second load on the same ship, and if they find there are two when they raid the ship, they will think Christmas has come early."

Sturrock said, "That complicates things a bit, you will have to be sure we identify the right load. Right, come and meet the team." He then phoned the rest of the team and they met in the hotel conference room. Mozart was impressed with the four men. Two looked tough enough to handle most situations, and the third and fourth were introduced at technical experts. Sturrock briefed the team, and Mozart added the details he had told Sturrock about a little earlier.

The meeting then broke up, with Sturrock saying, "We will meet here at 7p.m. this evening. I have arranged a table in the restaurant for six of us, and we can use the time after the meal to fit our equipment into the Armstrong's room. We need to act like work colleagues would when away from the office, conferences and a jolly." Sturrock then suggested Mozart to register and settle into his room. He was on the same floor as the Armstrong's, but Sturrock said, "I have the room next door to them and the Russians have a double suite on the other side, so we need to bug their room as well. We each have a balcony, which might be handy for access."

That evening, after the meal, they all went to Sturrocks room, and two of the men used the balcony to access the Armstrong's balcony. They were gone for half an hour, and reported that they had installed their equipment. They used the same method to access the Russian's room. They set up recording devices in Sturrock's room, and issued each of the team with an earpiece to enable silent monitoring. "This will let us listen to what they say when they are in the room. It's a double frequency, so we can switch from one to the other. I speak Russian so that should be no problem. I will have one man in the lobby to report on the arrivals of the Russians and the Armstrongs', and once they arrive we will monitor their conversations in their rooms."

The MV Santa Cruz docked that same evening, and began discharging its load of containers in the port. The Captain was Pakistani, as were his crew. He let them have shore leave for the two days the ship would be in port. One day to discharge cargo and the second day, for loading the fresh cargo. They were due to sail during the morning of the third day.

Sturrock took Mozart the following morning to a park overlooking the port facility. They walked to the far side of the park, where they had a view of the port and the sea. With a pair of binoculars, Mozart was able to see the MV Santa Cruz had docked, and Sturrock told him this was berth No. 2, of the Platonovsky jetty.

Sturrock said, "The ship is a medium size container ship, some 139 metres long. I looked it up in Lloyds and the size of the load suggests it can be unloaded in a day. The loading might take a bit longer."

As they watched the dockside cranes moved into position and the unloading began. Sturrock's mobile phone rang. He listened for a while and said, "Thanks. I will see you at the hotel later this morning."

He said, "The lorry has arrived from Russia, and the team have followed it all the way to the docks. It is currently alongside the offices of Marine Logistics. They have photographs of the container. It is blue, and its registration number is KS 51437. The lorry was driven by

Komorov and Siderov themselves. There is another lorry alongside the Marine Logistics Office which has another container on it. This one is Red, with white lettering, bearing the number KS 55674. This is not the one the team followed from Russia. It looks like they are the two containers we are expecting, but which one is the Armstrong's? Hopefully we will hear in due course, otherwise we might have to find the paperwork in the Marine Logistics Office." Mozart thought, Hell! This is getting so complicated. We need to know the right one.

Mozart said, "Let me make a call." He rang Annie Forbes and explained the problem. "I will ring you back," she said.

On the way back to the hotel Mozart's phone rang. "We have looked at the hacking transcripts," said Annie Forbes. The one destined for Zimbabwe is number KS51437 according to their computer records. This is the first consignment ordered by them, and two weeks later they added another consignment which their computer shows is destined for Mozambique." "Good work," said Mozart, "Thank you. I will see you when I get back." "I'll be waiting," she said.

They returned to the hotel to find the Armstrong's had arrived and had been shown to their room. Sturrock checked with his team and found that the Armstrong's had just received a call from Komorov, inviting them to view the load at Marine Logistics at their agency office in Odessa Docks. They were asked to bring payment for the load.

George Armstrong and his son John left the hotel by taxi for the docks, George carrying a large briefcase, and Sturrock and Mozart followed. At the dock gates the Armstrong's got out of the taxi and were met by a man Sturrock recognized as Siderov. They were allowed inside. Sturrock drove to a point where they could overlook Marine Logistics office, and saw through their binoculars Komorov and Siderov with the two Armstrong's. They opened the back of the container and showed its contents to the two Englishmen, who were handed documents, and then the four went into the Marine Logistics offices with George Armstrong still carrying a the briefcase. They remained in the office for about an hour, and when back in view Sturrock and Mozart saw through their binoculars that Siderov was now carrying the briefcase. They walked to the dock gates, and all four got into a taxi, which Sturrock and Mozart followed back to the hotel. The group shook hands in the lobby and were heard to make arrangements to meet for lunch in the hotel restaurant the Armstrong's went to the restaurant and booked a table for four in a booth at the back of the restaurant, and then they went to their room. Siderov and Komarov went to the bar for a drink and were later seen to go to their room.

Once in their room the Russians began talking. The MI6 agent listening to the conversation called Sturrock to the earpieces, which he shared with him.

Sturrock came away looking thoughtful, smiled and said, "The Russian's are trying to double deal Armstrong. Once the load gets to Beira, they are diverting both container loads to the Russian Forces in Mozabique. In effect they are ripping off the Armstrong's, because they have already been paid for both loads by Valkerie Security and the Armstrong's have paid them for the same load. So it looks like the Armstrong's are trying to rip off the Zimbabweans, by having the load hijacked on its way past Somalia, and having taken a substantial profit from them, they intend selling it to Hassan in Somalia, but they themselves are being ripped off by the Russians, who having had the Armstrong's pay for their consignment, are diverting it to Valkerie Secuirty in Mozambique. It's a double rip off."

They all laughed, and Mozart said, "I've got to tell them back in the office in London. They will never believe it. You couldn't make it up. It's a crookfest of double dealing. This alters our position somewhat though, we should put it to London that we intercept the ship and maybe remove both loads. We need to take instruction on it."

The following evening the MV Santa Cruz sailed. It was seen to be loaded to deck height with containers, and was towed out of the port by local tugs. The Armstrong's checked out of the hotel and went to the airport where they flew off in their private jet. It was to be a direct flight to London. Mozart said goodbye to Sturrock at the same airport and caught a scheduled flight to London Heathrow the same day, he had much to tell upon his return, and perhaps much more to learn from the various threads of the inquiry both in the case of drug importations, and arms dealing.

Chapter twenty three

Mozart had taken the Heathrow Express to central London, and from there he travelled by taxi and Dockland Light Railway to his home. It was now evening and getting dark. The lights were on in his flat, and as he let himself in through the front door, he was greeted by Annie Forbes with a warm smile of greeting. Mozart's heart gave a leap, there was nothing more he wanted just then than to see

Annie and wrap his arms around her. They kissed. It was more than just a greeting, it was an understanding they felt deeply about each other, and this was meant to be. No other woman had moved Mozart so completely, made him feel such passion and oneness. Her kiss of greeting lifted the weariness from his body, vigour returned to him. She had the key, and her presence and greeting made his body surge with energy and vitality. She pressed a glass of wine into his hand and said, "Supper is ready." She led him to the dining area where a table was set for two, candles were burning, and perfume filled the air. He breathed in her scent, and his olfactory organs made his body respond to her enticement. He sat, without saying a word, as she busied herself in the kitchen area. She took the lid off a steaming pot, and her scent was overpowered by delicious aromas. He was now very hungry, and she placed before him an aromatic lamb dish which had been cooking for hours, which he slowly devoured whilst looking deep into her eyes. They talked quietly and passionately making love with their eyes, sipped their wine, and lost themselves in each other and the moment. Mozart's troubles melted into the background. He was in another place, another time. With the last dish put away

Mozart found himself in her arms. He lay beside her, caressing and feeling her. Her skin was silken and delicate, they kissed deeply, longingly and gently made love and intertwined to climax in a melding of their bodies and souls, both falling into a soporific void, a feeling that neither of them had experienced before. It was complete and utter love. He fell slowly asleep in her arms, he was replete and the most content he had ever been, knowing without doubt that this woman was meant for him, and no other.

The following morning they went to the office together. All the way into the city he kept looking at her, with a small smile of contentment on his face. She looked at him in the same way, as if they were sharing a private joke.

Once at the office Mozart became business like. He asked DS Stevens to call all the people together for an update meeting, where he briefed them on what had taken place in Odessa.

It was the cause of much amusement when he told all present the details of the proposed arms deal double rip off.

Detective Inspector Dave Harley of SO11 told the meeting of the return of the Armstrong's to their home, and that the recovery of the recording of their conversation on their plane had revealed that they had discussed flying to Mogadishu on the 2nd of the following month to meet with their business contact, Abdirahim Halimo Mohammed, and the pirate chief Mohammed Umbedi Hassan to finalize the deal and to obtain the payment for the shipment of arms from the Santa Cruz. Harley also told the meeting they had discussed the drug shipment due to enter the country through the London Gateway on board the MV Castelo del Rodrigo, which was due in port on 3rd of the following month. This would put George and John Armstrong out of the country when the ship arrived, leaving Graham Armstrong to make the arrangements for the load to be transported to the Springhill Nursery in Balsham, Cambridgeshire, just north of Linton.

Mozart said to Richard Woodgate of HM Customs Investigations, "Can you and your team handle this drug importation."

Richard said, "Yes. We always visit ships when they dock, and we will put a tracker on the container and follow it to its destination. We can then arrest all the people."

Mozart said, "Dave Harley and his team from SO11 will assist in the surveillance. That is their forte, but we would like to bag Sam Leonard the owner of the Nursery, and Graham Armstrong on the spot if we can."

Woodgate said, "Leave it to me, I will liaise with Dave and sort it out. It should all happen whilst George and John Armstrong are in Somalia."

Mozart then said, "The latest on Ross-Harding is that he has made a full written confession to his part in using drugs, and money laundering for the Armstrong's. He is still in the safe house under armed guard, and will plead guilty to money laundering. We intend to use him as a witness, and hopefully he will get a lighter sentence for cooperating. He is still in fear of his life, but Detective Inspector Steve Easterbrook of the City of London Fraud Squad is dealing with him, and is in the process of identifying the accounts in which the Armstrong's have hidden their illicit cash. We will be able to bring this all before the courts in due time. The team at GCHQ have now managed to hack the Russian arms dealer's computers and the Armstrong's communications, even though they are now using a dark web site called Crypto Chat, an encrypted messaging network. GCHQ have cracked it, and are monitoring the Armstrong's use of it, and I have no doubt they are also feeding other agencies with titbits as they listen in."

"Lady and Gentlemen, we now need to concentrate on **Operation FORSYTH**. That is the interception of the Santa Cruz on the high seas off Somalia. We intend to recapture the ship after it has been pirated, and recover the arms intended for Zimbabwe. However we now know there are two container loads, and I suggest that we plan to recover both, as they are subject to a double rip off. However, this may well upset the Russians when they hear of it."

Admiral Vincent said, "Lady and Gentlemen. Let's talk through **Operation Forsyth**. The plan is to use a SBS team who are currently in Oman, and get them to Bahrain where they will join HMS Bulldog at the British Base, HMS Juffair. The MV Santa Cruz is expected in the Red Sea on the 2nd of the month, and HMS Bulldog, which is a Commando Assault ship and capable of creating an on board harbour for fast attack boats, needs to time an intercept on the Santa Cruz just after the Pirates have made their move. HMS Bulldog will be backed up by HMS Yarmouth, one of our latest frigates, which will keep out of sight but will be near enough to provide backup if required. Yarmouth is in the southern Indian Ocean and the moment, heading north. We intend using RAF Drones and AWACS to follow the Santa Cruise once it exits the Suez Canal.

We will also plot the pirate movement on radar once they are in range, and once they have shown that they have taken the ship. We will then move in under the cover of darkness, and our SBS team will carry out an assault on the ship, arrest and detain all the pirates. We expect them to be fully armed, and the SBS team will have full authority to respond in kind to any discharge of firearms, using lethal force if necessary. The pirates are not to escape. Our main target will be the pirate leader Mohhamed Umbedi Hassan, who sees himself as a reincarnation of the Mad Mullah, and who is intent upon insurrection in Somalia. We believe his ultimate goal is to overthrow the government and turn it into an Al Shabaab haven. This must not happen. If we miss him at sea, we have to try to eliminate him on land. If we don't get him, the consequences for Somalia and perhaps the whole of that part of Africa are dire. Once we have recovered the ship from the pirates, we have to off-load the consignment of arms. There is a complication in that there are now two container loads of arms expected to be on the ship and we have the details of the container markings. One load has the arms in it which the Armstrong's have bought and which were originally intended for Zimbabwe, which as you know is under a UN arms embargo, and this is the load the pirates intend taking in a rip off operation. The other container is one supplied by the Russians, and is intended for their forces in Mozambique where they are fighting in the north of the country against Al Shabaab. Both containers are destined to arrive in the Mozambique port of Beira, which is the nearest port to landlocked Zimbabwe and the load intended for Zimbabwe should then be taken by rail to Harare. The other load should be going up country to supply the Russian mercenary army. What the Armstrong's don't know is that Komorov and Siderov, the Russians who are supplying the arms, intend diverting both loads to their own forces in Mozambique, thus providing us with a double rip off situation."

There were smiles around the conference table at the perfidy of the plan devised by both the Armstrong's and the Russian's.

Admiral Vincent continued, "We have fitted a crane on HMS Bulldog to enable us to remove the container from the Santa Cruz at sea, not an easy operation, where it will be brought back to HMS Juffair in Bahrain. If it proves impossible then the arms will be dumped at sea. The problem arises about the container of arms the Russian's intend for their forces in Mozambique. There is no UN embargo on arms to Mozambique, and in any event, HM Government approve of the arms going to the Russian forces there because they are fighting Al Shabaab, By allowing the arms to go through that may help suppress terrorism in the area. What we do on the spot is a matter dictated by circumstances and instructions from our Government It may well be that our Government would see sense in allowing both containers of arms to proceed as planned to Beira, but instead of one load going to Zimbabwe, they might allow both consignments to go to the Russian forces in Mozambique. If that is the case I suspect that HMS Yarmouth might have to accompany the Santa Cruz to Beira to ensure that the all of the arms go in the right direction. If this is the case, I will change my flag to HMS Yarmouth to monitor the shipment and make sure it goes in the right direction once it is landed. Now, are there any questions."

Those sat round the table all had expressions of somewhere between amusement at the double rip-off, and amazement at the complexity of the disposal plan. There were no questions.

Peter Simpson then said, "Well, let's move on. Detective Chief Inspector Mozart has been driving this inquiry from the start and he is the most qualified to give an update on all the threads of the inquiry so far. Mr Mozart, please update us on progress."

DCI Mozart said, " With regards to the to the drug situation. HM Customs are dealing with the drug find at Felixstowe, which we know is connected to the Armstrong's, and they have already arrested the people in the yard at Grays, so they are out of the picture. They are going through the evidence to try to prove a connection with the Armstrong organization, but this could take some time. We have kept away from this find and left it entirely to HM Customs, because we want them to believe that this was a random Customs find at the port of entry, with subsequent follow up inquiries by the Customs."

"The remaining Nolan brother from the Whitechapel Cartel is out of business. He is in custody and inquiries are being made by Detective Inspector Steve Easterbrook of the City of London Fraud Office to trace and recover his assets for the court. He is being charged with drug supply, GBH and the attempted murder of Mungo Ross-Harding. We have recovered two firearms from them which ballistic matches tell us were used in drug related shootings, and there will be charges levied in relation to these finds as well. We have full forensic evidence from the Nolan's business premises, and it appears to be a straightforward case, and again appears to have no connections with the Armstrong's other than they beat up the Armstrong's banker and money launderer."

"As you have heard, Ross Harding remains in protection. Has recovered from his injuries, and has admitted his involvement in money laundering for the Armstrong's. He is being interviewed regularly by DI Easterbrook who is also tracing the Armstrong's assets and preparing evidence for court. He will be charged with drug use and money laundering, and we will be recommending a lighter sentence for his cooperation."

We now come to Samuel Leonard an old criminal associate of the Armstrong's. DI Dave Harley has tracked the Armstrong's to the Leonard's nursery in Cambridgeshire, and from intercepts, thanks to our friends from GCHQ, we know that whilst George Armstrong and his son John are in Somalia dealing with the pirates, his other son Graham, is organizing the disposal of another consignment of drugs hidden inside a container on a ship coming into the London Gateway. The container we have learned from intercepts, is supposed to house a consignment of oranges. They intend housing the load in the nursery until distribution. Our friends from HM Customs," and he smiled at Richard Woodgate HM Customs Investigations Branch as he said it, "has this in hand and DI Harley and his team will assist. They will raid the nursery and arrest all those responsible, including we hope, Graham Armstrong."

"The team which tried to eliminate Ross-Harding in Northampton are in custody. Those who survived anyway, and are being charged with firearms offences, attempted murder and conspiracy to commit murder. They were handed on to the local Police and are awaiting trial. We are to supply additional evidence where needed. It may well be we will pull them back to London for one big trial. That has yet to be decided."

"George and John Armstrong have arranged a flight in their own aircraft to Mogadishu to receive payment for the arms consignment of arms which will be hijacked at sea by Hassan and his pirate terror group. They have already been paid a substantial deposit by Hassan, and they will receive the balance on delivery. As you have been told, we are arranging an intercept using the Royal Navy and the SBS, in an operation code named **Operation Forsyth**. The Armstrong's are playing with fire, because there is another load of arms on the same ship as you have heard, which the Russian's are dispatching to their Security Forces in Mozambique. The Armstrong's don't know the Russian's have arranged this second load, but if

Hassan finds them both on the same ship he will, I am sure, try to take both."

Richard Woodgate reported that George and John Armstrong had arranged a flight to Mogadishu, from Manston for the next day. The flight would be via Cyprus again, landing the day after in Mogadishu.

Chapter Twenty four

The MV Castelo del Rodrigo docked at berth four at the London Gateway Thames side port located between Thames Haven and Stanford le Hope, in south Essex. It was nudged into place by two tugs, and brought gently to rest against the dockside, beneath the huge cranes which were a feature of the newish port built adjacent to the main A13 trunk road.

Boarding officers of HM Customs as a routine went on to the vessel where they carried out their regular inspections of the bills of lading. Dressed in the uniform of a Customs Officer, Richard Woodgate, accompanied the boarding party to get his first view of the ship and to be present when the Master, a Spaniard, Senor Miguel Martinez, was interviewed by the leader of the Customs group. They were offered drinks and ascertained that some of the load had come from Karachi in Pakistan and other parts from Cape Town in South Africa. Woodgate knew that Karachi offered a direct overland route to Afghanistan, which had a thriving drug supply, and he concentrated on the details on the bill of lading which showed they had been placed on board in that port. He spotted that container No. PK

79934 was the only consignment of oranges on board, the handling agents being MG International, of Kingsbridge Road, Barking, Essex. This must be the drug consignment. After the inspection of the bills of lading, the leader of the Customs unit, walked amongst the containers, with the paperwork in hand as if carrying out a routine check of the bill of lading against the load itself. He was able to fix a tracker device covertly to container PK 799334. He then cleared them for importation, and left the ship with a copy of the paperwork.

Richard Woodgate returned with the team to the port side customs office, where he linked up with DI Dave Harley of SO 11, and his own surveillance team. It was now a waiting game to identify the vehicle which would transport the load to Cambridge, and this could take up to 48 hours, which perhaps meant a long night or two, and perhaps working in shifts.

The following morning, with the ship off loaded to the dock, a lorry turned up at the dock gates and showed paperwork to collect Container PK 79934. The paperwork was issued by MG International, and showed a destination as a distribution centre on the A14 just east of Cambridge to be collected by driver Tony Collins of Collins Transport, Kingsbridge Road, Barking, driving articulated lorry, registration No. PE 09 TBC. The driver was directed to the Dock Office, where he produced the same paperwork, and one of Woodgate's under cover agents who had been placed in the dock office inspected the paperwork, and directed the driver to the area of the dock where the container had been stored. The Customs team watched as the driver pulled alongside the container, and a heavy duty forklift placed the container on his lorry. DI Harley's mixed team of Customs and armed Police, took the radio call from their position outside the dock gates and then activated the tracker unit. They were ready to follow the suspect vehicle when it came out of the gates.

DI Harley contacted his office for a check to be made on the Police National Computer (PNC)to check on the driver. A reply came back to him, revealing the driver of the lorry, who was a partner in the haulage firm, was known to the Police. He was born in the Whitechapel area of London, and had convictions for armed robbery in his youth. Records showed he had been convicted with George Armstrong, of a small time robbery at a shop, when both were teenagers, and had served a short term in the same Borstal, but nothing was on his record since that time. He had worked as a lorry driver and had set up his own business, with his younger brother Brian, starting with the purchase of two second hand lorries and working from home, but had expanded over the following years to now own a fleet of 8 lorries operating from the yard in Barking. He now lived in a large detached house in Chigwell, Essex. He had obviously come up in the world and appeared affluent.

Armed with this information, DI Harley arranged for another smaller surveillance team to watch the Collins Transport Yard in Barking, and he instructed them to await a call from him when the strike took place in Cambridgeshire, so they could act simultaneously.

The Collins Transport lorry left the London Gateway Port, and made its way to the A13. It was discreetly followed by Harley's surveillance team in various non- descript vehicles. They anticipated it would turn right onto the M25 towards the M11, and had plotted their forward vehicles in that direction. When the lorry got to the junction with the M25, it surprised them and turned left towards the Dartford Tunnel, which threw the following surveillance vehicles into turmoil. Harley called up a motor cycle and a van, and they followed the lorry onto the lorry and coach park on the Purfleet side of the M25, where it stopped. The driver sat in his cab and was seen to use his mobile phone. An hour later, with Harley contemplating changing the now re-positioned surveillance team, a black Range Rover 4 x 4, pulled up alongside the lorry, and Graham Armstrong got out. He went over and spoke to the driver of the lorry. He looked around for a while, reached back into the boot of his car and took out a cloth covered bundle. He locked his car and got into the cab of the lorry. He was seen to use his mobile phone and then the lorry moved and the team followed it onto the M25 where it headed north towards the M11 and as expected, Cambridge.

DI Harley, accompanied by Richard Woodgate, followed at a distance, allowing his team to precede and follow the lorry. As it neared Cambridge, Harley spoke on the radio. "Hunter One to Hunter three. Make your way to the Springhill Nursery, in the village of Balsham. Be a customer until we get in the vicinity. Keep in touch." The occupants of the car, Detective Constable 'Sooty' Coleman and his customs companion, Micky Hurst acknowledged, accelerated past the lorry and disappeared from view.

The two officers of Hunter three entered the car park of the nursery, and taking a plant barrow walked into the nursery, picking up plants on their way. They did a tour of the nursery acting as customers, and saw the main building was a vast space housing plants of all descriptions, as would be normal in that kind of business. There were a number of staff present, all dressed in green sweaters bearing the logo Springhill Nursery, and on their tour they identified the owner Sam Leonard, talking to a man in his late twenties. He looked the spitting image of Leonard Senior and they assumed him to be Leonard's son. They were holding an animated conversation, when Leonard's mobile phone rang. He answered it, but the officers could not hear what he said. Once the call had finished, Leonard and the young man with him walked away and went through a door marked staff only. The two officers moved through the shop area, outside to a plant growing area. Beyond the boundary they saw a field with multiple polytunnels and outbuildings, and they saw

Leonard walking through the tunnel area, to a large barn at the rear of the premises, where he opened the front doors. DC Coleman's earpiece activated and he heard a coded message which meant the lorry was approaching the nursery. The two officers replied to the call indicating they were in position. A short time later, they saw the lorry enter the goods delivery entrance which led directly to the poly tunnel area, and they saw the lorry back into the barn, being directed by Leonard. The doors were then closed but the younger man with Leonard stayed outside the barn. DC Coleman reported what he had seen.

DI Harley instructed in a coded message, "All units hold until I give the word." He issued the instruction for the team to don their bullet proof vests, and for the Police Officers in the team to have their firearms on view and ready for use.

After ten minutes, the younger Leonard, was still outside the barn, and Harley issued the order**, "All Hunters, Strike, Strike, Strike!"**

Six cars and one van, drove onto the site at speed, and pulled up surrounding the barn. Officers, led by Harley and Richard Woodgate, leapt from their vehicle, and charged toward the barn shouting "Armed Police. Stay where you are."

The younger Leonard looked startled, he turned and opened the barn door, running inside, closely followed by Harley and Woodgate, and the rest of the team. Woodgate rugby tackled young Leonard, wrestling him to the floor, where he struggled until Woodgate punched him hard to the side of his head. This subdued him enough for Woodgate to handcuff him. Meanwhile two Policemen and two Customs Officers ran to the rear of the barn and finding a back door, opened it. The two officers in the rear garden of the nursery, vaulted the fence and ran through the poly tunnel area towards the Barn to join their colleagues.

Inside the barn all was panic. Harley shouted again, "Armed Police. Stand Still!" holding his automatic pistol in his right hand. The elder Leonard froze, looked startled and stood blinking and very still. The driver of the lorry took off running towards the back door.

Those by the lorry heard a thump and the sound of a body hitting the floor. Graham Armstrong reacted by reaching into the cab of the lorry where he pulled out a Scorpion semi automatic machine gun. He sprayed bullets towards Harley, most went high and wide but two hit him in the chest knocking him to the ground. Woodgate was still grappling with the younger Leonard on the floor when four shots were fired at Graham Armstrong by the officers who had followed Harley into the barn. Two of these shots hit Armstrong one high on the right side of his chest and the other smashed through his right forearm. He spun round, dropping his gun as he did so and falling to the floor screaming with pain. These officers followed up by standing over the wounded Armstrong pointing their guns at him. Sam Leonard put his hands in the air, and Woodgate pulled his son onto his feet where he stood very still, with a sickened look on his face, alongside his father. More Officers ran into the barn, and took charge of those detained, handcuffing them and sitting them at the side of the building. The lorry driver was dragged, in a daze, back to the front of the lorry, held by two officers. He was handcuffed and made to sit down with the others. He had a vivid bruise on the side of his jaw and he was obviously still suffering the effects of a blow to the head. DI Harley laid on the floor groaning and gasping for breath.

DC Coleman looked down on Harley and said, "You alright guv'nor." "No I'm bloody not. It hurts like buggery. I think he's broken my ribs. Help me up!"

He managed to get to his feet with Coleman's help, and stood holding his chest still gasping for breath and in obvious pain. He said, "Someone get that bugger an ambulance" pointing to Armstrong, " Search him, and bag all his possessions, including his mobile and bag that gun separately," pointing to the Scorpion lying on the ground, "Don't forget to unload and deactivate it first." They searched the cab of the lorry and lying on the back seat was a sawn off double barreled shotgun, which was loaded. This was seized as evidence and placed inside an evidence bag.

The scene inside the barn had calmed down. A woman appeared from the house on the far side of the Nursery.

She screamed "What have you done to my husband."

Harley gasped "Who are you." She said, "I'm Mrs Leonard, what are you doing to my husband. " Harley gasped, "Get her out of here, and arrest her too." One of the officers took the woman to one of the Police Cars and sat her in the back seat still shouting hysterically.

The officers then took stock of the interior of the barn. The doors of the container on the back of the lorry were open, and several large cardboard boxes were on the floor, two of which were open. There were several identical empty cardboard boxes stacked at the side of the barn, and oranges were spilled on the floor. Woodgate emptied the contents of one box into a spare one and it contained only oranges. He did the same to all the other boxes on the floor of the barn and all they contained were oranges. These were the ones immediately at the front of the load. He climbed into the container, and shifted a few boxes, helped by his Customs team, and further into the load, they found boxes which had a cardboard partition halfway down and once this was removed they saw that there were a number of plastic covered oblong packages containing a light coloured powder. A second box revealed the same, as did the third and fourth. The remainder of the load was stacked inside the container on pallets.

Woodgate said, "We will reload the boxes onto the lorry and take it to our nearest Customs Depot to unload it and chart the evidence properly." He indicated to all the prisoners and said, "You are all under arrest on suspicion of importation, possession and supply of drugs and for firearms offences, you will be taken to Cambridge Police Station. He then cautioned them. Woodgate then took a series of pictures of the barn, the lorry and its load, then those arrested, plus the firearms found on his mobile phone for evidential purposes.

An ambulance arrived and Harley said, "I want two men to accompany me and Armstrong to hospital. One in the ambulance with me and the other can drive behind. Graham Armstrong was placed in the ambulance, and Harley climbed in with him. Both were given oxygen, and the ambulance crew worked on Armstrong as they drove off.

Two of the Customs officers got into the lorry, and were escorted to the Customs inspection area at Stansted Airport. The unloading of the lorry in the customs area was filmed, and it was discovered that most of the boxes of oranges contained packages of Heroin, to a street value of £40 million. A major drug consignment, which upon forensic examination was believed to have emanated from Afghanistan.

DI Harley was x-rayed at Hospital and it was discovered he had severe bruises to his chest which made it hard to breath without pain. His chest was black and blue. He was strapped up, given pain killers and released. Graham Armstrong had been shot high on the right side of his chest. The bullet had smashed his collar bone. The other bullet had broken his right radius and ulna. The bullets were extracted under anesthetic, and the arm bones repositioned and the arm plastered. His arm was bound to his chest by tape, and put into a sling to stop movement. Once he recovered consciousness he was given pain killers, kept overnight under escort, and the following day released to the custody of the two Officers guarding him. He was arrested and taken to Cambridge Police Station, to join the others who had been arrested at the nursery.

Full forensic examinations were carried out at the nursery. Spent bullets recovered and guns which had been fired were taken for examination. The Scorpion machine gun and the sawn off shotgun were taken for examination. It was later found that bullets from the Scorpion had been recovered at the scene of two drive by drug related shootings in the East End of London. The sawn off shotgun was identified as part of a haul from a burglary in Hertfordshire two years earlier. The burglary netted £150 worth of stolen goods, but the shotgun was a Purdy, and valued at £21,000. Someone had cut the barrels down and ruined a valuable and unique shotgun. There's no understanding the criminal mind thought Harley. The criminals had made a valuable shotgun worthless.

When Woodgate and his team had completed their interviews, they discovered from the younger Leonard that they intended to repack the oranges in the new boxes found in the barn, and deliver them to the distribution centre off the A14, which was their proper destination. In that way, although a delayed delivery the paperwork would show a genuine consignment of oranges delivered according to instructions. A good way to cover their tracks.

A message had been sent to the other surveillance team watching activity at the Collins Transport Yard in Barking shortly after the Cambridge raid. These officers detained Brian Collins as a suspect and he was brought o Cambridge to link up with the others arrested. A search of computer records by the Customs Investigation team showed previous loads of fruit had been collected from the London Gateway and taken eventually to the Cambridge distribution centre.

Richard Woodgate and his Customs Investigations team were given the task of interviewing the suspects, and charging them with criminal offences. This allowed Mozart and his team to concentrate on George and John Armstrong, who were on their way to Mogadishu whilst the arrests in Cambridgeshire were happening.

Chapter Twenty Five

Mozart walked through the control areas of Manama Airport into the public concourse, to find a man in naval uniform bearing a plaque with his name printed on it. He introduced himself as Able Seaman Matthews from HMS Juffair. The air conditioning kept the temperature at a comfortable level inside the building, but as soon as Mozart got outside the searing heat hit him. It must have been about 100 degrees or more. He walked quickly to the car immediately outside the airport building, and was grateful the naval rating had kept the engine running, as the air conditioning in the car emulated that inside the airport. Mozart stripped his jacket off, and loosened his tie, and was comfortable for the remainder of the 50 mile journey across the island of Bahrain, watching the scenery change from an urban sprawl of white houses and high rise hotels and business premises, to the broad and barren expanse of sandy desert. It was a land of heat and contrast. When they passed close to the sea there was no visibility to the horizon, the view was obscured by a steamy heat haze off the water which reminded Mozart of the steam from a hot bath. It was the middle of the day, and the streets were almost deserted. Later, when the heat of the day dissipated, the population would emerge from their air conditioned homes, the shops would open, and life in a more tolerable temperature would commence. The heat of the day forced everyone who could manage it, indoors. The Able Seaman Matthews, a lad from Liverpool, kept up a running commentary as they passed through various towns and villages, and he said even the Riffa Golf course had a lighting system, where the players would start their game at twilight to avoid the heat of the day, and finish under a million pound lighting system that turned the course to daylight. Most of the population lived a nocturnal life. The welfare system meant that not many Bahrainis worked, but they all had free housing, free health and dentistry, and pensions from the state, a welfare state which existed because of an oil income envied around the world. The ruler of Bahrain was an absolute ruler, who benevolently passed on the benefits of the oil income to his people. The manual labour was carried out by an immigrant work force, who pandered to the whims of the Bahraini population. There were many European businessmen in the Caliphate who lived in compounds in standard housing, and lived a life separated from the local population. It was in these compounds that a western lifestyle could be pursued provided it did not spill over to the local Muslim population. All this Able Seaman Matthews explained to Mozart on his journey south, so by the time they arrived at HMS Juffair, a British enclave port in the extreme south of the island, Mozart was aware of some of the do and don't in this strange new environment, new to Mozart that is.

At the gate to the base the car stopped, and Matthews identified himself and his passenger to the armed uniformed naval rating at the entry lodge. Mozart was given a pass to hang around his neck on a cord, the barrier was lifted. They drove to HMS Bulldog, a Royal Marine assault ship with internal floating dock, passing through a busy naval dock. Matthews directed Mozart to the gangway of the ship and said, "I will bring your case aboard sir".

As he got out of the car Mozart again felt the searing heat of the midday sun. He walked up the steeply angled gangway breaking out into a sweat as he did so. He was met at the head of the gangway by a Lieutenant in tropical gear who said, "Mr Mozart, I am Lieutenant Clive Foster, ADC to Admiral Vincent, will you follow me please."

He then took him into the comparative coolness of the ship, through grey steel corridors and up a flight of stairs where he knocked on a grey steel door, and entered immediately. He said, "Mr Mozart sir," he saluted and left. Mozart saw he was in a large conference room, with a long conference table and chairs all around. There were a number of people present, including Admiral Vincent, who came forward and shook Mozart's hand.

Admiral Vincent raised his voice and said, "Gentlemen, please be seated. Mr Mozart, please sit next to me." There was a scraping of chairs and everyone sat around a large conference table. Coffee was placed beside Mozart by a naval rating, who then quietly left the room.

Admiral Vincent said, "Gentlemen, for those of you who don't know him, this is Detective Chief Inspector Joseph Mozart. He started this whole escapade by delving into the activities of a family of criminals back in England and I will let him tell you why we are all here."

DCI Mozart, looked around the room, recognizing the familiar face of a Royal Marine Major, whom he nodded at and smiled, receiving a nod and smile in return.

He said, " The family we are talking about are George Armstrong and his sons, John and Graham. They were small time criminals until they got into the supply and then importation of drugs, obtaining bulk supplies of drugs from Afghanistan and South America. They have, over the years become very wealthy, so much so, they have managed to finance so called legitimate businesses in transport, property, plant hire, and the buying and selling of second hand plant to overseas customers. They are a major crime family and feared for their violent methods, even by other criminal gangs. They are what we might term Crime Overlords and have so far been untouchable. They own a garage or two, and we know they have financed other criminal enterprizes. They have become so wealthy they have now purchased two private aircraft and set up a private hire company operating out of Manston Airport. They have however, used the services of a private banker whom they had a drug hold over, to launder their illegitimate profits and they have salted away millions in secret accounts around the world. Lately we have managed to cut off two consignments of drugs they have imported and have made arrests in Felixstowe, Grays, and most recently in Cambridgeshire."

"All I have mentioned so far would be the province of us, the Police and HM Customs, however they have now got involved with arms dealing. At this very moment there is a ship on the high seas, the MV Santa Cruz, which is en route from Odessa in the Ukraine, via Alexandria, to the port of Beira in Mozambique. There are two containers of arms and ammunition, everything from machine guns, AK47's, pistols, mortars, anti-tank weapons etc. on board. One of the containers is intended for delivery to Zimbabwe, arranged by the Armstrong's, which as you might know has a UN embargo in force forbidding the supply of arms to the country. The other container, which is nothing to do with the Armstrong's, is due to be delivered to Russian Security Forces, in effect a private army, who are currently employed by the Mozambique government to help the fight against Al Shabaab, in the north of that country. Both container loads of arms were supplied by the same two Russian Arms dealers, who intend ripping off the Armstrong's by diverting both container loads of arms currently on that ship, to Russian forces in Mozambique."

"However the Armstrong's having obtained a substantial deposit from the Zimbabwean's, have done a side deal with a Pirate and Terrorist leader named Mohammed Umbedi Hassan in Somalia and have made arrangements for him to hijack the ship to remove the arms at sea. Neither the pirates nor the Armstrong's are aware there is a second consignment of arms on the same ship and should the pirates find both, they will probably be better armed that the Somali army. We know Hassan has political ambitions and if he had these arms he could move to take over the country and depose the government. The country, already wild in places, could then become a haven for terrorists exiting the middle east and Afghanistan. We obviously can't allow this to happen."

Admiral Vincent said, "Thank you for the update Mr Mozart. Let me tell you Gentlemen, that HM Government has decreed that the arms shipments on board that vessel cannot be allowed to fall into Hassan's hands. The consequences would be too horrific for North East Africa. We must stop the pirating operation, arrest or eliminate the pirates themselves, and prevent the arms from getting into the hands of the Zimbabwean's. To that end we have formulated a plan which we call **Operation Forsyth**. Major James McKay and his SBS team have been brought over from Oman, and we intend to intercept and board the Santa Cruz at sea, and retake the ship from the Pirates thus preventing the arms ending up in Somalia."

We are aware that the Russians have a naval presence in the Indian Ocean. We know of a surveillance ship off Deigo Garcia watching the Americans there, and we know one of their latest Frigates, the Admiral Gordinski, is in the southern Indian Ocean. They may know about the consignment of arms intended for Mozambique because it has the confidential approval of their own government. "

"Mr. Mozart has prepared a briefing document to go along with the documented Operation Forsyth and the Prime Minister has a copy and has been briefed."

"We are monitoring the progress of the MV Santa Cruz, and at present she is making her way through the Suez Canal, and is expected to travel through the Red Sea, into the Arabian Sea, where it should detour around the island of Suqutra to make a loop around the High Risk Area (HRA) where pirating has been rife. From information we have received, we believe the pirates intend to launch an attack from the northern shore of Somalia, when the ship is nearest to land, and before it has to turn east to avoid the HRA. Once they have the ship, they intend to sail it further down the coast of Somalia, to their enclave and off-load the arms there. I suspect they intend then to ransom the ship and crew, which is a pretty novel way for them to pay for the arms. We are monitoring the ship by drone and AWAC's, and they will communicate direct to us on this ship. We have also arranged for backup to the operation, and HMS Yarmouth one of our latest Frigates will be patrolling nearby to assist if required. Any questions."

Major McKay said, "I presume we attack at night sir."

"Preferably" said Admiral Vincent, "It would make the task easier for you and more difficult for the pirates."

Major McKay then said, "How do we know which containers have the arms inside." Admiral Vincent said, "The details are in your operational orders. Please study them whilst we are en route. We will sail this afternoon. Meantime it is lunchtime, and we have all been invited to the wardroom to get to know one another."

The meeting broke up and Admiral Vincent said to Mozart, "I will have you shown to your cabin, so you can freshen up before lunch."

As he was speaking, Major McKay approached, smiling, and said, "Excuse me Admiral" he then turned to Mozart and said, "Hallo Joe, long time no see."

" James, how are you. You've made another step since I last saw you. You made Major." Admiral Vincent looked amazed and said, "You two know each other?" McKay said, "Joe and I were Captains together in the Corps." "You were in the SBS?" said Admiral Vincent to Mozart, with amazement in his voice. "Yes" said Mozart." James and I served together for a number of years. I was wounded in the back on one of our operations, and left the corps after rehabilitation, and then joined the Police."

Vincent with a raised eyebrow and a half smile said, "That explains a lot. You two will obviously have a lot of catching up to do. Now let's get you settled, then lunch."

At 1600hours that day HMS Bulldog sailed from HMS Juffair, Bahrain. It proceeded slowly south down the Persian Gulf, following many oil tankers coming from Saudi Arabia and Iran, and its offshore facilities. The ship then transited the Straits of Hormuz, keeping as close as possible to the United Arab Emirates to avoid confrontation with the Iraqi forces, and then gathering speed entered the Arabian Sea, where it rendezvoused with HMS Yarmouth. Admiral Vincent ordered the Captain of the Yarmouth to come aboard Bulldog and his barge came alongside a short time later.

Captain Miles Henderson presented himself to the Admiral and was taken to the conference room, where he met all the officers of the ship, the SBS Assault team, plus Mozart. There Admiral Vincent briefed Captain Henderson on his role, asking that he kept station well out of sight over the horizon from Bulldog for the duration of Operation Forsyth, and be ready to assist if required. They discussed communication, and at the end of the briefing Captain Henderson was clear on his role and the duty expected of him. Major James McKay and Mozart then concentrated on briefing the assault team who were brought into the conference room. Major McKay asked Mozart to explain the situation and history of Operation Forsyth to his team, at the end of which he discussed in detail the plans to assault the Santa Cruz, and how they would accomplish the rescue of the ship and crew and the recovery of the consignment of arms.

McKay asked for any questions and listened to his men. He was not the only one with ideas. His men were trained to think independently and he leaned heavily on their experience. Admiral Vincent was impressed with the way that the SBS planned their assault. He then realized it was because everyone on the operation had an input, that success was more certain. At the end of the briefing Captain Henderson left Bulldog and rejoined his ship feeling confident that the assault was well planned. His ship steamed away over the horizon, maintaining a radar and radio contact.

An Airbourne Warning and Control System (AWAC) aircraft took off from Akriteri Airbase in Cyprus, heading for the Red Sea. Its mission was to identify the MV Santa Cruz, as it exited the Suez Canal, and track it down the Red Sea, as it travelled south. The AWAC was in early contact with HMS Bulldog and quickly identified the Santa Cruz from the myriad of ships using those waters, giving Bulldog its course and speed. Once the ship was in the Red Sea, a Reaper Drone, took off from RAFO Musannah in Oman. The drone was piloted remotely from the United Kingdom, and it took over the surveillance of the Santa Cruz, following it and circling widely over it from a height of 30,000 feet. These two aircraft would maintain constant surveillance on the craft until interception, reporting its movements to HMS Bulldog.

Chapter Twenty Six

Mohammed Umbedi Hassan stood on raised ground in front of his assembled disciples. He was in full rant. His eyes bulged with fervour, the veins on his neck and forehead stood proud of his flesh and throbbed to the pulsating of his passion fueled heart. His arms were gesticulating wildly causing his robes to swing and flow like the rhythm of a bat's wings. He was shouting his cause to the ensemble before him, with spittle discharging into his beard at the force of every word. He was preaching death and destruction to all who would not follow his holy cause. His disciples were mesmerized by his charisma, swaying to the tempo of his messianic energy. He had them in the palm of his hand, they were clay for his molding. His voice rose in crescendo, climaxing as he raised his arms in crucifix. "Follow me to victory" he screamed, as his audience pointed their guns to the sky, their rolling volley adding thunder to his finale. Their chants of "Victory, Victory" echoing over the valley. They stamped in feverish rhythm as Hassan conducted his audience like an orchestral leader, the dust rising to head height as they stomped out their allegiance. Once he had them to fever pitch he waved his arms north, and bounded with demonic energy to a fleet of waiting trucks, each mounted with an RPG machine gun over the cab.

His followers kept chanting his name, their voices louder and ever louder, "Hassan, Hassan, The chosen one." Each was captured by the force of his harangue , each willing to follow him even to death.

"We go to arm ourselves, to eliminate the oppressors of our women, our children, our faith. Death to the infidel," he shouted, an echo which was repeated by those who followed him.

He had his army, he would arm them with guns and righteous faith. They were guarded by his shield of invincibility. He was a disciple of the true, the only way. This was his mission. He and his followers would move soon to free Somalia from corruption, vice, and oppression of its people. He would return the country to the religion of old. He would wage Holy War. Was he not the reincarnation of Mohammed Abdullah Hassan, the messianic deliverer, did he not have the power of the Djinns with him. Was he not impervious to bullets. Was he not the deliverer of miracles. Would he not establish himself as the head of a new Caliphate.

The truck convoy drove north to the town of Bandabela where their mother ship, a large Dhow was based. The vessel was fitted with an old radar set, but it worked, and it had mounted RPG machine guns fore and aft. It was fitted with a powerful diesel engine which gave it a maximum speed of 18 knots, but it was sound and weatherly, and would provide a good base for the raiders. The Captain was an old hand, a follower of Hassan and he was well paid for his expertise, his share of ransom money assured that. He was an experienced pilot in the northern waters of the Indian Ocean, The Red Sea, the Gulf of Aden and the Arabian Sea. He knew the places to intercept ships coming from Suez, and the Persian Gulf. The places where they would turn east to avoid the so called HRA –

the High Risk Area, designated because of the frequent acts of piracy in those waters.

Hassan and a score of his followers, all armed with AK47's, boarded the Dhow, which immediately put to sea. It followed the coast north, into the Gulf of Aden, pulling into a bay near the port of Caluula, where sea going skiffs were moored ready. Five of the skiffs were unmoored, and fitted with powerful twin 40hp outboard motors. Each had extra fuel on board, and each was fitted with a bow mounted RPG. The Dhow towed the five shallow drafted skiffs to sea, making for the rendezvous point. There was just hours to go before action according to their information.

Hours later the Dhow's radar picked up a blip. It was a ship coming from the right direction, and at the right speed. It coordinated with the information the Dhow Captain had. It moved steadily along the Gulf of Aden, towards the pinch point between the Yemen and north Somalia. If it was the right ship, it should soon turn east to skirt around the HRA. The radar operator saw it make the turn east. By now the Dhow had closed to within 20 miles of the target vessel. It was time to launch the high powered skiffs. The sea was calm, the weather good, and visibility only marred by the surface heat haze.

The five skiffs each had a four man crew. All heavily armed with AK47's and full belts of ammunition. Each crew had radio for communication. Each skiff was fitted with grappling irons and ropes. One had a rocket launcher on board. They expected some resistance from the crew, but they would have two skiffs to each side of the ship. It could not escape them.

They tore across the sea at 25 knots, the twin outboard engines screaming as the skiffs planed towards the ship which they quickly identified as their target, the Santa Cruz. The radar on the ship picked them up five miles out, but there was little those on board could do to avoid the pirate incursion. The Captain ordered his crew to the port side hoses and he also readied them on the starboard side. He would turn the ship at the last minute port side on to the invaders. He knew what was coming and knew there was little he could do to stop it. He told his crew not to take chances. If fired upon to come inboard immediately. He did not want unnecessary loss of life on his conscience. He had the radio room send out a mayday call, in his own language and English which was to be repeated for a long as possible. This was picked up on HMS Bulldog, which was over 100 miles away. The Captain of Bulldog ordered full speed ahead, wishing to close within 20 miles of the Santa Cruz by nightfall. The Captain of HMS Yarmouth also heard the call and knew that Operation Forsyth would be activated. His ship was nearly 200 nautical miles away, and he too demanded full speed ahead. The Captain of the Admiral Gordinski, was far to the south of the Santa Cruz and would have to steam over 500 nautical miles. He heard the call and ordered full speed ahead.

The skiffs closed with the Santa Cruz, and the ship turned, showing its port side to the invaders. Six of the crew readied the port side hoses, and the rest were ordered to the mess deck to await developments. There was no use in throwing lives away to an armed and determined assault. As the Santa Cruz made its turn, the high pressure hoses were activated, but the skiffs divided and went into to attack mode, two to the port side, keeping just out of range of the high pressure stream, and the other two to starboard where the pirate crews grappled the taffrail, and started to climb aboard. On the port side a burst of AK47 fire at the fire hose party soon had them scurrying for cover, wounding one crew member, and another burst of automatic fire at the bridge windows, made the ship heave too. The crews of the port side skiffs also grappled the side rail and climbed aboard. The armed insurgents quickly moved through the containers, firing bursts into the air as they made their way to the bridge where they took control of the ship. The Captain and the helmsman were threatened with guns, and held in situ, whilst the remainder of the pirates sought the crew. The radio officer was secured and taken to the mess deck, where he was made to join the remainder of the crew, and the ship was secured in an almost bloodless operation.

The ship's ladder was put over the side and Mohammad Umbedi Hassan boarded in imperious style. In English he told the Captain that the ship was now his, and would be taken to the coast of Somalia, where some of the cargo would be unloaded and he and his ship would be held for ransom from the owners. He then dispatched four of his men to look for a blue container number KS51437, and asked for the bills of lading, which the Captain produced from the safe in his day cabin. This manifest showed two containers with similar numbers and similarly described loads. One due for Harare in Zimbabwe and another KS 55674 for Mozambique. This peeked Hassan's interest, and he radioed his crew to look for both. Meanwhile he ordered them to feed both his own crew and Hassan's followers. The on board chef was taken to the galley and put to work. It was now late afternoon and his men were hungry.

A short time later his men reported they had found both containers, and Hassan went on deck to see. He found one container at deck level and the other stacked on top of the first. He had his men smash the customs seal on the lower container, and open it. Inside he saw a stack of spare motor vehicle parts, and machinery. He had his men pull this out of the load, and behind he saw wooden boxes. On opening two of them he discovered AK 47's and handguns. He was satisfied that he had found the load he wanted. He had his men climb up to the container above the first, and again after removing mechanical parts, similar boxes were found, and these contained more AK47's and handguns. He had found the double haul. Taking a sample from each, he saw that the weapons were in good condition and in their greased packaging,

Hassan returned to the bridge and in the gathering twilight, he saw the Dhow mother ship had joined them. He pointed to his first lieutenant, Mohammed Obanguli and said, "You know the compass bearing, and the place near Bandabeyla where you must anchor the ship off shore. The Dhow will guide you, and I will be aboard it to make sure we get there. I leave you in charge, and I will see you ashore. Just follow our lights." Hassan then climbed down the ladder to his own skiff, and returned to the Dhow. In line astern the two vessels headed toward the Somali shore.

The overhead Reaper drone saw the whole operation from 30,000 feet, and filmed the pirating operation. The film was relayed to operational control at a secret airbase in England, and relayed from there to the COBR incident room in London. The drone was able to supply information on the change of course and speed of the Santa Cruz to the pursuing HMS Bulldog, which was capable of twice the speed of the other vessel.

As the Reaper Drone ran out of time over its target, and night fell, it was replaced by an AWAC from the Royal Air Force, which had the capability of radar interruption as well as night vision and infra red detection. Communication between the AWAC and Bulldog led her to within 10 miles of the Santa Cruz, where the bridge party could see their target with night vision. HMS Bulldog was a unique ship in the British Naval fleet, it had the capability of flooding special tanks in its structure, which lowered the back of the vessel in the water. At the rear of the ship there was a large drop down ramp which when lowered allowed the sea to enter what was in effect a sea going dock for shallow draft boats such as landing craft and fast attack craft. This meant that assault craft could leave the ship at speed and fully loaded with arms, equipment and personnel, and were ready for instant use. Once operations were concluded, the rear ramp could be closed and the water pumped from the interior harbour. The ship also had space for helicopters, and was carrying an Augusta/Westland Merlin Mk 2 with troop carrying capability, and an Augusta/Westland Wildcat Attack helicopter fitted with harpoon missiles. The ship was well equipped for purpose.

The Captain of Bulldog ordered flooding of the at sea harbour on board, and the SBS team lead by Major James McKay boarded their fast attack ribs, with twin 50hp outboards. Mozart was there to see them off and wish them luck. No matter how much he itched to join his old colleague, he would not be allowed to, he was now a civilian. Being ex-SBS, was just that, he was no longer part of that elite unit, and he would be a liability to those trained and honed for just this sort of operation. The equipment they now used was more advanced than that used when he was in the unit. He was only on hand to gather evidence which might help the overall investigation back in the UK. He found it highly frustrating, but understood all the reasoning behind the decision to exclude him. The remainder of the SBS team boarded the Merlin helicopter and would follow when called by the assault commander.

The fast attack ribs were shallow drafted, skimmed the surface of the water and could attain speeds of 30 knots when pushed on a flat sea. There were four ribs, with a 4 man crew on board each. One man was designated coxswain of the boat and a reserve for the boarding party, and the other three were part of the assault team. Each man was equipped with night vision goggles, radio communication, light weight flak jackets, and rubber soled boots. They were each armed with a suppressed Heckler and Koch semi automatic weapon, and a Glock side arm. One in every two men had a stun gun, and a supply of cable ties. They were the best of the best. Trained to the highest degree, and all capable of operating independently under extreme conditions. They were also well practiced at ship assault, and anti piracy operations.

The harbour on Bulldog was now fully flooded, the team had been fully briefed, and they left their ship at speed heading for the Santa Cruz. The moon had not yet risen, and the craft skimmed across the water, slowing down to the speed of their target ship and dividing port and starboard around it. Rubber coated grappling hooks were thrown to the deck rails, as the assault boats bobbed up and down and to and fro alongside the ship which looked mountainous with its containers stacked two or three container height above its deck level. The advantage of boarding such a ship was that the containers shielded the assault team from the bridge, and provided a maze of cover once on board.

Major James McKay was the first to climb the grappling rope and plant his feet firmly on the deck. He was soon joined by the rest of his team, as they assembled at the rear of the ship. They were lucky, the two pirates who had been designated as lookouts had not yet moved into position. At hand signals, the team divided in port starboard and centre, McKay leading the centre group. They all had throat microphones, and earpieces, and their night vision goggles showed a clear as day image of the ship. They worked carefully along the length of the ship toward the bridge. McKay was the first to startle a pirate in the lee of the bridge structure, who when he saw McKay raised his AK47 to fire. McKay fired twice with his silenced Heckler & Koch and the man went down. He was dead before he hit the deck. McKay led his team to the starboard steps, leading to the bridge. Captain Ian Thacker led his team to the port side steps. They crouched below the glass paneled door leading to the bridge, and saw a man they assumed to be the ships' Captain in his uniform, standing with a pirate pointing an

AK47 at him. The crew member steering the ship, had another pirate holding a gun on him. All appeared fairly calm. McKay pulled a flash grenade from his belt, and whispered for Captain Thacker, through his radio to do the same on the other side of the bridge. "On a count of three" he ordered. "One, two, three." One of each team jerked the door open and two flash grenades were thrown onto the bridge. The assault team averted their eyes, and switched off their night vision, as the two grenades exploded with a searing white light and a very loud noise. The door was jerked open again, and the assault team ran in clubbing the two pirates to unconsciousness. Another man appeared from a door which led from the Captains' day cabin, he was raising his AK47 and pointing it at McKay. Ian Thacker took him out with two shots to the chest. He died on his way to the floor. The bridge was secure, but they had to find the rest of the pirate team. McKay asked the Captain how many there were and where they were on the ship. It was now obvious that their cover was blown, the remainder of the pirates would have heard the twin explosions. They would have to be hunted down and their threat eliminated.

McKay ordered the reinforcements from MHS Bulldog, and a short time later helicopter rotors were heard at the rear of the ship. Two of the original assault group covered the reinforcements as they abseiled from the machine to the top of the container stack at the rear deck of the ship.

The hunt through the remainder of the ship commenced. The engine room was the first to be entered. There were two pirates identified holding guns on the Chief Engineer. Flash grenades were deployed once again, and one of the pirates was subdued by the swipe of a Heckler & Koch to the side of the head. The other ran behind machinery. He fired his weapon hitting one of the assault team and knocking him to the ground. Fortunately his Kevlar vest took the impact, and whilst it made him breathless, and bruised, it did no further damage. When the pirate exposed himself to finish the job, he was shot by the other assault team member, and as he died he emptied his magazine spraying around the engine room. One of the bullets penetrated a steam pipe, and the engine room became foggy. The SBS changed their goggles to infrared mode and were able to clear the room. The engine room staff soon had the situation under control and gradually the fog cleared.

"Lock the engine room off and stay here. We will clear the rest of the ship and come back for you," said the Commando. "The bridge has been secured, and the Captain is now back in charge there. We have to clear the rest of the ship. Do you know where the rest of the pirates are?"

The Chief Engineer said, "They took us all to the mess deck. I expect that's where most of them are."

He then reported this to Major McKay. "Can you turn the lights off throughout the ship from the engine room," said the Commando." Yes, we have a master switch." He reported this to Major McKay, who instructed, "Tell him to switch off the lights, we can operate by night vision and infrared. This might give us an advantage. "

Leaving the reinforcements to search the container area and deck, they began a systematic search below decks. They heard another explosion, which turned out to be two members of the assault team clearing the radio room. One more dead pirate and one wounded and detained.

Major McKay studied a plan of the ship. He saw there were three entrances to the mess deck. He was also told about a small door at the back of a pantry, which led from a store room. He gave instructions by radio, for two man teams to cover each entrance, whilst he and his assault partner went to the store room shown on the ships plan. He found the small door, which was bolted on his side. He slid the bolt back very carefully, and looked into the mess deck. He saw numerous men sitting on the floor, lit in the dim glow of a torch held by one of the pirates, and four men with AK47's standing, menacing the crew with their guns. McKay and his backup threw flash grenades into the room, turning their heads away as they exploded. This totally disorientated the pirates inside as well as their hostages. The two SBS men jumped into the room, which was now in total darkness, and others from the SBS team entered through main doors. All four pirates were shot. Two were killed and the other two were seriously wounded. The SBS men who had poured through the three other doors at the first explosion checked on the dead and wounded and then shouted "SBS. Stay where you are. Do not move." This reassured the crew and told them they had been rescued. McKay radioed his men still on the bridge and a short time later the lights came back on.

McKay addressed the crew, "I am Major McKay of the British SBS. We have accounted for most if not all of the pirates. Please stay where you are. I will leave some of my men here, and we will search the rest of the ship. I will tell you when you can go back to your normal duties." A systematic search of the ship then took place. One other Pirate was found hiding between containers on deck, and he surrendered without offering any resistance."

Major McKay radioed HMS Bulldog and reported the Santa Cruz secured, listing the dead and injured and asking for medical assistance for the wounded pirates. He requested that the ships Wildcat Helicopter be dispatched to detain the Dhow mother ship, and then learned that a small radar blip had been seen making off from the Dhow earlier at high speed towards the shore which was now only 25 miles away. The Merlin from HMS Bulldog hovered just above the aft deck of the Dhow with a powerful searchlight illuminating the bridge. As it hovered above the Dhow, a loud speaker voice demanded it heave too, or be blown out of the water. The Dhow stopped only after the helicopter had fired a burst across its bows from its rapid fire machine gun and threatened to fire a missile. Four SBS officers abseiled onto its deck, whilst the Wildcat helicopter hovered in a threating posture, and they quickly took command of the Dhow, securing its Captain and crew.

The Dhow was brought under the lee of the Santa Cruz, and awaited the arrival of HMS Bulldog. The prisoners were placed in the hold of the Dhow, under armed guard, and the ships Doctor and his medical team came aboard the Santa Cruz and started administering to the wounded. One of the wounded Somali Pirates died of his injuries.

McKay learned through an interpreter, that Mohammed Umbedi Hassan had escaped from the Dhow in his high speed skiff. The Wildcat Helicopter was dispatched to give chase, but was under instructions not to violate Somali Waters. They nearly caught him, the crew could see him through their high resolution infra red cameras. They saw the skiff run ashore, and a man in white robes jump out. They couldn't pursue any further as they had been instructed not to violate Somali sovereignty.

As dawn broke, the SBS on board found the open containers, and identified that both contained large consignments of arms and ammunition. It had been a very successful anti- piracy operation.

HMS Bulldog's radar operator contacted the bridge. " I have a ship coming up fast from the south. It is about an hour out. It is not HMS Yarmouth, that's closer and to the east." The Captain called Admiral Vincent to the bridge and gave him the news. Vincent said, "This might be trouble. It could be the Russians. Have the Wildcat have a look and let us know if it is and inform Yarmouth."

Chapter Twenty Seven

The Russian Frigate, Admiral Gordinski came at speed toward the stationary HMS Bulldog with the Dhow alongside. It hove to, two cables from Bulldog rocking wildly as its following wake hit the rear of the ship. Its guns swung and zeroed on the British ship.

The radio operator called the bridge and said, "The Russian's are hailing us Captain. They sound threatening."

Admiral Vincent said, "Don't react Captain, we won't show any aggression at the moment. Please get Major McKay to the bridge, he speaks Russian. Get the radio operator to patch the call through to the bridge, and warn Yarmouth to come closer."

James McKay rushed onto the bridge and Admiral Vincent said, "Ask them what they want. Politely of course." McKay spoke into the radio mike and listened for their reply.

He said, "They want to know what we are up to sir. They said they have been ordered to meet the Santa Cruz and escort it to Beira in Mozambique. It is carrying Russian cargo, which is essential to their government, and they want to know why we have stopped the ship on the high seas. They see this as an act of aggression, and their orders are clear. They are to defend the ship and its cargo, with force if necessary. They demand that we release the ship."

"Tell them we have just rescued the ship from pirates who wanted the cargo on board. We have now taken over the Dhow which they used as a mother ship, and have the pirates in custody."

"The Captain of the Russian ship says they are here now and will take over the ship. They threaten to blow us out of the water if we do not comply. Their orders come direct from their Minister of Defense."

Admiral Vincent said, "Tell them that if they escalate their threat, then we will have to retaliate in kind. Our mission was merely to stop the ship being pirated and prevent a shipment of arms falling into pirate hands. Tell them to back off or face the consequences, and warn them that we have reinforcements approaching."

The Admiral then said, "Captain, have our guns pointed at the Russians. Then tell them that we are in international waters, carrying out a policing action, because as far as we understand a consignment of arms was due for delivery to

Zimbabwe, which as he should know has a UN embargo on such cargoes."

The radar operator said, "Sir, the Yarmouth is making best speed towards us, it will be in visual range in fifteen minutes. The Russians must know this ship is our expected reinforcements."

Admiral Vincent thought for a minute and said, "Captain, report what is going on to the Ministry of Defense. Major McKay, suggest to the Captain of the Russian Frigate that we meet in my barge halfway between the ships. See if he agrees."

McKay said, "That has made them think. They have asked for time to consult their government."

"Agree to their request and we will await results."

The telephone rang in the Prime Minister's office. He listened to the call and said, "Get me the Russian President on the hot line." The two heads of government spoke at length and the Russian President agreed to have his ship cease aggressive action whilst they took action to resolve the situation amicably. The Prime Minister called a COBR meeting immediately, and on advice he again telephoned the Russian President and said, "The situation is clearer now. It appears that there are two loads of arms on the ship. One destined for Zimbabwe and another for your forces in Mozambique. We cannot allow the arms to go to Zimbabwe, there is a UN embargo. We could allow both loads to proceed to your forces in Mozambique, if you agree."

The Russian President said, "I agree, and will instruct my warship to escort the Santa Cruz to its destination. Perhaps, in a spirit of cooperation, one of your ships could also accompany the Santa Cruz and that way you can be sure that the arms go to our forces and not Zimbabwe. Is that not a solution to our problem."

"Mr President, "said the Prime Minister, "That I believe to be a good solution and I will issue the instruction. Please tell your Captain that Admiral Vincent, who is in charge of the British Forces, will speak to him and make the arrangements. I am grateful for your assistance."

On board HMS Bulldog, the radio operator said, "Admiral, I have instructions coming from our government. I will patch it through to the bridge."

The Prime Minister's voice came on. He said, "Admiral, I have spoken to the Russian's. They tell me that the arms are urgently wanted by their forces in Mozambique, where they are fighting Al Shabab terrorists. This is why they are taking the matter so seriously because the situation in that country is critical. They know about the two shipments, and we have agreed the one destined for Zimbabwe will now be diverted to their troops in Mozambique. They are happy they are getting a second consignment of arms for their forces, for free. They have agreed we can escort the Santa Cruz together with the Russian Frigate in convoy to Beira to ensure both loads go in the right direction. I have also issued a D notice to the press, so the story will not break until the matter is resolved. "

" I will talk to the Russian Frigate Captain sir, and make the arrangements. They should have had their orders by now."

Admiral Vincent said, "Hail the Russians again. McKay tell them what the PM has said, and arrange a meeting if they will go for it."

McKay relayed the Admiral's message and saw the Russian Frigate's guns move to midships, their normal resting position. Admiral Vincent reciprocated.

The Russian reply came, "Our President has ordered our cooperation and he thanks you for your timely action in dealing with the pirates. He has requested we escort the Santa Cruz to the port of Beira in company with you, so you can monitor the shipment being taken to our forces in Mozambique. None of the arms will be going to Zimbabwe. I would also, in the spirit of détente, like to invite you and some of your officers aboard my ship, in order to plan our mutual escort."

The Admiral's barge was manned and the Admiral, with Major McKay and Mozart went to the Russian ship, where they were received with all naval courtesy, and taken to the wardroom. Greetings became profuse and vodka was produced. Toasts were made to the two countries. Captain Valerie Andreyev became the amiable host. He introduced a Major from the Russian Spetsnaz and during the conversations it became apparent that the Russians were on a similar mission.

HMS Yarmouth steamed up. Admiral Vincent asked the Russian Captain if he would contact the British ship, and he would speak to the Captain.

"Captain Henderson, " said the Admiral, "The situation is now under control, we have orders from the PM agreed by the Russian President that we will jointly escort the Santa Cruz to Beria in Mozambique. Please come aboard the Russian ship and join us."

A short time later Captain Miles Henderson boarded, and was introduced to the Russians, Mozart and Major McKay. A glass of vodka was put in his hand and toasts were given to the new détente.

Admiral Vincent said to Henderson, "Miles, I will be shifting my flag to your ship, we are ordered to escort the Santa Cruz together with the Russians' to Beira and see that the two consignments of arms on board are dispatched to north Mozambique. He then turned to the Russian Captain, raised his glass and said, "Gentlemen, here's to the success of our mission. Nostrovia!"

They all raised their glasses and downed the contents in one, in the Russian fashion.

McKay said in Russian, "Our Admiral means Na Zdorovie."

The Russian Captain replied, "You understand our language very well Major, but Nostrovia will do."

McKay in his turn had a very interesting conversation with his Spetsnaz opposite number. He introduced Mozart as an ex-SBS Captain now a British Policeman and they, as soldiers do, found common ground and cemented a professional relationship, each recognizing the courage and expertise of the other. They discussed the operational details of how the SBS had reclaimed the Santa Cruz from the pirates, and the tactics used. They found mutual ground, in that the Spetsnaz training included such operations, where tactics were similar. A professional respect grew out of this discussion.

Admiral Vincent returned to HMS Bulldog with Major McKay and Mozart. He called for the Captain and in the wardroom laid out his plans. HMS Bulldog, with Mozart on board would take the Somali prisoners to Mogadishu and hand them over to the authorities there. The Captain of Bulldog would contact the British Embassy there to make the arrangements with their government. Mozart told the Admiral that Detective Sergeant Stevens was on his way to Mogadishu following the Armstrong's, who were expecting to meet Hassan to receive final payment for the arms shipment and he needed to be there if possible." " Well you are going with Bulldog so you can join up with him. I will have our embassy in Mogadishu make all the arrangements.

George and John Amstrong flew in their private jet via Cyprus to Mogadishu. They were to attend a meeting with Hassan, to get the final payment for the shipment of arms.

Detective Sergeant Steven preceded the Armstrong's by catching a direct flight to Mogadishu, where he was met again by Major Jonathan Barwood, the Military Attache to the British Embassy.

Barwood said, "I have booked you into the Palm Beerta Palace Hotel again. You must be careful this time because you have stayed in the same hotel in Harare as the Armstrong's and we don't want them recognizing you. I have booked a room adjacent to them and you are on the floor above. I propose we bug the room again so we know what's going on. We know that Hassan got away from the hijack scene because one of our helicopters chased him ashore and couldn't stop him. If the Armstrong's intend meeting Hassan to get the final payment for the arms I expect it will be at Abdirahim Halimo Mohammed's office in the Jaziira Road. They will have a nasty shock coming to them, because I anticipate that Hassan will want his deposit back, and if he doesn't get it there could be trouble. Our Ambassador has contacted the Somali Government at a high level, and told them of the incident at sea. They are very keen to get their hands on Hassan, because if he had collected the arms there is no doubt he would have used them to further his political ambitions. That might have turned the country into a terrorists haven, and who knows what problems would ensue if that were to take place. As a result we may need backup and we have been offered the assistance of government forces. You and I have an appointment this afternoon with Colonel Milton Ndege of the Presidential Guard. We can have lunch and then go see him."

Stevens and Barwood walked into the offices of Colonel Ndege at the main barracks on the outskirts of Mogadishu. They were expected and taken to the Colonels' office.

Barwood introduced themselves said, "Colonel, Mr Stevens is a British Police Officer and he has been investigating a family called Armstrong in the UK, who are into drug supply and have now made an attempt to get into arms dealing. They purchased a container load of arms and ammunition from dealers in Russia, having it loaded onto a ship, the Santa Cruz, in the port of Odessa. They intended the load for Zimbabwe, which as you know has UN sanctions imposed on it, but they did a side deal with Mohammed Umbedi Hassan to pirate the consignment at sea. What they didn't know was the Russians from whom they bought the arms, put another container on the same ship intended for their forces in Mozambique, so the pirates might have got access to two container loads of arms, which we couldn't allow. The Armstrong's are crooks in the UK, and intended to rip off the Zimbabweans' having taken a substantial deposit from them, by giving Hassan all the information he wanted about the load and the ship's schedule. They arranged for Hassan and his pirates' to board the vessel at sea. but our forces were waiting for them. Our special forces assaulted the ship after they had taken it over and we have detained most and killed some of the pirates at sea. Our HMS Bulldog is on its way as we speak to bring the pirates here to Mogadishu, although some are in body bags. It is due to dock probably tomorrow or at the latest the day after, and we would like to hand those we have arrested over to you to deal with under Somali law as they are citizens of your country. I believe that this course of action has the approval of your government."

Colonel Ndege said, "Yes, our Minister of Defense has phoned me earlier and briefed me. Of course we would be delighted to take them off your hands, and we would be delighted to let HMS Bulldog dock here for that purpose."

Barwood continued, "Unfortunately Hassan got away from us after the hijack and made it back to shore. It is suspected that he is coming here, probably the day after tomorrow to meet the Armstrong's because he paid them a substantial deposit for the supply of the arms which are now in our hands. His mission failed and he will want his money back. Things could get nasty. We believe he will turn up here in Mogadishu, probably to Abdirahim Halimo Mohammed's office and compound in the Jaziira Road. Halimo is a business contact of the Armstrong's and the person who set up the meeting to discuss arms supplies between the Armstrong's and Hassan, so he is part of the conspiracy. The meeting, if it takes place, and hopefully we will know by tomorrow, could provide us with an opportunity to arrest Hassan and some more of his followers. I suspect however, he will come armed and there might be shooting. Of course Somalia is your country, we have no jurisdiction here, so we cannot take any action to arrest or detain anyone here, but we are more than willing to assist you and your forces."

Colonel Ndege said, " That's no problem. We have been wanting to get our hands on Hassan. He has become a growing problem for our country. I can have a platoon of Paratroops deployed nearby, ready and waiting. I will take a look at the premises, and develop a plan."

Barwood said, "We will know more by tomorrow once the Armstrong's arrive. Perhaps we could come to see you again and finalize a plan." "Good idea "said the Colonel, "See you tomorrow."

Stevens and Barwood returned to the hotel for a nightcap. Barwood discovered that the room next door was unoccupied for that night. They both went up to his room, and Barwood managed to jump to the adjoining balcony, get through the patio doors and plant a bug in the room.

He returned and said, “I have a recording device and we can hear what is being said in their room through these earpieces.” He then produced a small box, and from it took the recorder, plugging in to a socket. The same box contained two ear pieces. Steven’s said, “They are coming via Cyprus, and should arrive tomorrow. I suspect that they will have a meeting arranged for the day after. My boss DCI Mozart is on HMS Bulldog bringing the Somali Pirate prisoners here. He will want to be in on this. They started out from the Arabian Sea two days ago. It’s about 1400 miles, at say an average of 20 knots. They should arrive some time tomorrow. If they are delayed perhaps the day after. I will phone my boss and update him.”

Chapter Twenty Eight

The following day Detective Sergeant Steven's phone rang. "Win," said a familiar voice. Thanks for your call. We have been delayed because we have a Dhow with us. It's slowed us down, so much so, that we are now towing it. They were using it as a Mother ship. We probably won't dock until tomorrow now. However the Captain has said he can get me there by helicopter, so I can be there tomorrow afternoon."

Stevens said, "Mr Barwood from the embassy and I are seeing Colonel Ndege again tomorrow at his barracks near the Mogadishu sports stadium. I'll ask him if you can land there. I will book a room for you for tomorrow night at my hotel. I'll ring you after I have spoken to the Colonel."

At lunchtime the following day the George and John Armstrong arrived at the hotel. They were shown to their suite next to Barwood's room. Just after their arrival Barwood knocked on Steven's bedroom door to find him with his earpiece in listening to the conversation from the floor below.

"They have said already they are going to see Halimo. They are having dinner with him here in the hotel tonight. They are talking about going down to lunch soon. It doesn't look likely they know anything about how the hijack went, but they are expecting to get paid," said Stevens.

Barwood said, "I will cover the restaurant, perhaps you can do room service."

Barwood got to the hotel restaurant ahead of the Armstrong's and saw them enter. They sat at the table they had used on their previous visit. Obviously creatures of habit. After lunch they returned to their room, and Barwood switched the recorder on. Stevens and Barwood then left for the army barracks.

Colonel Ndege readily agreed that Mozart could land in the barracks, and he said, "I have arranged for a platoon of Para's to be available tomorrow. We will deploy with our light amoured vehicles fitted with machine guns. There will be six vehicles, with three soldiers in each. I will be in my car. We need a forward spotter to give us the go."

"We can do that Colonel," said Barwood. "We can plot up ahead of the meeting and watch them arrive, and give you the go, when we think the timing is right. Knowing Hassan he will fight. He's slippery, he managed to escape our forces in the Arabian Sea, so we have to be prepared." They then discussed communications, exchanged mobile phone numbers, and a plan was conceived.

Barwood and Stevens drove to the Jaziira Road to view the premises of the Halimo Road Plant (HRP) offices and compound. They found a spot just off an adjacent road on higher ground with a good view of the compound which was about 100 metres away. The trees around the view point gave good cover, but with the aid of a pair of good binoculars they could see the whole front of the building. The compound was fenced with chain link fencing and had gates of similar material. There were workshops, and barn like structures inside the compound and a number of staff moving around, most in overalls. It was an ideal forward observation point. They telephoned Colonel Ndege and briefed him. Stevens and Barwood then returned to the hotel. They listened to the recordings from Steven's room and discovered that the Armstrong's had talked to Halimo on the telephone and they were meeting at 8pm that evening for dinner in the hotel. Barwood went to the restaurant to book a table. He saw the Head Waiter and pointed to the table the Armstrong's had used earlier. Can I book that table for this evening."

The Head Waiter said, "I'm sorry sir, that table is booked by Mr Armstrong."

"Okay," said Barwood, "How about that one, "pointing to a similar table on the other side of the room."

The Head Waiter said, "That would be fine." Barwood gave the man a generous tip, and the Waiter went into the kitchen. This gave Barwood enough time to slip a recording device beneath the Armstrong table.

That evening Barwood was in the restaurant at 7.30pm and had started his meal, when George Armstrong, his son John and Halimo walked into the restaurant and sat at their usual table. He had left Stevens to use room service again. Barwood put his earpiece in and listened to the conversation. Amongst the business talk he heard that

Hassan was due to arrive at Halimo's compound at 4pm the next day, and assumed the purpose of the meeting was for Hassan to pay the agreed balance for the arms consignment. They obviously did not know of the failed hijack yet. There was some discussion that Hassan might not pay up, but Halimo assured them that Hassan wanted further shipments, so he would keep his end of the bargain to ensure future business. They did not seem concerned. This was all good news to Barwood, who finished his meal. Upon returning to Stevens' room he briefed him and they passed this information on to Colonel Ndege. Stevens then updated Mozart by phone.

"I will arrive at the barracks by helicopter at 10am," said Mozart. "Bulldog will probably not dock until mid evening." "We will arrange everything, and meet you at the barracks," said Stevens.

At 9am the following day, Barwood and Stevens were again at the barracks, with Colonel Ndege. They briefed him on what they had learned from their intercepts.

Colonel Ndege raised his eyebrows and said, "I will not embarrass you by asking how you know all this, but well done. It makes life much easier."

They then discussed the refinements of their plan, and just before 10am heard the sound of rotors, as the Bulldog's Merlin Helicopter made its final approach and landed within the barracks. Mozart got out and the helicopter took off again to return to its ship. He shook hands with Barwood, and Stevens and was introduced to Colonel Ndege, shaking his hand as the introduction was made. They returned to the Colonel's office where Mozart was briefed. He could see no flaws in the plan. They agreed that they would be in their allotted positions at 2p.m. Colonel Ndege invited them all to the officer's mess for brunch, where they continued their discussion and at 1p.m. they left to take up their observation position overlooking the Halimo Road Plant (HRP) compound. They were in direct radio contact with Colonel Ndege and his forces.

At 3.30pm. the Armstrong's arrived at the compound by taxi and were seen to enter Halimo's office. They waited impatiently, as 4p.m. came and went. Halimo came out looked around just after four, and then went back inside. He was obviously anxious. At 4.30pm a convoy of four trucks, each fitted with RPG machine guns on top of the cab, drove at speed into the compound and stopped with a screech of brakes and a cloud of dust. They formed an arc in front of the office building. Men got out, each holding an AK47, and one climbed onto the back of each truck to man the machine gun, which was pointed at the offices. Once his guard had deployed, a white robed Hassan got out of the lead truck and walked purposely towards the offices, disappearing inside with a swirl of his flowing robes. Barwood reported events to Colonel Ndege by radio. His troops were deployed nearby only a short drive away.

Hassan entered the offices. He saw Halimo, George and John Armstrong. He was in a rage. His eyes bulged, his mouth set in a snarl.

He pointed at Halimo and without preamble shouted, "You, you cost me money. You cost me men. You betrayed me."

He then produced a machete from within his robes and in one swipe, cut into Halimo's neck almost severing his head from his body. Blood spurted over his robes. George Armstrong stood transfixed, in total shock, frozen in horror. Even in his own cruel criminal world this was the most savage of acts.

Hassan turned on George Armstrong, "You betrayed me. A British Warship was waiting for us. They kill my men." He waved the now bloody machete at George. "I want my money back. You traitor, you try to sell me to the British. I kill you!"

He then swiped at George with his machete, George put up his hand to defend himself and the machete severed his right wrist. More blood spurted over Hassan's now crimson stained robe. John Armstrong backed off. He drew a pistol from under his coat, and shot Hassan twice in the chest. The bullets knocked Hassan backwards, but adrenalin was coursing through his frame, and he lunged at John seemingly unaffected by the impact of the bullets. John backed away further and shot twice more. One of the bullets hit Hassan in the right shoulder and he dropped the machete. He turned and ran outside, shouting to his men "Shoot them. Kill them all. They are traitors".

At the first sound of shots, Barwood shouted into his radio to Colonel Ndege, **"Strike, Strike, Strike!** There's a shootout going on."

Hassan's gunmen, outside the offices, started to run towards the offices, and the RPG's on each of the trucks swung towards the building. The blood spattered Hassan ran towards his men holding his bloody shoulder, and raging at his men to open fire. They sprayed the front of the offices with bullets, smashing windows, taking chunks out of the façade, splintering wood. John Armstrong hit the floor. His father was prone on the floor, writhing in pain and bleeding from his severed wrist. John pulled his fathers' belt off and made a tourniquet which stopped most of the heavy bleeding as bullets smashed into walls and furniture over his head filling the room with chunks of masonry, shards of glass and splinters of wood.

A convoy of army vehicles roared into the compound, with machine guns blazing. The first swathe of bullets knocked over half the pirate force. The second swathe eliminated the threat from the truck mounted RPG's. Hassan ran to the lead truck, and the government troops concentrated their fire on the cab of this truck, which accelerated away.

The driver slumped over the wheel as the windscreen shattered and bullets hit him in the head and chest. The truck swerved out of control and crashed into the front of the office building. Hassan climbed out with an AK47 in his hands which he leveled and started to fire, his teeth bared in a rictus of determination and pain. His bullets bounced off the armoured car in front of him. The heavy machine gun mounted on the turret returned fire and sprayed a long burst of fire which lifted Hassan off his feet. His robes were now a mass of red, and it pooled around him as he lay inert on the ground. The Government troops jumped from their vehicles, more shots were fired and out of the pirate force just five survived, three of whom were seriously wounded. The troop leader, with another soldier at his shoulder ran into the building. It was a scene of carnage. Halimo's body laid in a vast pool of blood, his head at a grotesque angle. George Armstrong was on the floor, covered in his own blood and holding his right arm where his hand used to be with the belt tourniquet wrapped around it. John Armstrong was unwounded but thoroughly cowed. As soon as he saw the soldiers with guns he threw his pistol to the ground and surrendered.

Colonel Ndege walked into the compound in his pristine uniform carrying his swagger stick. He looked immaculate, presenting an unperturbed and calm detachment. A commander in absolute control. He walked over to Hassan's body and turned it over disdainfully with his foot. He was dead. He had been hit in the head, and body, but it was the head shot which killed him. When his troops searched the body they found that Hassan was wearing body armour. So much for the divine, the supposed supernatural powers of the deliverer, the man who was supposed to be impervious to bullets. The Djinn's had deserted him. The so called reincarnation of the Mad Mullah was dead and his cause would die with him.

Barwood, Stevens and Mozart drove into the compound to be greeted by a smiling Colonel Ndege. He congratulated them on the turn of events. They had helped eliminate the current greatest threat to his country, and a lot of his followers were either captured or dead. It was, from his point of view a very successful operation, and would lead to a mop up operation in the northern districts of the country. The Colonel arranged for an army medic to attend the compound and he administered to George Armstrong's wound. Armstrong was then taken under escort to Mogadishu City Hospital in the Bandir district, where the doctors dealt with his amputated limb. Mozart contacted Admiral Vincent on board HMS Yarmouth and updated him with the news. Vincent passed the message on to the Ministry of Defense in London.

Colonel Ndege took Mozart, Barwood and Stevens to the officers' mess in his barracks. They toasted a very successful operation. The Colonel insisted on hosting them to dinner that evening. He turned out to be a very generous host. His kudos with his own government had risen substantially, and he had been told that his President was very happy at the outcome. A substantial threat to his government had been removed. Later that evening Mozart and Stevens were taken by Army Staff Car to their hotel. Barwood went home.

The following morning Barwood returned. He took the other two to breakfast after first recovering his bugging devices. Their flight did not leave until the following day, so he took them sight seeing. When they returned to the hotel there was a message for Mozart to contact the

Colonel once more. Again the Colonel was profuse in his praise of the officers and their part in the successful elimination of the pirate threat. The Colonel told them he had much to tell them, so Mozart said, "Would you care to join us for dinner at the hotel, we can discuss matters there." The Colonel said, "I would be delighted." Mozart telephoned Barwood and invited him, and at 8pm that evening they shared a very convivial supper. The Colonel told them that HMS Bulldog had docked and the prisoners had been handed over and were now in prison awaiting trial. George Armstrong would be released from hospital in a few days, and when released he would join his son in custody in Mogadishu's infamous prison. His clothing would be taken from him and he would be issued with standard prison uniform. A tee shirt, baggy linen trousers and flip flops. He would be sharing a cell with ten or more other prisoners.

Mozart briefed the Colonel on how the inquiry had started and how it had progressed, making the Colonel understand the Armstrong's were major criminals in the UK, and feared by many in the criminal fraternity. They used violence and intimidation to achieve their aims, and it had made them very rich in the process. However, he assured the Colonel his team were working on tracing all their assets, which had been gained through crime, to bring evidence before a court hearing where they hoped the courts would issue a confiscation order. The Colonel told them that the Armstrong's would stand trial in Mogadishu, but would be held in prison until then. Once sentenced, and Colonel Ndege expected the Armstrong's to serve at least ten years without parole, they would then be deported to the UK where they would then be again subject to British Law.

The following morning Mozart and Stevens were at the reception desk and about to leave the hotel, expecting Barwood to drive them to the airport, when a cavalcade of official looking vehicles pulled up at the main entrance. Two men jumped out of the lead vehicle and opened the rear door. Out stepped the Somali Minister of Defense, Aabid Mahbeer Mohammed, behind him was Colonel Ndege. Colonel Ndege introduced the Minister to Mozart and Stevens, who shook their hands profusely.

The Minister said, "Please wait a minute gentlemen." He went to the reception desk and said, "Please send the bill for these gentlemen to me. Our government will pay." He then turned to Mozart and Stevens and said, "Gentlemen. Brigadier Ndege has briefed me on what took place yesterday, and what you have done for our country. We will be eternally grateful to you, and I intend to let your Government know what you have done for Somalia and the relations between our two countries. You will be welcome here at any time. Now I understand that you have a plane to catch. Please join me in my car and I will give you a lift to the airport. The Brigadier will join us." The two British Officers smiled at Brigadier Ndege offering their congratulations on his overnight promotion.

Barwood appeared in the doorway, stood to one side smiling, and as they passed him he shook their hands and said, "I can't compete with your VIP treatment Gentlemen. Enjoy and Bon Voyage."

The cavalcade swept imperiously into the VIP area of the airport, and they were taken to the first class lounge by the Minister himself.

The Minister said, "Excuse me a minute." He returned a short time later with an airline executive in tow, and said, "This Gentleman will look after you. Once again, my

Government thanks you, and I will let your Government know what great assistance you have been to us. Have a good flight." He then left.

Brigadier Ndege shook their hands and simply said, "Well done and thank you gentlemen." And he walked out in the Ministers wake.

Left alone in the first class lounge, looking mystified, Mozart and Stevens were waited on by the First Class Lounge staff. A short time later they were called to board their flight to London, and were escorted on board by the Lounge Manager. They were shown to the front of the aircraft into first class where they discovered they had silver service meals to look forward to, comfortable seating and a real bed. This would be the trip of a lifetime. Once settled in, Mozart rang Peter Simpson and briefed him on all the occurrences in Somalia, and Simpson said they would have a debrief in full, with all members of the team, once they returned to the UK.

Chapter Twenty Nine

HMS Yarmouth docked at the port of Beira in Mozambique, in company with the MV Santa Cruz, and the Russian Frigate the Admiral Gordinski. The dock authorities had been notified in advance of their arrival and had cleared a berth for the ships. Admiral Vincent went aboard the Russian ship and he and its Captain agreed they would remain in port until the Santa Cruz was offloaded. They also agreed that Captain Miles Henderson of the Yarmouth and Captain Valerie Andreyev of the Admiral Gordinski, and some of their staff would oversee the discharge of the arms containers, and see them safely on their way to the Russian forces in the north of the country. Admiral Vincent arranged with the port authorities that should any Zimbabweans turn up to claim one of the containers, they were to be handed on to the Mozambique authorities for questioning. In the event no Zimbabweans turned up and the containers were placed on a flat railway cart which headed north. Its destination Nampula, where the Russian Forces awaited its arrival.

Admiral Vincent received a telephone call from Mozart, made whilst he was sitting on his plane awaiting takeoff. Mozart updated the Admiral on events in Mogadishu, explaining how the Armstrong's and Hassan had been dealt with. The Admiral was satisfied with the outcome. He also told the Admiral HMS Bulldog had delivered the pirate prisoners to the Somali authorities, and had now sailed for Bahrain.

Admiral Vincent invited the Captain and his officers, including the officers of the Spetznaz, from the Admiral Gordinski, to a reception in the wardroom of HMS Yarmouth. The gathering was convivial, and they toasted a successful mission, and the détente established between the two countries.

The Russian's thanked the Admiral for dealing with the pirates, and Admiral Vincent was able to update the

Russian's on what had occurred in Mogadishu. This news caused general delight and led to more toasting. Although the Russian political masters, once they learned of the outcome, may not have proved to be quite so happy, as the outcome might thwart their long term ambitions for Somalia. However the Russians' personnel on the ship, being non political, left HMS Yarmouth happy at the outcome of what had turned into a successful joint mission, and as HMS Yarmouth left port they saw the Russians had dressed their ship, with all the crew standing to attention around the deck. The British reciprocated, and the Admiral saluted, the crew of Yarmouth lining the deck cheering, and the White Ensign dipped as they passed the Russian ship, with sirens blaring in farewell.

Mozart and Stevens landed at Heathrow after an overnight flight direct from Mogadishu. They had been treated royally on their flight and felt refreshed. They went straight to their office in the City of London. On his arrival Mozart was told that a conference for all parties involved in the inquiry had been arranged for that afternoon, where updates would be given by everyone involved.

That afternoon Annie Forbes came into Mozart's office. She smiled causing Mozart's heart to a leap. He sprang to his feet and disregarding any protocol, instinctively threw his arms around her and greeted her with a long and lingering kiss. He blushed with embarrassment when he looked up, most of the office staff were staring at the couple and laughing, some even applauded. Their secret, if it was a secret at all, was out. All Mozart could do was to grin a sickly grin in response, managing to look totally embarrassed in the realization of what he had just done. Knowing policemen being policemen, it would come back at him some time. Annie did not look at all perturbed, she giggled but was delighted and showed it.

Shortly after the room began to fill with people from HM Customs, the National Crime Agency and MI5 and 6. Forensic officers and DI Harley limped in, his breathing shallow and laboured, obviously protecting his very bruised and black and blue chest. Coffee was served and they all moved into the conference room.

Peter Simpson opened the meeting and called for DI Harley to give an update on the joint Police/Customs operation at the nursery in Cambridgeshire. Harley stood, in obvious discomfort, detailing the incident which resulted in the arrest of a wounded Graham Armstrong. The arrest of the Leonard's, senior and junior, and his wife, plus the driver of the lorry. The Leonards' remained in custody, as did Graham Armstrong who was recovering from his wounds. Forensic examination of the nursery and personal accounts were taking place to trace assets and to see if there was an unexplained income from drug distribution. It was expected there would be a financial link to the Armstrong's and their organization.

"Mr Mozart" said Simpson, "Tell us about the Nolan's, and how the inquiry first started."

Mozart then repeated the story of how the Nolan's had kidnapped and beaten Ross-Harding, which had started a chain of events leading to the uncovering of a connection to the Armstrong's crime family, then to shootings, drug importations, money laundering and finally arms dealing and pirating.

Mr Simpson then called upon Richard Woodgate to give an account of the Customs drug find at Felixstowe Docks. He told the meeting the find had led to the arrest of the lorry driver and to a raid on the Purfleet Transport

Company (PTC) based in Grays, Essex. where the owners, the brothers Trevor and Michael Burns, together with the lorry driver had been arrested for conspiracy to import class A drugs. The company was being investigated for a link to the Armstrong's who were believed to be behind financing the company and setting the brother's up in business. Company finances were being scrutinized by HM Customs and Nick Braithwaite and his team from the National Crime Agency.

Peter Simpson called on DI Harley again to update the meeting on the attempt on Ross-Harding's life in Northampton. Harley told the meeting that a four man hit team had travelled on the orders of the Armstrong's to Northampton, where they had attempted to silence Ross-Harding. The SO11 team had followed the hit team from the Armstrong's farm to a hotel near Ross-Hardings' safe house, and from there to the clinic, where a Northamptonshire Police Firearms team was waiting. One man was shot and killed, another wounded and two others arrested. They were all employees of the Armstrong's. Those who survived were being dealt with by the Northamptonshire Police for conspiracy to murder.

They were found in possession of Scorpion Machine guns, similar to one recovered from Graham Armstrong in Cambridgeshire, and obviously from the same batch. Detective Chief Inspector Mozart was liaising with the Northampton Police in relation to this incident.

Mozart was then called to give details of, Operation Forsyth, the proposed arms deal in Russia to supply arms to Zimbabwe, and of the Armstrong's rip off attempt to have the arms hijacked in the Arabian Sea by the pirate leader Mohammed Umbedi Hassan. He told of how the arms had been shipped from Russia via the port of Odessa in the Ukraine, where they were taken aboard a The MV Santa Cruz bound for the port of Beira in Mozambique. He explained how the Special Boat Service and the Royal Navy had been used to intercept the pirates, shooting some and arresting others. He told how the Russian Navy had forced a confrontation at sea believing that the British Forces had intercepted a load of Russian arms heading for their forces in Mozambique. He described the final meeting in Mogadishu where Hassan was killed by Somali Troops in a planned operation, and how George Armstrong was injured and both he and his son John arrested by the

Somali authorities. The Armstrong's were being held in Somalia and would face trial there, and were expect to serve at least 10 years imprisonment, after which they would be deported to face British justice.

Detective Inspector Steve Easterbrook of the City of London Fraud office gave a report of his progress in tracing the world wide assets of the Armstrongs' together with colleagues from the National Crime Agency. He was still working on tracking assets in Mexico, Panama and the Cayman Islands.

Simpson concluded the whole operation had been a triumph of cooperation between government departments, HM Forces, and forces of law and order both in the UK and overseas. He congratulated all the various agencies present, and picked out Mozart and Stevens for special praise for rising to the challenge of coordinating and driving the whole inquiry. However, he pointed out there was still much work to do and he requested that the Police Forensic Teams subject the Armstrong's farm and land to intensive forensic scrutiny. Mozart said he would arrange for a warrant to be obtained for a large team of scientists including IT experts to visit the farm with a

Police Search Team, and carry out an intensive forensic search.

Peter Simpson asked for any questions. None came, all were amazed at the complexity of the case, and how it was drawing to a conclusion. What was very apparent was that a major crime family had been brought to justice, together with a large number of their associates. They had been put out of business, and should further inquiries prove successful more charges would be laid in the future. A very satisfactory result. He then invited Mozart to say a few words in conclusion.

Mozart then said, "We still have much work to do in tying up all the loose ends. We have much paperwork to do, and a lot of forensic work has to be carried out before we can call it a day, so I suggest we get on with it . We have a number of prisoners to process and take before a court, but I don't think we will be seeing George and John Armstrong for a number of years, so in their case we have time on our side, but the pressure is now on to deal with the others in custody. We will probably recommend to the Director of Public Prosecutions that we bring all the various cases together, to be heard in one big trial in

London. In that way the enormity of the case will be brought out and how the threads intertwine will become very apparent"

Mozart took Annie Forbes into his office to make personal arrangements with her, when Commander John Russell walked in on them.

"Mr Mozart" he said, "You and DS Stevens are to report to the Commissioners' office at 2p.m. this afternoon. Don't be late." Mozart looked at Annie Forbes and shrugged his shoulders, "Can we meet later?" She said, "I will wait for you at your flat. Don't be late," she quipped with a smile.

Mozart and Stevens walked into New Scotland Yard at 1.45p.m, and were shown to the Commissioner's suite. They waited in the outer office and at 2p.m. Commander Russell walked out, and said, "You can go in now."

They marched in and stood stiffly in front of the Commissioners' desk. He looked up and said, "Sit down gentlemen. Well you've had quite a time lately. You have both impressed me with the way you have handled what turned out to be a very complex inquiry. Mr Stevens. You await the results of your inspector's exam. I can tell you now that you have passed. Congratulations. With immediate effect you will be promoted to Detective Inspector, working under Commander Russell in SO15 – Counter Terrorist Command.

Mr Mozart, you and Detective Inspector Stevens have brought great credit to the force. You will remain posted to SO15 under Commander Russell and I will recommend you for a Command Course once you have put this case to bed. Well done both of you."

Mozart and Stevens walked out of the Commissioner's office, with a lot lighter step than when they entered.

Once they were in the outer office Mozart said, " Congratulations Winston, your promotion is well deserved and I am glad that we will be working together at SO15 once we have put this case to bed. You have worked hard over these last few months and have been great to work with. Well done," and he shook Steven's hand warmly. " Now go home and tell your wife the good news. I'll see you in the morning."

Mozart went home, and just as he was letting himself in through the front door his mobile phone rang. It was Peter Simpson.

"Congratulations to you and Mr Stevens. "

Mozart said, "How did you know sir." Simpson said, "It's on a need to know basis," and he chuckled. "However" he continued, that's not the end of it. Tomorrow afternoon, you, Mr Stevens and the rest of the team are invited to meet the Prime Minister at 5p.m. at number 10 for cocktails and canapes. He wants you to brief him on all that has happened in Somalia and Mozambique, and with the Russians. He thinks you have done our international relationships the world of good and he is anxious to get the inside story. He is also secretly chuffed that by your actions the Russian influence they expected to further in Somalia has suffered a serious setback. He is arranging a major press conference and wants all the details. This will look very good for his re-election prospects so he is well pleased. I will see you there. Don't be late."

Mozart entered his flat pulling off his jacket as he did so. His senses were hit as he walked into his living room with the most delicious smell of cooking. Out from the kitchen came the love of his life, looking radiant. Annie placed a glass of red wine into his hand and gave him a lingering kiss of welcome. He responded in kind, and his tensions evaporated under her attention. They looked deep into each other's eyes with complete fulfillment. He sighed with pleasure at the feel of her lips and her body against his.

She pushed him away, "Down tiger," she said, "I've slaved over a hot stove to feed you. I expect you to do justice to my cooking."

He meekly followed her to the table and sat. She then brought in a steaming dish, which she placed in the middle of the table. "This is my version of aromatic goat. It is made of vegetables, with aromatic spices, and has dates and apricots in it, as well of course slow cooked goat. It has been cooking now for hours. I thought as you had been in Africa, that goat would be appropriate although it took me ages to find the meat. It's very hard to find. There is rice as well. You had better be hungry. I'm famished. Now light the candle and eat."

They lingered over the most delicious meal. She was a fantastic cook, and Mozart realized how hungry he had been. They talked and sipped their wine, and reveled in each other's company, losing themselves in each other again, ignorant of time. He showered, and she joined him. They explored each other all over again, and renewed their deepening relationship. It was natural and nature took over. They held each other, nuzzled and brushed their lips, then they were lost in their want and need for each other. Tensions disappeared. Perfection was sought and found. They then slept a peaceful and untroubled gentle slumber, wound in each other's arms.

Detective Inspector Harley of SO11 was a seconded Essex Officer, whose period of secondment was to end in two months time. He took a telephone call from the Head of CID for Essex.

"Mr. Harley," he said, "You have an appointment to see the Chief Constable at 10am in the morning at Police Headquarters."

Harley wondered what the Chief wanted. He went home concerned.

The following morning at 10am he was admitted to the presence of the Chief Constable, the head of CID was sitting next to the Chief. He walked stiffly to the Chief's desk and stood, taking shallow breaths and grimacing in discomfort.

The Chief saw his obvious discomfort, took pity on him and said, "Please sit.". Now I want you to tell us what you have been up to lately in regard to the Armstrong case. I have heard that the case started off as a drug case, and went to gun running in Africa. Tell me all about it."

DI Harley then spent the next hour briefing his Chief and his head of CID on details of the case.

At the end, the Chief said, " Congratulations, you have represented our force extremely well. I hear that even the PM was involved."

"Yes," said Harley, "He was called upon to speak to the Russians to prevent an armed confrontation between our Navy and theirs in the Arabian Sea. It took a diplomatic two step to take the tension out of the situation. The PM is holding a press conference later and the story should then hit the headlines."

The Chief then said, “Well, now we need to talk about your future. I understand that your secondment is due to expire in two months time. Do you want to extend that.”

Harley said, “Well I have enjoyed the work.”

The Chief said, “Well I had intended to have you back here, but if you really wanted to stay with SO11?”

Harley said, “I am happy to go where you think I’m needed sir.”

“Very diplomatic and the right answer” said the Chief looking at his head of CID and smiling a knowledgeable smile, “Because I was thinking of having you back here and promoting you.”

Harley looked at the two behind the desk as they burst out laughing, self satisfied at their tease. They became serious again and the Chief said, “ We have a problem and you have been selected to sort it out. We are recalling you early. I have squared it with SO11. You will take over as Detective Chief Inspector, commanding the CID at Colchester starting next Monday. Congratulations”.

They stood and both senior officers shook Harley’s hand. The head of CID said, “I know you have an appointment at the PM's office this afternoon, but walk with me to my office, I want to brief you on your new appointment."

Harley said to the Chief, "Thank you sir. I am sure my wife will be delighted to have me home again." He then walked with the head of CID to his office on the 4th floor of the headquarters building. Once inside his office, he called in his deputy head of CID and they sat down to brief Harley on his new appointment.

" Between these four walls I want to tell you, your new appointment will be no sinecure. We have trouble at Colchester CID at the moment, and you are being sent there to sort matters out. The incumbent DCI is on retirement leave. This leaves the CID being run by two Detective Inspectors. One of the Inspector's is a drunk and has no control over the staff at all, and the other is very disappointing as his attitude is all wrong. He has turned into a ruthless social climber who appears only interested in self aggrandizement. His dictatorial, self serving and oppressive attitude has caused a real morale problem with the staff. You are going there to sort this out. It will not be easy, as you will find out, but we expect you to sort things out and very quickly. The staff are totally demoralized and we want you to fix it, and quickly. If you want to get rid of people to achieve this end, you will find us very supportive. We must have a good working unit and at the moment that isn't the case. The rest is down to you. Do you think you can do it."

Harley said, "I know the two men involved and I have heard about the problem there. The staff are very unhappy and the unit is in chaos so I understand. The two DI's are like chalk and cheese. It's the dictatorial one who is the main problem, he has an attitude problem, and is totally ruthless, confrontational and critical. Even before I get there, from what I hear, I feel he is the one whose megalomania is ruining the department and will have to go. However, I will go there with an open mind, assess the situation and then get rid of him. Where you would put him, I don't know. If he gets pushed out he could become even worse. The other one would also have to go if he can't give up the drink. He might be worth saving. We will see."

The two men said, "Good luck. Keep us in the loop." "I will sir, " said Harley, and left the office half glad and half concerned about his future. He shrugged his shoulders, determination etched on his face and he strode carefully, but purposefully from the building into his new life.

Mozart, Stevens and the rest of the team, with a full team of Police searchers, and Forensic scientists descended on the Armstrong farm. They carried out a thorough search of the house and outbuildings, including the animal pens. They found guns in one of the barns hidden in an underground cellar, which had a trapdoor entrance hidden under hay. This provided an arsenal of weapons, all which would have to be tested for ballistics. They found some packages of a brownish powder which when tested proved to be Heroin. They also found vehicle parts from high value vehicles which would have to be checked against stolen vehicle registers, but above all the forensic team found the remains of human bones in the pig pens, which would have to be subject of DNA testing against missing persons. The search provided a myriad of material which would have to be checked, but the Armstrong's would not be coming home any time soon. Computers, laptops and mobile phones were seized, and all these would have to checked by IT experts. It would take months of painstaking research by the Police to follow every clue to its end. What the final outcome would be it was hard to tell. Certainly more arrests and more criminal charges. Mozart and Stevens left the forensic team to their labours. They had an appointment to keep.

Epilogue

The whole of the Operation Forsyth team entered 10 Downing Street at 5p.m. They were met inside the entrance by a uniformed Police Officer, who directed them to the cabinet room for a look round, and then into a conference room. Mozart walked in with Annie Forbes and Stevens. They took drinks off a young lady, dressed in waitresses uniform, with a tray of glasses. They immediately saw that the Minister of Defense, The Home Secretary and the Foreign Secretary were already there with drinks in their hands, and they shook everybody's hand in greeting as they entered.

The Home Secretary said, "The PM will be down in a minute, he is talking to the Russian President at the moment, probably about you," and he smiled. Mozart with Annie Forbes at his side, looked around at the grandeur of the building and was awed by it's palpable aura of history.

"Mr. Mozart, "said the Home Secretary. You started this I believe." Mozart said, "Yes sir. It started quite simply. I was called to deal with a person found beaten up and left tied up in a puddle at Barking Creek, and it escalated from there."

The Home secretary said, "Then it went to international drug dealing, arms smuggling, pirating and shootouts at sea and in Somalia I believe."

Mozart said, "Yes sir, it kind of got out of hand."

The Home Secretary said, "Come with me a moment. He ushered Mozart and Annie Forbes to the other side of the room, and said, "Let me introduce you to the Somali Ambassador. He wants a word with you."

The Ambassador, after introductions said, "Mr. Mozart. My government wish very much to express their thanks for what you did for our country. Hassan was determined to turn Somalia into a terrorist hotbed, which would have set the whole of North East Africa alight. By removing him you have done us a great favour, and we will be eternally grateful. His removal will allow our government to flourish and stave off foreign intervention" He then shook Mozart's hand whilst giving him a knowing look and a nod of confidentiality.

The room hushed as the Prime Minister strode into the room. He called for silence, and then said, "I would like to thank the whole Operation Forsyth team on a job well done. By your actions, not only have you removed major criminals from circulation in our country, but you have removed an international terror threat from the East of Africa, especially Somalia. We are grateful to you all. I would especially like to mention Detective Chief Inspector Joseph Mozart and Detective Inspector Winston Stevens, who started the whole thing off. You should all know that as a result of your efforts our kudos on the African continent has reached an all time high, and our relationship with the Russians has improved immensely, although we may have thwarted their political ambitions for a while. In fact I have just been speaking to the Russian President and have updated him on the outcome in Somalia, and he is pleased because his forces in Mozambique have now got the arms required to put down Al Shabaab who were causing so much trouble. I will be holding a press conference later this evening, so be warned to expect some press attention and to be in tomorrows' headlines. The good publicity will undoubtedly boost our chances at the next election." He chuckled at his whimsy, " Now, welcome all, and please enjoy yourself. Oh. One thing more. Mr Mozart, I am curious. Why was this operation called Operation Forsyth."

Mozart said, "Well sir. The arms shipment from Russia was put on a ship in the port of Odessa. Frederick Forsyth wrote the spy novel "The Odessa File". It seemed an appropriate title. The PM laughed, "I will have to tell him next time I see him." The ensemble laughed at the joke and the party started. The Prime Minister then whispered to Mozart and Stevens, "Well done both of you. I will be recommending that you both receive the Queens' Police Medal, as a mark of your country's debt to you. Well done." He then shook their hands, leaving them stunned, as the PM then concentrated on working around the rest of the room.

The following morning a letter arrived at Mozart's flat. He was in his dressing gown, as was Annie. The letter looked official. He opened it. It was from a firm of solicitors, Trainer, Temple and Kline, of Eastcheap, in the City of London. The letter was short, and asked Mozart to telephone a Mr Kline at their office as soon as possible.

Mozart and Annie showered and dressed and went to the City Office. Once there Mozart made the telephone call. He was invited to the solicitors office to meet the Mr Kline mentioned in the letter. He arranged to go later that day. His phone rang a short time later, it was Mozart's father. "Joseph," said his father, "You are going to a solicitor's office this afternoon I understand." Mozart said, "Yes. It's a bit of a mystery." "Well" said his father, I will see you there. I got a letter as well. They are seeing us together."

At the solicitor's office , Mozart was shown into a wood panelled Dickensian looking office with an antique polished desk behind which sat Mr. Kline. Also sitting there was Mozart's father Manfred.

After introductions Kline said, "We have received a communication from a firm of lawyers in Vienna. Gruber, Bauer & Schmidt of Rotenturmstrasse, Vienna. They wished us to find you both and to give you their contact details for you to make an appointment to go to their offices and see a Herr Schwarbe. First I must be sure that you are the right Mozart's, so will you tell me about your family history. Mozart Senior said, "This is most unusual." Mr Kline said, "I assure you it is to your advantage." Mozart Senior then related his family history to Kline, who then said, "Well you appear to be the Mr. Manfred and Mr Joseph Mozart we are looking for. May I suggest that you telephone Mr Schwarbe from this office and make an appointment to see him.

Mozart Senior used the telephone and made an appointment to go to Vienna the following week. A date which was mutually convenient for him and his son. They were told to bring their birth certificates and passports. Mozart Junior would take some well earned leave, and spend a few days in this beautiful city. Perhaps Annie would come with him and treat it as a short holiday. They both left the solicitors office wondering what it was all about. Joseph told his father that he would be taking his girlfriend, and staying at an hotel for a few days. Manfred said, "I will arrange a room at the same hotel. It would be nice to meet Annie, at last."

Joseph Mozart returned to his office and spoke to Annie Forbes. "I have to go to Vienna next week and so does my Dad and Mum. Would you come with me?"

She said, "I am due some leave, of course. It would be a wonderful break. I've never been to Vienna. I am told it's a beautiful city. It is the home of the Lippizana Horses, and has beautiful buildings, a State Opera House and the Schonbrunn Palace. It's on the Danube as well. It would be nice to be with you and share it, and also meet your parents as well."

Mozart telephoned Commander Russell who readily agreed to him taking time off. He then booked a flight for four people from Heathrow to Vienna for the following week. He looked up Hotels in Vienna and settled on the Vienna Plaza Hotel in the Shottenring, and booked a double room with balcony and en suite for four days for himself and another for his mother and father. He told Annie and she was delighted. He then told Winston Stevens what his plans were and said, "Will you hold the fort while I am away." Winston smiled and said, "Yes, of course. Is Annie going with you." Mozart nodded and Winston's smiled broadened.

Mozart said, putting on a pretend serious expression, "I don't know what you're grinning at Mr Stevens, we have a lot of hard work to do putting this case together, and while I'm away, it's you who'll be running the show." Steven's grin disappeared as he realized the enormity of the task ahead.

Mozart said, "Don't worry Win, one step at a time. We can do it. But next week, you will do it alone."

Mozart with Annie Forbes and Manfred and his wife Joan , landed at Vienna Airport. They hailed a taxi, which took them on the most hair raising ride they had ever experienced into the City centre. The driver was of Lebanese extraction, who spoke bad German and even worse English. He kept a conversation going in his unique version of English as he drove, often with one hand on the steering wheel. He must have trained as a rally driver, how he missed other traffic was a mystery. He seemed totally unconcerned as they weaved in and out of the traffic at high speed causing vehicles to swerve and sound their horns at his bullying tactics and his several near misses. Eventually they screeched to a halt outside the front of the hotel. Annie was pale and trembling as she got out of the cab, her legs almost giving way and she let out a huge sigh of relief, and even Mozart's right foot ached where he had been inadvertently emergency braking on the front passenger side, with his eyes closed, for most of the journey. His parents remained deathly silent. They were in a total state of shock and very relieved to get out of the vehicle in one piece. Mozart paid the driver, with no tip, and he shot off as fast as he had arrived shouting about ungrateful foreigners, with a huge screech of tyres and a smell of burnt rubber. Mozart said, "I don't know if he expected a tip for getting us here so fast, but I wasn't giving him one. He scared us all to death."

They walked into the Vienna Plaza Hotel and went straight to the bar for a nerve calmer. They then returned to the reception desk where they were all expected, and were shown to their rooms. Each room had a balcony, was large and airy, and Annie loved it.

Mozart said, "I have a surprise for you." He then produced tickets for that evening at the Vienna State Opera House. We need an early evening meal. The show starts at 7.30pm. Annie moved into his arms and said, "This is perfect. "

Mozart said, "Mum and Dad will have an early night. They didn't want to come. Perhaps they were being diplomatic."

They ate early in the hotel restaurant and then took another taxi to the State Opera House. Fortunately this driver was older and more sedate, for which they were eternally grateful and tipped him handsomely. The Opera House was beautiful. The Performance and music was ethereal. It was a wonderful introduction to the beauty and sophistication of Vienna. They walked back to the hotel with the opera still playing in their minds.

The following morning Mozart left Annie to her leisure and to link up with his Mother, suggesting they shopped until he and his father returned. The men took a taxi to the offices of Gruber, Bauer and Schmidt, Lawyers located in Rotenturmstrasse. There they asked for Herr Schwarbe. The Mozart's were admitted to his office in short time.

Herr Schwarbe asked them to sit and then said to Mozart Senior, "You are Manfred Mozart." Mozart said, "Yes." "The son of Joseph Eckart Mozart." Manfred said, "Yes."

"Have you brought your birth certificate with you Mr Mozart." Mozart produced the document which Schwarbe examined. He said, "Have you brought your passport." Again Manfred produced the document. Schwarbe said, "Would you mind if I photocopied these." Manfred said, "Not if you tell me what all this is about." Schwarbe said, "In a minute."

He then said to Joseph Mozart, "You are Joseph Mozart, son of Manfred Mozart." Joseph said, "Yes." He then asked for Mozart's passport and birth certificate. "I will photocopy these as well."

Manfred said, "What's this all about.

Schwarbe said, "Your Father," indicating Manfred and your Grandfather indicating Joseph, Joseph Eckart Mozart, was in the German Airforce during the war." "Yes" said Manfred. He was shot down in Holland and taken prisoner, and moved to a prisoner of war camp in England." Manfred said, "Yes." "Where he met your mother whilst working on a farm. They moved him when they found out about the relationship to another camp in Scotland. He was returned to Austria from there after the war leaving your Mother pregnant with you Manfred."

Manfred said, "So I believe." "Your Father did not know of your birth for many years, and when he returned to Austria he eventually married an Austrian girl and they had a son. That son was killed in his late teens in Vienna in a road accident and your Father and his wife had no more children. Joseph's wife died a few years ago, she was a wealthy woman in her own right, and left her estate to her surviving husband. I now have to tell you that your Father died 3 months ago, he lived a long and full life. He was 93 when he passed, and he has named you and his Grandson Joseph as his heirs. So let's deal with your bequest."

The Mozart's took a moment to take this information in.

The lawyer continued, "Your Father was an architect, and dabbled in fine art. He was a well respected businessman in Vienna, and he left a considerable estate. There was a house , standing in 1.4acres of ground in Baden. There was also a large amount of money from his wife' estate. He instructed that everything had to be sold except the family photographs and other items of sentimental value, which he wants to go to you both. His iron cross, which he again wants to go to you Manfred and half a dozen paintings. Which he wants split between the two of you. The sale has now been completed and the value of the entire estate after taxes and all fees is over 6.3 million euros. Half goes to you Manfred and half to you Joseph. You will benefit to the sum of 3.15 million euros, just under £3 million. If you both give me your Bank account details in the UK I can arrange to transfer the money to you today. Both Mozart's were stunned. This was a game changer. They were lost for words momentarily.

Manfred said, "Can you tell me where my Father's grave is, I would like to pay my respects while I am here."

Schwarbe said, "He and his wife are buried in Evangelische Pfarrgemeinde Church, in Baden bei Wien." He then gave Manfred the telephone number and said, "The Priest will direct you to the grave."

Both Mozart's left the lawyer's office in a daze. They were suddenly wealthy. They walked to the nearest taxi rank and took a taxi back to their hotel. Annie and Mozart's mother were not there, so they went to the bar. A short time later the ladies appeared with several bags each. They all sat in the bar and Manfred told the ladies what had happened. They were amazed, delighted and shocked. Especially Manfred who had suffered all his life for not having a Father figure involved in it. The money would ensure a comfortable old age for both him and his wife. Joseph Mozart on the other hand had the intention of starting a family life with his beloved Annie, and when she went for a comfort break he told his parents of his intentions. His Mother and Father were delighted. Annie had been a hit with both of them right away. She was a delightful girl and Joseph and Annie, in their view were ideally suited. Mozart told his parents that he saw this break in Vienna as an ideal opportunity to propose. They were even more delighted at this news and Mozart had to quieten them down before Annie returned. The two couples parted Joseph and Annie going to their room. Manfred and his wife told their son of their intention to return home the following day. Joseph told his parents he intended to stay a few days with Annie and see the sights. Joseph arranged to meet his parents later for dinner and then he and Annie went to their room. Once there Mozart said, "Annie I love you. I now know I have never loved anyone else." Annie responded, "You must know I love you my darling man."

Mozart said, "Let's go shopping". He dragged her out of the room and out of Annie's hearing asked the hotel receptionist to recommend a jewellers. The receptionist told him of one just round the corner from the hotel. They almost ran there. Mozart spoke to the man behind the counter and he produced a tray for rings showing no price tag. Mozart asked Annie to chose one. She took some time selecting the right one, but finally made a choice which Mozart approved of.

He then dropped to his knee right in the shop. "Annie Forbes, will you marry me." Presenting the ring to her. She was stunned at the suddenness of the proposal, and breathlessly whispered, "Yes, my darling, Yes." They kissed to the applause of the shop staff and customers. Slightly embarrassed Mozart placed the ring on her finger. They returned to the hotel and told Manfred and his wife the news. There were tears and joy, and much celebration. That evening they found a nearby restaurant and over dinner Annie showed off her ring.

Mozart said to Annie, with a twinkle in his eye and a half smile on his face, "I wanted to ask you to marry me before you knew about the money, because I didn't want money to influence your decision, but as they say money talks."

She hit him playfully on the shoulder and said whilst flashing her ring in the light of the overhead chandeliers, "I'm glad, you know I only agreed to marry you for the money."

They then both laughed at their private joke, joined in their merriment by Mozart's mother and father. The dinner was a great success. Annie would quickly became a valued member of the Mozart family.

The following day Joseph Mozart with Annie, and his mother and father, stood somberly in front of the grave. They laid flowers just in front of the headstone, and stood in respectful silence hand in hand, reading the headstone. **JOSEPH ECKART MOZART. 1923 – 2016. AUF WIEDERSEHEN. RUHE IN FRIEDEN.**

Schedule of Characters

Detective Inspector Joseph Mozart	Met Police. SO15
Detective Sergeant Winston Stevens	Met Police. SO15
John Brice/ Sally O'Brian	Finders of Ross- Harding at Barking Creek
Horace Dounne	Manager – Graves & Co. Tailors
Mr Anderson	MI5
Mr Adam Brocklehurst	MI5
Peter Simpson	Director – MI5
George Armstrong John Armstrong Graham Armstrong	Head of The Family Eldest son Youngest son
John Nolan James Nolan	Whitechapel Cartel Whitechapel Cartel
Mohammed Umbedi Hassan	Somali Pirate Chief
Nick Braithwaite	National Crime Agency - NCA
Commander John Russell	Head of Counter Terrorist Command SO15

Detective Inspector Steve Easterbrook	City of London Fraud Squad –Asset tracer
Pc Noel Griggs	Police Officer assigned to guard Ross-Harding in Hospital
Pc Paul Pascale	Intelligence Officer – Bethnal Green Police
Detective Superintendent McMillain	Head of CID – Bethnal Green
Commander Bertram Whalley	District Commander – Bethnal Green
Detective Chief Superintendent Beare	Directorate – Professional Standards Dept.
Inspector Steve Williams	Met Police – Firearms Team SO19
Paul Lanscombe	Head of Private Banking. Grindley's Bank
Mike Hornsby	MI6
Detective Inspector Dave Harley	Essex Officer attached to SO11
PC Robert Cook	Local Beat Officer - Kent

Major Angus McKay	Ex Army Intelligence Corps.
Detective Constable Don Ambrose	SO11
Detective Constable "Dick" Barton	SO11
Valerie Reynolds	Graham Armstrong's girlfriend
Greg Murrison	HM Customs - Dover
Richard Woodgate	Customs Investigation Branch
Charles Bishop	Head of HM Customs
Annie Forbes	GCHQ – Mozart's girlfriend
Dr Michael Carrington	Forensic Scientist
Donald Baxter	Employee of Armstrongs Driver of black Jaguar
Detective Constable Alan Smith	SO11
Inspector Ron Stovell	Northampton Police – Firearms team
Duncan McKenzie	Military Attache – Harare

	Brother of Brigadier McKenzie
Milton Ombegwe	Zimbabwe Government official
Horatio Wamadie	Armstrong's business contact – Harare
Joseph Eckart Mozart	WWII German Pilot Mozart's Grandfather
Margaret Judd/Mozart	Mozart's Grandmother
Manfred Joseph Mozart	Mozart's Father
Joan Mozart	Mozart's Mother
Major Jonathan Barwood	Military Attache - Somalia
Abdirahim Halimo Mohammed	Business contact of Armstrong's Mogadishu
Brigadier Athol McKenzie	Ministry of Defense Brother of Duncan – Military Attache - Harare
Admiral James Vincent	Royal Navy
Senor Miguel Martinez	Master – MV Castelo del Rodrigo

Tony Collins Brian Collins	Collins Transport, Barking
Detective Constable "Sooty" Coleman	SO11
Lieutenant Clive Foster	ADC to Admiral Vincent
Major James McKay Rtd.	SBS Commander. Son of Major McKay, ex Army Intelligence
Captain Miles Henderson	HMS Yarmouth
Captain Ian Thacker	SBS
Captain Valerie Andreyev	Russian Frigate "Admiral Gordinski"
Sam Leonard	Springhill Nursery – Balsham, Cambs.
Colonel Ndege	Presidential Guard - Somalia
Aabid Mahbeer Mohammed	Somali Minister of Defense

GLOSSARY OF TERMS

CO - New Scotland Yard

SO11 - Metropolitan Police Intelligence
and

Surveillance Squad.

SO 15 - Counter Terrorist Command. Met Police

SO 19 - Met Police Firearms Department

MI5 - Military Intelligence - Domestic to UK

MI6 - Military Intelligence – Foreign – effecting

UK

GCHQ - Government Communications HQ – Code

Breaking etc.

Millbank House - Home of MI5

NCA - National Crime Agency (UK's equivalent of FBI)

SBS - Special Boat Service (equivalent of SAS)

AWAC - Airbourne Warning and Control System

Drone - Unmanned surveillance aircraft

COBR - Cabinet Office Briefing Room

PNC - Police National Computer

Djinn - Supernatural creatures In early pre-historic mythology and theology

Acknowledgements

This debut novel was conceived during the Corona Virus lockdown. It came about as a result of my grandson, Scott, suggesting I should write a crime novel. It would give me something to occupy my time, and engage my brain, he said. He suggested the name of a hero – Joe Mozart. He had thrown down the gauntlet.

Having previously written a children's story in the first lockdown I felt compelled to write a grown up story in the second., I thought about it and said to myself, why not. So Mozart was born.

I would be writing of what I knew, and of some of the experiences I had over twenty seven years as a detective. Not all the experiences are mine. Some were those of friends and ex-colleagues, whose stories I have adapted and used in the text. However a great deal is from my imagination, based on collective experiences.

I am deeply indebted to my wife, for putting up with hours of isolation, as I wrote and rewrote plots. At least this left her to pursue her own hobby of quilting in peace.

I am also deeply indebted to my particular friend Dave, who not only is a friend but an ex-colleague, whom I have based a character in the story on. He has been a constant source of information, encouragement and detail, and volunteered to be my critic and editor, as did his wife Sue who valiantly stuck to her editing although she would not normally enjoy a crime novel with descriptions of such graphic violence. Many of their amendments and suggestions have been included and I am grateful for their valued input.

It is my hope that you, the reader may enjoy the tale. If you do, perhaps Mozart will rise again.

Jeff Murray

January 2021

Printed in Great Britain
by Amazon

64373361R00241